Unconditional Love

J.M. CLARK

iUniverse, Inc.
New York   Bloomington

Unconditional Love

iUniverse books may be ordered through booksellers or by contacting:

iUniverse
1663 Liberty Drive
Bloomington, IN 47403
www.iuniverse.com
1-800-Authors (1-800-288-4677)

Because of the dynamic nature of the Internet, any Web addresses or links contained in this book may have changed since publication and may no longer be valid. The views expressed in this work are solely those of the author and do not necessarily reflect the views of the publisher, and the publisher hereby disclaims any responsibility for them.

ISBN: 978-1-4502-3591-4 (sc)
ISBN: 978-1-4502-3592-1 (ebook)
ISBN: 978-1-4502-3593-8 (dj)

Printed in the United States of America

iUniverse rev. date: 8/11/2010

Gina sat there in the musty room waiting for the man to come back. She had been sitting there for over an hour and still he hadn't returned. She looked around the motel room and nearly threw up at smell and sight of all the garbage and mold. There were dirty clothes laying in a pile and some gym shoes which should have been burned ages ago. The sheets on the bed were dirty and the room smelled of urine. She checked her watch she had been sitting there over an hour and the man had not returned yet to the room. Gina wondered how much longer she going to have to sit there before he returned. "Have I lost my mind? I have got to find a better way to live man!"

Fifteen more minutes went by before she heard the key going into the door. Gina stood and pointed the gun at the door and waited for the man to come inside and turn on the light.

When he saw her he reached for his gun and Gina let off two shots to his head and he fell to the floor. It seemed right to looked at him lying there Gina laughed, it was true justice that he fell into the pile of garbage he had lived his life like a total pig. Gina put the gun back in the holster and then straighten her jacket and stepped over the body, Gina opened the door and walked out closing it behind her. Gina looked up and down the hallway to make sure no one was out or saw her then she went down the stairs and headed to the car.

When she got inside of her car then she turned on the radio and rolled down the window started the car and headed for home. She needed a shower she smelled of the room and it disgusted her. When she went into her apartment she took off the clothes she had on and placed them in the garbage and then went and got into the shower and turned the hot water on. For a few minutes she just stood there her face distance and empty, then she picked up the soap and started to lather her body and soon the room was filled with the scent of lavender and roses.

Gina scrubbed hard to get the smell of the room and all of the grime off her skin. A ritual she soon had gotten use to yet it didn't seem to remove anything. After about twenty minutes she turned the water off and walked out of the bathroom and wrapped a towel around her hair. She slipped on the silk robe and went to the phone and started dialing a number. A deep voice answered the phone "Hello" Gina waited then spoke "Meet me over at Charlie's on Fort Street I'll be there in twenty minutes." She hung up and went to get dress right before Gina walked out the door she looked at her reflection in the mirror. She stood there staring at herself and then straighten the dress making sure her gun wasn't showing. She checked her watch then took another quick look and headed for the car.

She didn't like what her life had become yet it was all she knew since she had taken her first life back in her teens. Often she wondered what her life would have been like had she only stayed home and not move out and try to make it on her own. Her parents now dead and her an only child, left her life seemed rather empty. She stared at herself and then pulled her gun out and made sure the clip was full. When she walked out the door the men across the street who were talking in front of the store hollered and Gina smiled and waved, then got into the car.

When she pulled up in front of Charlie's Bar the parking lot was full of men standing around smoking and talking. Gina opened the car door and swung her legs out and they started to hoot and yell at her as she closed the door and started to walk by. The blue dress fitted her like a glove and her blond hair flowed in the breeze. Gina was use to men hollering and cutting up about her figure they had done so all her life and she had become accustom to it. She wondered what it would be like to walk by and not have men noticing her.

Derrick was sitting in the Cadillac and motion for her to come to him, the man standing by the door of the car open it and Gina got inside the car. Derrick handed her a joint he was smoking and Gina took it and inhaled the smoke and then blew it out in his direction. Derrick handed her an envelope with five grand in it; that was what Gina charged to get rid of "special" problems for some of the local dealers and loan sharks in town. She had become known for being fast and accurate with her gun. In her younger days she had been quite taken by all the fame which came with her ability to use the gun. Now Gina felt like it was time for her to change her life, she had taken to many lives to feel justified. She needed to change and she knew it wouldn't be long if she didn't before her luck ran out. Gina opened the envelope and looked at the money then went to get out of the car.

"Have you eaten Gina?" Gina turned and looked at him and smiled as Derrick looked at her thick thighs and shook his head and grinned. "Not yet I was planning on having a steak what you treating? Derrick looked at Gina standing there in the tight blue dress and wondered where she had her gun hidden. He knew she didn't carry it in her purse and she didn't have on a shoulder holster so where was it? Gina bent over to straighten her stocking and he saw the leg holster and he smiled.

Damn she was so beautiful it was hard to believe she was so deadly and dangerous. "I'll take you to Carl's Chop House if it pleases you." Derrick looked over at Gina and smiled and winked in approval at how she looked. Gina said she would go as soon as she had spoken to someone inside the bar. Derrick started the car up he knew what she was getting ready to do and he wanted to get the hell out of there once she did. Gina had been hassled the night before by Teddy, an oversized weight lifter who thought he had the hook on every girl around. Last night he had slapped Gina on the ass and grabbed her breasts in front of his boys. Gina had told him she would be back so he could try it again. The one thing Derrick had learned about Gina was that when she said she would be back you could count on it.

When she walked into the bar Teddy saw her and yelled for her to bring her fat ass back there and let him finish getting his feel on. Tom, the bartender, knew he was asking for trouble and ducked behind the bar as Gina walked by him. Gina smelled heavenly as she walked by and one of the customers told her she smelled good. Gina stopped and stroked his cheek with her finger and blew him a kiss. No matter what Gina was doing she always took time out to thank men who were polite or sweet to her. Maybe it was because she remembered how polite and sweet her father would be to women he met. It was her way of showing her love for him to others she encountered. Her memories of her parents were soon fading yet she knew that she wanted to cherish them. Strange how the things in her life she wanted to cherish soon disappeared or changed.

Teddy got up and walked over to her and grabbed her and before he could turn her around Gina had pulled the gun and had it pointed at his forehead. Everyone in the bar stood back as she pulled back the trigger and she turned and winked at them and told the Tom to set everyone up a drink on her. "I do believe you owe me an apology Teddy and it had better be sincere or else I think I might get trigger happy." Teddy stood there speechless he looked at Gina his anger was apparent but he knew better than to try Gina. He looked at his boys staring at him then he chucked and apologized and told her he would not do it again. "Well now Tom do you think he's sorry?" Gina backed up and still had the gun pointed at him she picked up the shot from off the counter and down it. Teddy was watching her every move as Gina reached into her purse and pulled out two one hundred bills and laid them on the bar and then started to back out the door. Teddy went to rush her and she fired straight between his legs Gina was an accurate target so the men in the bar began to laugh at Teddy they knew Gina could have shot him if she wanted to.

Teddy froze and his face went white as a ghost and he grabbed his pants and checked to see if she had hit him. "Damn I miss the little thing, be grateful next time I won't miss!" Gina said as she went out and got into the car and Derrick drove off. Derrick was laughing so hard he was crying. He said Teddy probably shit on his self, he knew he would have. Gina looked over at Derrick he really wasn't that bad a looking guy. He was six feet with blond wavy hair that hung on his shoulders. He had firm muscles and thick thighs and he probably could have passed for a model.

Gina smiled and laughed when she noticed he was sexually attracted to her. "Don't tell me I'm turning you on?" She said as she lit a cigarette and blew out the smoke. "You would turn any man on especially in that dress. Gina did he talk before you quiet him?" Derrick stopped at a red light and turned and looked at Gina waiting for an answer. Gina didn't say anything for a minute "No I don't give anyone time to talk; a person might change their mind if they listen."

Derrick raised his eyebrow then focused back on the traffic as he drove to Carl's. He had known Gina for over a year now and she had done over six hits for him and not once had she ever missed her target. They pulled into Carl's and the valet came and got the car to park it. When he opened the door for Gina he smiled and she winked at him. "Hi Gina I see you're still looking beautiful." He went to get the door for her and then hurried to park the car.

Carl's was one of Gina's favorite places to eat steak; they had a way of making it melt in your mouth. Gina wasn't much of a cook. She loved to eat good food but she never seemed to have time to learn how to learn how to prepare it. Derrick was a regular and when the waiter saw Gina he took them to one of the better tables. The waiter whispered in Gina's ear that John was sitting in the back and wanted to see her. Gina looked back over at him and nodded, and then whispered to Derrick she would be right back. John stood as she approached the table and Gina held out her hand and looked at the other two men that were sitting with him. "Gentlemen this is Gina Davis or as I call her Gina the problem solver." Gina extended her hand and shook the men's hands and gave them a smile and wink. She leaned over and told John to call her later he nodded and then ordered her a bottle of her special wine and had it sent to her table.

As Gina turned to walk away the men watched her behind move from side to side and they smiled. "Don't underestimate her gentlemen she's as deadly as she is beautiful" John remarked and the men returned to their talking. When she got back to the table Derrick looked at her and smiled "I didn't know you knew John he's a hard person to befriend." Gina smiled and winked "so am I but that doesn't seem to bother you." Derrick thought back to the day when he first met Gina it seems like only yesterday. Gina was going with Miguel then He ran several houses on the Southwest side of Detroit. They were a deadly team and were building up quite a reputation in the streets. Miguel got into it with one on the local gangsters on the East Side of town about crossing over into his territory one evening at a dance hall.

Gina had gone inside to get them some drinks when she heard the shots coming from the parking lot. She dropped the glasses she was holding and fought through the crowd of people to the door. She pulled her gun and opened the door and went outside. By the time she got there to protect Miguel the gunmen had already shot him and were speeding off in their car. Gina ran to Miguel's side and knelt down and picked up his head and laid it in her lap. Blood was flooding the parking lot as Miguel looked into her eyes, his last words were "Don't let William get away with it baby...I love you." His eyes closed and Gina held him to her chest and cried out in pain. It was the first time anyone had seen Gina cry and it was the last. Gina tried hard not to show emotion she felt it was a weakness and she didn't like to be weak in anything.

It took three men to pull Gina off Miguel and let the morgue men take him away that night. She looked cold and distant as the police officers question her about what had happen. Gina didn't like police so they got nowhere with her and after a month of bringing her in for questioning they finally dropped it. Gina didn't, she was a blond then and she dyed her hair a fire red, and started working out every day. When she wasn't working out she was out at the gun range practicing. Gina practice getting faster and with each draw of the gun she vision William as her target. Her feeling for him had her hating him more and more and she knew she was wrong but revenge was what she wanted and she intended to get it. It didn't matter what she felt she knew that she would not have peace without revenge, or would she? Gina had been feeling strange lately, she was unable to determine what was going on inside of her mind. Revenge is deadly and dangerous, and in Gina's case it was truth. Yet somehow she was beginning to have feelings she could not explain, she knew it was time for her to change her life.

William and his crew were having this big party down at an old abandon warehouse one weekend. They had the place jumping with music and people dancing and clowning around. No one had any idea what was about to happen. When Gina heard that the party was going to be at the warehouse she decided that she would pay William a visit and put an end to his breathing.

Gina pulled up in a red mustang and got out showing off those long legs and thick thighs. Every man standing around had to look at her she was breathtaking. She had on a red velvet dress that looked like someone had painted it on. It was low cut accenting her full round breasts and that small waist of hers.

When William saw her he quit talking to the girls he was standing with and walked over to Gina. "Damn I thought I knew all the ladies here, I'm William and you are? He held out his hand and took Gina's and kissed it. "Damn baby you smell too good. Who you with baby?" Gina still hadn't said anything she smiled and started to walk over to the bar and ordered a drink. William watched as every inch of her body seem to move with the rhythm of the music her round behind seemed to have a beat of its own. Gina dropped her purse and William smiled as she bent over to get it. "I don't care who you came with you're going with me home baby!" He shouted at her.

Some man asked Gina to dance and she agreed and went out on the dance floor they were doing a salsa and Gina was good. She worked the crowd up with her moves and shakes when the music stopped William walked up behind her and told her to come with him he had just the thing she needed to tame that wiggle. He slapped her on the behind and Gina laughed and went with him upstairs to and empty room with a dirty mattress on the floor. William pulled Gina to him and kissed her passionately then started stripping his clothes off. Gina reached down on her thigh and pulled out the gun from the holster and pointed it at him.

When William looked up he laughed and said she would never get out of the warehouse alive. Gina smiled and told him she had a present for him from Miguel and shot him in the head. William fell to the floor and blood splattered everywhere, Gina stood there for a few minutes looking at him. She felt nothing only justice for what he had done to Miguel she turned to go out the door and then stopped and turned and looked down at him again and spit on the floor.

The music was so loud that no one heard the shot, but Gina knew she couldn't go down the way she came up. She walked over to the window and saw the ladder she took off her shoes and then climbed out on the edge and slowly walked towards the ladder and grabbed it. When she got down to the ground she put her shoes back on and straighten her dress then walked around the side of the building to where she had left her car. As she drove off she heard some men yelling for them to stop her but it was too late Gina headed down Jefferson towards Fort Street and was leaving a trail of smoke behind. Word got out that someone had did a hit on William the only description they had was she was a fine red head that drove a red mustang.

Gina had the mustang painted blue and dyed her hair back blond the next day after the shooting. When she walked into Tom's bar everyone looked at her and smiled. They knew Gina had done what Miguel wanted her to do and got justice for him. Derrick befriended Gina that evening she told him she wasn't interested in dating anyone. He told her he had something else in mind for her and they sat down in the back booth and started talking. Derrick had a few houses but mostly he ran numbers and needed someone to watch his back. He liked Gina's style and asked her to be his bodyguard. At first Gina laughed and told him he was crazy but after a little thought she agreed. Where Derrick went Gina was always close by watching his back.

One evening he was coming out of the shop after picking up the take. The count was unusually high that night and Derrick had to get a suitcase to carry it all. He was headed to the car when Gina saw the two men walking up fast behind him. There was no time to think, She opened the car door and told Derrick to duck and before the men knew what happen she had shot both of them. Derrick turned and looked at the men lying in the puddle of blood they both had guns lying by their sides. Gina had shot one man through the heart and the other dead center through the eyes. Derrick tried to adjust to the shock of what had just happen, no one was to know they were carrying a case full of money. Gina told him to come on and get into the car unless he wanted to explain to the police about the suitcase he was carrying. Derrick got in and she did a U-turn and headed up the street she was about a mile away when she stopped the car and asked Derrick did he want to drive.

He told Gina to drive the rest of the way for him his nerves had been rattled he hadn't gotten that close to death before. The truth of the matter was he was shocked he had hired Gina to do many hits but this was the first time he had seen her in action and he now knew she was worth every penny of the money she charged.

He looked over at Gina she was cool it was as though nothing had happen. When he got to the drop house he told Peter what had happen and he told Gina to come there. Derrick explained that if not for her he would have lost his money and told him what he owed Gina. Peter handed her five grand and told her he had a place for her in his operation. He hired Gina to watch over his pick up men and soon took a fancy to her. He started buying her clothes and jewelry and even got her a new mustang. Gina soon after became Peter's girl but she kept her friendship with Derrick.

Derrick pulled Gina to the side one night and told her he wished he had asked her to be his woman before Peter. Gina smiled at him then kissed him on the cheek and told him that they were better off being just friends. Gina didn't like rushing and more important she didn't like just accepting being someone's girl. She was sure the right man would one day be in her life and she would find true love, but in her heart Gina doubted rather anyone man would want such a woman as herself.

Gina would look at Peter sometimes she really didn't think she wanted him but she needed love. It was this thing with her she needed to feel the presence of a man by her side. She didn't think she would ever find true love so she settled for whatever. It was the most unusual relationship she had ever been in. She felt like Peter was always hiding something from her and that he really didn't like her, but Peter she thought did put up a good show and so she put up with him. Gina figured the sex was okay so what did it matter if she didn't love him like in the storybook. Gina had this dream of one day meeting her true love and them having a host of children and bringing them up in love and happiness. She made sure no man knew it though she didn't trust men she felt like they were not worthy of true trust. If she ever trusted a man it was her father. Gina called him a man of great strength and she often based her acceptance on any man off of what she admired in him. Peter had none of the qualities of her father so she knew that what was between them would soon end.

Peter kept Gina busy doing odds and ends for him but mostly he kept Gina by his side. He lived out in Livonia in a four bedroom ranch a few blocks from the freeway. The house was set up for both living and business as you walked into the front door you entered the living room. It was a huge room with white carpet and black leather furniture. There was a fireplace and some large white statues of naked women holding water vases in their arms. The dining room was formal with a crystal chandelier hanging over the antique wooden table. The pictures on the wall had been purchased at an Art Gallery in Paris on one of his trips there.

The kitchen was off from the dining room and it was a cook's delight with all the utensils and modern appliances. Gina laughed when she thought of herself in there trying to prepare food. She didn't know what half the items were used for and she sure didn't know much about anything else when it came to a kitchen. There was a glass door, which lead to the patio and the swimming pool and garage. The bedrooms were set up for business the first one was where he kept the computers and the records of what came in and out. The second bedroom was the money room it had a large table with chairs around it. Always there were piles of cash to be sorted and counted Peter usually worked in there until two or three in the morning making sure the tally was right.

The bedroom across the money room was a gym Peter had mirrors installed on all of the walls and had a bike, a bench with weights and some other gym equipment and a massage table set up in there. The last bedroom was the master bedroom and it was just that. It had a canopy bed with sheer white curtains hanging from the sides. There were marble end tables on both sides of the bed with matching lamps of naked women holding a white ball. There was plush white carpet and a fireplace that had two high back Victorian chairs sitting in front with a glass table with some flowers sitting on it.

Gina wondered what woman had set up the bedroom for she could feel the presence of her. She knew a woman's touch and the place smelled of it, Peter had brushed her off by saying a friend had helped decorated it for him. Gina smiled when she walked into the bathroom and saw the Jacuzzi and the phone sitting next to it. The whole house was beautiful and when Peter told Gina to move in with him and be his lady she found it hard to resist. She thought for a minute Peter was joking, and that he had a woman but when he insisted she move in she decide he didn't have anyone.

Peter was thirty five with broad shoulders and the body of a twenty year old. He had long silver black hair and a mustache and side burns. He was really a good looking man for his age and he didn't lack in the romance department. Peter would watch

Gina lifting the weights and would smile at her as she pressed in a steady motion. She could lift one twenty without even breaking a sweat. He took her down to the gun range and let her practice twice a week and even the cops would stand around watching her. One of the officers had commented that they needed more cops with her talent with a gun.

One afternoon they were heading back to the south side to pick up some money and slips when Gina noticed they were being followed. She had him pull the car into River Rouge Park and pull over to the bushes. "Stay put and lay down and don't get out of the car" she told Peter as she got out and ran to the bushes and lifted her dress up like she was going to take a quick pee. The car slowed and Gina saw the gun in the hand of the man on the passenger side. "Peter lie down and don't come up till I tell you" she hollered as she pulled her gun and shot the man in the head and the car did a U-turn and headed back for them.

Gina jumped in front of the car and took aim and shot and then dived on the hood of the car and shot again as it drove off into the ditch. She jumped off the car and ran and opened the door and checked for identification and pulled both of their wallets and then ran back to the car and got inside. "Let's get the hell out of here!" She said as Peter headed out of the park and she tossed the wallets back on the seat. She was bleeding and Peter saw she was shot in the side close to her shoulder. She told him to go to the club not to the house and she would clean up. Peter ran into the club and had two of his boys come out and help her inside the club and back to his office. He locked the doors and ran back to the office to see how she was doing. Blood was everywhere and Gina was lying on the sofa and they told him she had passed out.

Gina woke up and looked around the room then she felt her side and stood up and told them to back up off her. She pulled off the dress and then she pulled out the wallets she had picked up off the seat right before she had passed out. Gina tossed the wallets over to Peter and told him to find out who the fuck they were. She went into the bathroom to check on the wound she saw that the bullet had gone straight through. She reached into the cabinet and pulled out some cotton and alcohol and then started fixing up the wound.

Peter looked at the wallets they were from New York they had Manhattan addresses each man had about seven grand on them. Peter was lost he had no idea who would order a hit on him from New York and put word out that there was a ten thousand dollar reward for the first person who could tell him what was going on.

It didn't take but two days and they found out that the hit was done by William's brother. He was after both he and the girl who had shot his brother and so Gina decided to pay him a visit. Peter told her she was walking into dangerous ground going after William's brother but she laughed and told him she liked sleeping at night. She left that Friday evening after they had made love. "Baby don't go it's a suicide mission, let me get someone else to take care of it." Gina told him the hit was because of her and she would settle it and be back as soon as she could. Peter felt his heart drop as she drove off down the street towards the expressway.

A gold impala pulled up into the lot and Peter walked over and got into the car and it took off. Some of the men sitting in the parking lot looked and asked who it was that Peter had taken off with in the car. Derrick was coming out of the bar and asked what they were taking about and they told him that Gina had just left and that Peter had gotten into a strange car and went the other way. Derrick asked did anyone see who it was that Peter was with and they said no and went back to talking. Derrick stood looking down the street smoking a cigarette he wondered where and what Peter was up to.

When Gina got to Manhattan she got a room at a hotel not far from where William's brother lived. She had it planned how she was going to meet him but the rest was going to be sheer luck and skill. Paul and his boys were standing outside the apartment when the taxi pulled up and Gina got out. "Damn who the hell is that!" one of the men asked as she headed inside the pool hall. Paul ran across the street and grabbed her hand and asked could he help her with anything. Gina laughed and tossed her hair out of her face she told him she just wanted to get a game of pool in and he open the door and followed her inside.

She had found out he liked blue so she wore the blue leather outfit that Peter had given her so he would notice her. Paul was on her like a dog in heat and Gina told him she wanted to play pool "do you know how to use a stick?" She asked as she walked into the pool hall and picked up the pool clue and then walked over to the table and racked the balls. The men gathered around when she sat five hundred on the table and called eight ball. Paul laughed "now just what makes you think I'm going to play you for that?" He asked as he looked at her walking around the table. Gina behind seemed to move in motion to the music and he was definitely turned on. "Let's play for something better than money then" she put her hands on her hips and slowly unbutton her jacket revealing a pale blue sheer blouse. Her round breast poked through the material "if you think you're good enough you can play for me."

Paul took off his jacket and told her to break the balls she had that bet. He ordered a drink from the barmaid and asked what she was drinking. Gina turned and looked at him "Killer's brew" the barmaid asked what the hell was that. Gina laughed "one shot of Jack Daniels, two shots of napoleon brandy and a twist of lime, no ice" Paul raised his eyebrows he had never had it before and told the barmaid to make him one too. Gina drunk it down and set the glass back on the counter and then walked over to the table and broke the balls. Paul was still nursing the first drink when Gina finished her second and one and she walked back over to the table and won the game.

She ran her tongue around her lips and then took off the jacket and tossed it on a chair. "Still want to try and get into these panties?" She asked as she racked the balls again. Paul was anxious and told her he could handle just about anything she ditched out.

"Really now that sounds like a challenge and I love a challenge."
She broke the balls and once again didn't miss a shot. Paul had
taken off his jacket and Gina saw he was wearing a holster. She
smiled and told him she had an ideal if he won the game she
would give him the best thrill of his life, but if she won he had to
agree to the terms she wanted. Paul looked at her for a long time
then he laughed and asked what was it she wanted. Gina laughed,
"you'll see I'm not the one making the challenge."

Paul looked at her "Shit no bitch is that good" he said as
she walked around the table and stroked his face. The smell of
lavender and roses turned him on and he went to kiss her and
she moved backward "Remember you have to win first." Gina
walked over to the jukebox and put on a song and started dancing
and swaying her hips to the music, and the men in the pool hall
gathered around to see what Paul would do. Paul asked her what
did she want from him and she jokingly said "your life baby boy."
Everyone thought she was playing and they started laughing as
Paul told her to rack the balls.

They stood around and watched as the game took on heat.
Gina let Paul win but it didn't come easy for him when he won he
raised his hands and pranced around the room. He pulled Gina
towards him and placed his hands on her ass and squeezed as Gina
brushed up against him.

"Let me grab my jacket and we can go someplace for your
prize." Paul told his boys to stay put and they walked out across
the street up inside the high rise apartment building and took the
elevator up. He lived on the ninth floor and there were only two
elevators Gina made sure no one was in the hallway and when she
went inside she checked the apartment out.

"Let me freshen up a bit" she said as she went into the
bathroom. She took off her clothes and put the gun inside the
jacket sleeve she made sure the safety was off and then splash some
water on her blouse and made the blouse stick to her skin. She
needed to distract him long enough for him to relax and for her
to rid herself of a problem. When she came out of the bathroom

Paul was already in bed Gina smiled and walked over to the table and took a hit of the cocaine that was lying by the lamp. Gina saw his gun lying on the pillow next to him and she noticed that he had the safety off.

She laid her clothes on the foot of the bed and climbed on top of him and started stroking his chest and licking his nipples. Paul closed his eyes as Gina climbed up on him and began to make love to him. She was hot and wet and he shouted as she began to grind him. Paul was lost in the moment he hadn't notice Gina reaching back for her jacket and gun with the silencer, it wasn't until she had it pointed at his head that he realized he was in trouble.

Gina looked at him then said "question why did you send someone to hit me for killing that piece of shit of a brother of yours?" Paul tried to move but Gina had him firmly held to the bed with her knees and the trigger was pulled back and Gina was pointing the gun directly at him. "Bitch do you really think you can get away with killing me? My boys will track you down and kill your fucking ass!" Gina started grinding him harder and Paul found he couldn't help himself he ejaculated and Gina shot him in the head. The blood splash on her and the wall behind and Gina looked at him for a minute then got up and rushed into the bathroom and threw up. She showered and put her clothes back on. She was about to open the door when she heard the elevator doors open. She peeked through the keyhole and saw it was two of Paul's boys.

She opened the door and told them Paul was back in the bedroom sleeping it off. They headed towards the back and Gina pulled her gun and shot both of them in the back of the head. Gina checked the peek hole to make sure the hall was clear then opened the door and got on the elevator and went back downstairs. A cab was just dropping off a fare and Gina flagged him and got inside and she told him to take her to the hotel. She paid the maid extra to clean the room extra well and then she went out to her car and headed back to Detroit. On the way back to Detroit, Gina thought about a lot of things. She no longer felt like she was doing the right things in life. It was becoming harder for her to look at herself in the mirror. She knew she would soon have to change, she only wondered how she would do it. She spent many hours talking to God about what she was doing and asking him how she would ever be able to undo all the wrong she had done. She was feeling sad but the emotions were not for the hit she had just completed. She was feeling a lost and today more than anything she was missing Miguel.

When she walked into the club Peter jumped up and ran and grabbed her and twirled her around. "Drinks on me tonight my baby's back!" Everyone rushed up to the bar and he took Gina to the back booth and she told him how she managed to get rid of the problem. Peter had a strange look on his face and Gina laughed "now tell me if you had to go wouldn't you like to take it hot and tight?" Peter broke out laughing and told the barmaid to bring them a bottle of champagne he felt like celebrating. Word came from New York that someone had ordered a hit on Paul and no one had any ideal who it was. Gina had left no clues only the scent of her cologne lingered in the room. Word was out that he got off, before he got off.

For the next few months Peter and Gina stayed together like glue there was something different about him but Gina couldn't but her finger on it. Where one was the other followed Peter had Gina taking care of all the loose ends for him. Word got around that Gina was both dangerous and beautiful and that she had the police in her pocket. Peter asked Gina about her relationship with Patrick an undercover cop on the south end of town. She told him she knew him from the hood and that it pays to have someone watching her back. He smiled and told her to be careful Patrick was hungry to make Captain and that he didn't trust him. Gina looked at Peter she knew better, if she could trust anyone she knew she could trust Patrick to have her back. They had ties which no one could tear not even a badge. Peter didn't like the relationship he kept on her about it and Gina told him she would have Patrick back up some if it would make him feel better.

One night she was out alone and she pulled up to the squad car and smiled "Hey Patrick I hear you been looking for me what's up baby?" She winked and he told her to pull the car over to the side. He got out and got into the car with her "Gina I hear that you took out a fellow over on Fort the other night. Now you know if I find out you did it I'm going to have to arrest you" he looked at Gina sitting there in the red dress and reached over and put his hand on her thigh. "I sure would hate to have all this fine shit locked away" he started to run his hands between her legs and Gina stopped him and winked. "Now Patrick if I let you touch it you're going to have the right to get it and you know that's a no." Gina smiled and reached over and kissed him on the cheek "one favor takes another remember that" she whispered and he looked at her and smiled and got out of the car. "Be safe baby you know I'm watching your back" he walked over to the squad car and got in and then took off.

Gina knew Patrick wanted to make love to her again but they had made a promise years ago that they would only be friends. Patrick had tried to kill a man over her one night after he had tried to hurt Gina. It was right before he decided to become a police officer and Gina had told him that she thought they should be friends and not lovers anymore. Patrick looked at her then after a while agreed and since then they had been watching each other's back. Gina had saved his life a couple of times and he told her there was nothing on earth that would make him turn against her and Gina knew he was telling her the truth.

When she got to the club Peter had already heard about her and Patrick he asked what she was up to. Gina kissed him and told him just making sure that her back was covered that's all. Peter pulled her down close to him and whispered "don't fuck him Gina I swear it'll be his death warrant." Gina stood up and reached down and picked up the cigarette from off the ashtray and inhaled the smoke and then blew it out. She looked at Peter but didn't answer him she didn't like the fact he was threatening her friend. Roscoe came into the club and came back to Peter and whispered something in his ear and Peter stood and told Gina to follow him.

Outside was three police cars they had his boys lined up against the cars and were searching them. When Gina saw Patrick she froze she knew what everyone was thinking that she had set them up. Patrick looked at her then turned and told the man on the hood to lay flat and spread his feet apart. He patted him down then told them they could go once they found out they were clean. Peter stood watching him and then pulled Gina to him and passionately kissed her. Patrick slammed the car door and did a U-turn and took off Peter asked Gina had he told her anything about doing a search on his people today. Gina told him no and that she would find out what the fuck was up she got into her car and took off after the police car.

She came back three hours later and she had a gunshot wound in her side. She walked into the club and fell to the floor she was calling for Peter. Peter called his boys and told them to take her back to the office. Gina refused to go to the hospital she had the men bring her some supplies and told them how to pack the wound. Peter was worried he asked what had happen and she told him that Roscoe had set her up. She had shot him and two of his boys outside the pool hall once Patrick had told her who the snitch was. Peter picked Gina up and took her to the car and had one of his boy's go check out the pool hall and find out what the fuck was going on.

When his boy came back he confirmed that Gina had shot all three of them and that they had the pay off money still on them when the cops checked. The cops were looking for the other shooter they had no idea it was Gina. Peter had them take her home and then posted a guard outside the house just in case trouble came their way. Gina was up and on her feet in a few days and she told him she owed Patrick. He had saved her life she hadn't seen Roscoe until the last minute that was how she had gotten shot. Patrick had shot Roscoe and called for backup and let her get away. His partner was in the restaurant and hadn't seen what happen by the time he came out Gina was gone.

Peter looked at her she was so calm but he knew better Gina was angry she felt that Roscoe had someone behind him. There was no way he could have planned the shit by himself he had no courage for the game. Gina met Patrick over at the restaurant on Dix and they talked for about an hour. He didn't know who it was behind Roscoe but he did know that they were pumping information into the cops. They planned on raiding Peter's house that weekend and he told her to make sure there was nothing around. Gina went back and told Peter and he went into action. He had his boys move all the take and tickets to a special house they had over on the east side. Gina took all the money and put it in a safe deposit box at the bank.

When the raid trucks came in and surrounded the house Gina and Peter were making love. Peter asked to see the warrant and asked what they expected to find in his home. He called his attorney and told him he wanted to press charges against them. Peter knew someone had talked they went straight to the money room and knew where the safe was. Peter agreed with Gina something was up and he decided to take a trip and find out just what the hell was going on. He sent Gina out shopping and when she came back there were three men sitting in the front room. Gina could tell by the clothes they had on that they were money. Peter introduced her and they stood and shook her hand.

They were from New York and New Jersey and were here to discuss the problem he was having. They had narrowed the problem down to one guy and they had to catch him before he disappeared. Delano one of the men from New York asked how good was Gina. Gina looked at him there was something about him he made her heart flutter when he spoke. She looked at him and then at Peter as he asked him a series of questions about her. Peter said she was better than the death angel she could sneak up and attack a man without him even feeling the bullet. Delano looked to be in his forties and he was the headman for he spoke and Peter jumped. Gina looked at him and for a moment she thought he looked like Peter but she put her mind back on the business at hand. Gina had gone into the weight room it was something she did right before she knew she was going to have to go out. Delano went back in to where Gina was and closed the door and started talking to her.

"I hear you're good I need to know how good you are. I have a major problem that is causing side effects here in Detroit. It'll take a strong person to get inside the house and leave it clean. Do you think you can do it? There is no room for mistakes?" Gina looked at him then smiled she walked up to him and within seconds had the gun pointed at his head. Delano smiled and told her she was hired and gave her an address to where the problem lived. When they came out of the bedroom Delano gave the okay to Peter and the other men. "She's perfect only I can't figure how she's going to get into the house." Peter told him not to worry if Gina says she can get inside then she will. Gina walked over to Peter and jumped up on him and wrapped her legs around his waist. "When I come back I want you to ride my brains out" she passionately kissed him then got down and headed for the door.

"Gina there are seven men in the house" Delano said as he lit a cigarette he looked at her and his heart fluttered "we'll wait to see if you come back." Gina turned and looked at him "I'll be back in an hour you have my steak and lobster sitting on the table and make sure my champagne is cold." She usually didn't talk to strangers, but for some reason she felt a strange connection to this man. Delano looked at her then he smiled "Deal, but I am not sure Peter is the one who should be getting the reward" he winked and she turned and walked out the door and got into the car. Delano looked over at Peter and lit another cigarette "she's seemed overly confident, are you sure she can handle the job?" Peter laughed "very sure we better get her food on the table because you haven't seen nothing like her after she finished a job man." Gina had been known to eat two steaks, a lobster, potatoes and salad, then would often ask for dessert. He couldn't understand how she could eat after seeing so much blood but Gina had told him that the food was her reward for herself.

Peter looked at Delano and then went to the phone Delano asked him what he was doing. Peter explained she worked out before and afterwards, " she likes eating" he went to the phone and ordered some food from Carl Chop House. When he told them it was for Gina they said they would have it ready by the time the driver got there. Delano looked at Peter he had known him all his life and he made sure he was protected because of a promise. He asked Peter how long had he known Gina and he said for a little while. "Why you want to play the game?" He winked at Delano and sat down in the chair. Delano told the other men to go back to the hotel and finish making sure everything was ready for them to go home.

Delano looked over at Peter and then smiled and told him that he didn't think Gina should be played with. Delano looked at him for a while then asked did she always wear a dress like that when she went to do a hit. Peter told him Gina always wore a dress he had only seen her wear jeans or pants twice since they had been together. Delano said she looked like angel in that damn dress he asked did she have any flaws. Peter laughed and told him she had a weak spot she wanted someone to love her. Delano looked at him he knew then that Peter didn't love Gina and he laughed and sat down in the chair and they started talking. He knew Peter and it bothered him that he was keeping a secret from him especially now with all that was going on. Delano didn't say it out loud but he wished Gina would come back, he wanted more than anything to get to know her. He watched Peter set the table and prepare for Gina and when the food arrived he took it and put it in the oven. He put the champagne on ice and then he set up a tray with cocaine and two joints on it. "What's that?" Delano asked him and Peter told him that Gina was strange she usually did three lines and smoked the joints before diving into the food. "She is an odd one alright" Delano remarked then he noticed that Peter was watching his watch. "Do you have somewhere to be?" Delano asked him but Peter told him he was timing Gina.

Gina pulled up over on Steel street and parked a few houses from the house and watched the traffic coming in and out. When she saw the last two customers leave she walked up to the door and knocked. "Hey baby I need something bad cans you fix a girl up?" She held her head down and rubbed her nose and was shaking. The man opened the door and told her to come inside Gina stepped in and she looked around the room. There were three men sitting to a table playing cards and one was in the kitchen frying some bacon all of them had guns inside of their holsters. Gina could hear some people up stairs and she watched as the man went to get the drugs.

When he came back she pulled her gun and shot him and the three men at the table through the head. The man from the kitchen came out with a shotgun and Gina ducked down and shot him in the chest and then turned and shot the man coming down the stairs in the head.

She rolled over behind the chair and reloaded as the man came from the basement she fired and hit him in the leg first, then shot the man she had shot in the chest in the head, and then turned back and caught the man she had shot in the leg in the head. She heard the steps of someone coming fast as the other men came downstairs with guns they aimed at her and Gina rolled her body as she shot both of them in the head she counted and knew she was missing one man. She reloaded the gun and then she listen the house was quiet but she could feel the man's presence. Gina rolled over to the door by the hall and opened the door and then closed it hard and the last man came downstairs thinking he was alone and she shot him in the head. The room was full of blood and bullet holes and she could hear the police sirens she reached into her pocket and pulled out a wig and put it on her head. Gina went quickly through the house then open the back door and checked to see if anyone was outside. Once she saw it was clear she ran and jumped the fence and ran across the yard then jumped the next fence and walked around to the side of the house and then to her car.

She was just driving off when she saw the police cars tearing down the street to the house. She turned the corner and went three blocks and then stopped and pulled off the wig and tucked it under the seat and got out of the car and went into the store. A police car pulled up next to her car as she was coming out of the store and she asked was there a problem. Gina tossed her long blond hair back and smiled at them. They smiled and said no they were looking for a car similar to hers that had just left the scene of a crime. Gina smiled "Well I hope you find who you're looking for" the officer told her to be careful and she got into the car and drove off.

When she got back to the house Peter smiled and winked then picked her up and twirled her around the room the table was set and he popped the cork on the champagne. Delano turned on the television and listen to the news about a shootout at a house on Steel and the killers getting away. Delano looked at her and smiled then nodded at her and pointed to the table. They sat down and started eating and listening to the news. Delano shook his head and told her that he knew now just how special she was. Gina looked at him and she felt herself feeling something she didn't want to feel she liked Delano and for one minute she felt she should be going in the back with him. She got up and then pulled Peter by the collar back to the bedroom and pushed him on the bed. "You're not even going to wait for our guest to leave huh?" Gina was out of her clothes and on top of him "Does that answer your question?"

Peter went back out front and Delano asked how long had he been with Gina again. "Not long enough why?" Delano said he could use her at home but Peter said no way she was his woman and he wouldn't trade her for anything. After that night Peter kept an eye on Delano when he was around Gina, Delano usually got what he wanted and he wanted Gina. Peter looked at Delano looking at Gina and laughed to himself. Gina had seen him and she didn't like the way he looked at them. Gina for the first time in a long time wondered should she be with Peter. Something wasn't right she thought as her and Delano talked she kept an eye on Peter she knew he was up to something and she wondered why she had a feeling Delano had something to do with it.

Gina noticed the change in Peter right away and she knew it had to do with Delano she no longer had to question that she just had to find out what it was. Delano left that next afternoon on the evening plane to New York with the other men. Peter was restless he kept Gina by his side for the rest of the week. Gina asked him what was bothering him so much but he didn't answer. He smiled and told her that his best days had been with her by his side. Gina looked at him and smiled and wondered why he said his best days did he know something she didn't? When she came home the next evening the house was flooded with red and yellow roses and white carnations and daisies. Gina asked Peter what was the occasion and he told her to read the card. "My offer still stands I want you here beside me...Delano."

Gina tossed the card into the fireplace and walked over and sat on Peter's lap. "What's going on baby you have to talk to me for me to understand" she kissed him passionately and then laid her head on his shoulder. Peter said Delano sent a plane ticket for her and that she was to meet him in New York in a week. Gina asked was he going and he said no the invitation was just for her. Gina didn't like the fact that Delano thought he could order her around but Peter told her it was in his favor if she went and saw what the hell he wanted. Gina looked at Peter he seemed different now as he talked as though he had been knifed in the heart. "Peter I will not leave you baby, no matter what happens I'll come home to you." Gina started taking off his shirt and slowly started kissing his neck and shoulders.

Peter sat back in the chair as she relaxed him and then he stood and took her to the bedroom. "Gina if he asks you to stay will you?" Gina walked up to Peter and put her arms around his neck and kissed him. "Baby I belong to you there is nothing or no one who can change that." She took off his pants and laid him back on the bed and slowly started making love to him. Peter screamed out in passion and He pulled her up into his arms and looked at her then flipped her over on the bed and pinned her hands over her head and started kissing her. The passion between them was hot and furious and Peter held on to Gina. She didn't know what it was but something was different about him. Was he faking?

Afterwards he held her in his arms and listen to her breathing. "Gina I love you please come back to me" he whispered as she drifted off to sleep Gina felt strange she didn't think Peter was telling her the truth He almost sounded like he wanted her to hurry and leave. Peter was saying one thing but his actions were saying another. Peter took Gina to the airport and stood there watching as she boarded the plane. Gina didn't understand why she had to go see Delano or what power he had over Peter but she intended to find out. She like having control of her life and her affairs. On the plane she had a chance to think about Delano and she realized that she was happy she was going to see him again. She could not explain it but she felt a certain warmth when she was around him, something which she could not explain and she wanted to know more about him.

What was going on with her, she didn't think Peter was telling her the truth about being in love with her and now she found herself happy to be going to meet with a stranger. Gina turned and stared out at the clouds and wondered if it was some kind of sign. She knew she trusted her feelings and always had when it came to men. Peter had been anxious for her to leave and she knew he was up to something. They had made love but she didn't think he was really in the bed with her. There were moments when she could have sworn he was thinking about someone else. She looked up at the stewardess as she handed her a drink and then turned and looked back out the window. What was this she was feeling for this strange man? Here she was going to New York to be with him and she didn't know why. Peter had told her she had to go and she agreed since it was so important to him. Did Delano think he could control her? Gina wondered if she would be recognized she hadn't been to New York since she had done Paul in and now she was having second thoughts.

Chapter Two

All the way to New York Gina kept seeing the hurt look in Peter's face and the fear she would not return home to him. Why didn't she believe him? She wondered what Delano wanted with her and why it was so important for her to come see him. When she got through customs Delano met her with a limo and a dozen of red roses. There was champagne and clavier waiting inside chilling on ice. Gina smiled and then asked why it was so important for her to make the trip. Delano didn't answer her at first he poured her a glass of champagne and handed it to her. He offered her a tray with some cocaine on it and Gina did a few lines and then looked at him.

"I like to keep up with whom my men socialize with. Peter seems to be quite taken with you maybe I just want to get to know you." Gina looked at him and his smug attitude and smiled "You could have gotten to know me in Detroit so let's cut the bullshit. Why am I here?" Delano laughed and told her he wasn't use to a woman being so frank. "I'm uncomfortable I don't have my gun with me Peter made me leave it at home." Delano reached over on the seat and handed her a box Gina looked at him and wondered what was in it. She opened it and inside was a twenty-five automatic with a thigh holster. She looked at him and smiled then put the gun on and picked up the glass of champagne and toasted him.

"To what might turn out to be an interesting trip" Gina looked at him and once again she thought he looked like Peter. "Are you more comfortable now?" He asked and Gina smiled and told him she was real comfortable and that was not natural for her. Delano smiled and told the driver to stop at Tiffany's before going home. "I'll only be a second" he said as he got out and went inside. After a few minutes he came out and got back inside the limo. He handed Gina a diamond necklace and she asked what it was for as he took it out of the case and put it around her neck. "I like giving surprises I hope you like accepting them" he smiled and looked at her then said the necklace suited her.

Gina took another hit of the cocaine and leaned back on the seat and started listening to the music. Delano stayed on Lexington Avenue and Gina was quite impressed with how he had the place decorated. There were paintings on the walls and statues everywhere she smiled when she saw the roses and the card on the front table "Welcome home Gina." He had the butler take her up to her room to shower and change for dinner he said they would be dining out tonight.

"I hear you like the salsa I know a great spot we'll have some fun before we get down to business." Finally Delano had slipped he did have her there for business but what business? She went to the phone and called Peter and he seem happy to hear from her.

"Honey what business can he have for me here?" She asked and waited for him to answer. Peter said he couldn't talk on the phone but that she was to do whatever he asked and come home he missed her. Gina hung up and went to take the shower when she came out Delano was sitting on the bed. He had a box in his hand "It's for you to wear tonight I want to surprise a few people with your presence." Gina open the box and raised her eyebrow the dress was red and made in a very sheer material. Gina told him she would wear it but she didn't feel comfortable with him in the bedroom right now. Delano laughed "that will soon change I guarantee you."

Delano stood to leave the room and turned and looked at her he smiled then commented that Peter was a fool and didn't deserve her and left the room.

Gina slipped the dress on and looked in the mirror. Her golden skin and hair made the dress come to life she turned around and laughed she liked it. She put on the necklace he had given her and strapped her gun to her thigh and turned this time to make sure the gun didn't show. When she came down into the living room Delano stood and smiled "you're breath taking come here I have something to top off that necklace." Delano held out a pair of diamond drop earrings when Gina put them on he signaled for the butler to bring her wrap. He had gotten her a white fur jacket, as he put it on he asked Gina what was the name of her cologne that it suited her very well. "I don't wear cologne its lavender and rose oil" she turned and kissed him on the cheek and thanked him for the gifts.

They were just about to leave and Delano turned her around and looked at her and Gina felt it again a flutter in her heart. Delano told her again the dress suited her along with the jewelry. He open the door and he extended his hand for her to go pass as she did he felt his heart flutter. They laughed and talked all the way through the ride to the club. It was easy to talk to Delano he seemed so open, Gina looked over at him and smiled then turned and looked out the window. Delano seemed like an old friend and that made Gina uncomfortable, she usually didn't befriend anyone as quickly as she had done him. She had many questions that she needed answered, the top one being why was she here.

When they arrived at the club the valet open the door and Delano got out and then extended his hand for Gina to take it. Some photographers took their pictures as they went into the club. Delano told her not to worry about it they were always doing that. Gina got close to him and whispered "I don't like people taking my picture Delano can you get it back from them? He looked at her then smiled and told her to wait a minute and he went over to the photographers and talked to them. He pulled out a wad of money and handed it to them and they gave him the film from their cameras. He walked up and gave the film to Gina and she smiled and kissed him on the cheek and said thank you.

Delano was meeting four other men there when they saw Gina they stood up and smiled. "Delano you didn't mention you were bringing an angel with you" one of the gentlemen said as they sat down. Delano signaled for the waitress to take Gina jacket and ordered a bottle of champagne. Gina was getting into the music already and Delano told her in her ear to watch each man very carefully tonight for him. Gina looked at him then smiled and kissed him on the lips and whispered in his ear "what am I looking for?"

Delano smiled and sipped some water and then leaned over and whispered as he kissed her on the cheek "a traitor." One of the gentlemen asked if she would like to dance Gina stood and went out on the dance floor, the drummer noticed her right away and began to beat with the sway of her hips. Gina floated as she moved and danced with the man she put her hands on his body as she danced and check for wires and guns. Gina was good the man hadn't even noticed his attention was on her. He asked her how she knew Delano and she told him she was a guest visiting from out of town. The man took her hand and started twirling her around and Gina flowed with the music. A few of the people on the floor stopped and watched her move and smiled as she began to tease the man with her hips. Gina tossed her hair from side to side and wiggled and laughed as the music took her to a higher level. She loved the Salsa it was a dance which let her emotions flow freely.

When they went back to the table Delano kissed her on the cheek and told her to sit the next dance out and to pay attention to what was being said. Most of the talk was over Gina's head they talked of mergers and bank transfers then Gina noticed something one of the men wasn't talking he was watching a man standing at the door. Gina asked to go to the restroom and Delano looked at her, she whispered that she felt uncomfortable about the third guy. Delano smiled and told her to do her thing then sat back down and started talking to the men. The man the other man had been signaling to during the night moved towards the door and Gina saw the imprint of a gun but she noticed something else a mike in his ear. He was taping the conversation at the table.

When she came back she told the gentlemen to excuse her but Delano had promised her a dance. Once on the floor she warned him that they were being taped. He asked how did she know and she told him the guy at the bar had a recorder and mike hooked to his ear. Delano started turning her around and looked at the man at the door he wondered how she had noticed him with all these people in the club. Delano smiled and he kissed her on the cheek and told her to go back to the table and not to mention anything to anyone. Delano leaned over and whispered something in the man's ear that was sitting in front of him and he laughed and asked Gina to dance.

"Delano said for you to cause the room to look at us so let's give them a show shall we."

He picked Gina up and then they began to dance Gina picked up the hem of her dress and winked at the drummer who began to beat a rhythm to each of her moves. The people started watching as she danced and the man twirled her around when the music stopped, she noticed the man at the table and the man by the bar were no longer there. Delano came up and kissed her and winked let's go eat I'm starved." When Gina got into the limo she saw both men sitting with bullet holes in their heads. "Tell me something Gina how did you know he was taping the conversation?" Delano asked as he told the driver to head to the warehouse. Gina explained she had seen the mike and receiver before and that she had a good memory for recalling things that could get her in trouble. Delano smiled and told her he had to change limos and give out some orders then they would go to dinner.

Gina watched as they placed the men in cement and dropped them into the river. She wondered who they were and why they were taping Delano. After they had eaten and got back to the house he pulled Gina into his arms and kissed her. Gina slapped him and told him if she wanted to be kissed she'll let him know. Delano laughed and told her to go to the den he had a surprise for her. The room was filled with roses and carnations and there was a Jacuzzi with lavender and rose oil. Gina smiled he had gone through a lot of trouble to make her happy and yet she still didn't want to make love to him. Or did she? Gina wasn't sure what she was feeling inside and it made her nervous. She didn't get nervous often and it was confusing to her that she was feeling all these strange emotions around Delano.

When Delano came into the room with the tray of Napoleon Brandy and Jack Daniels Gina laughed then suddenly she caught a chill. The only time she had told anyone about the drink was Miguel and the barmaid the day she shot Paul and his boys. She turned and looked at him and he smiled and told her to relax. "Sit down and I'll make both of us a Killer's Brew" he looked over at Gina who was now holding the gun on him. "I'm not going to hurt you if I was I would have done it when I found out it was you who killed by boys. I just wanted to understand why you did it that's all."

He handed Gina a drink and she sat down and placed the gun in her lap. "You could have asked me that in Detroit so why all the pretense?" Delano looked at her and smiled "let's just say I took a special interest in you okay, I want to be your friend not your enemy." He lifted the glass up and took a shallow and Gina drunk it down and sat the glass on the table. Delano lit a joint and walked over and handed it to her and Gina looked at him and smiled. He wanted something and she was waiting to find out what it was. He made her another drink and then took off his clothes and climbed into the Jacuzzi. Gina looked at him he was so firm and muscles were bulging out everywhere. She was turned on and she knew it and suddenly she wondered what Delano really wanted with her.

"Come over here and get in the water with me I hate to play alone." Delano motions for her to come and she down the drink and slipped out of the dress. As she climbed into the water he pulled her to him and this time she didn't resist his kisses. The door to the room open and Gina did a flip out of the Jacuzzi and picked up the gun and had it pointed at the butler's head. "Damn!" Delano said "Gina he's only bringing in some clavier and champagne I told him too." The butler was shaking and Gina walked up to him and took the tray and gave him a kiss on the cheek. The butler blushed and turned and hurried out of the room and Gina took Delano the tray and sat it on the edge of the Jacuzzi.

"Are you always so fast to pull that gun?" He asked as he poured her a glass of champagne and handed it to her. Gina took it and walked over and sat the gun back on the clothes and made herself another drink and down it. She took a hit of the cocaine and then told him that it was force of habit. She liked staying alive and didn't take chances when it came to herself or people she liked. Delano looked at her and smiled he understood now why Peter wanted her and needed her. Gina was good with that gun and for a woman that was a rare quality. They enjoyed an evening of getting high and playing but Gina didn't make love with him and for that he gained respect for her. As the evening progress he found himself becoming even more taken with her inner beauty.

When he took her to the airport to go back to Detroit he asked if she would come and visit him again. Gina turned and smiled "who knows I might even let you make love to me" she kissed him on the cheek and then turned and walked towards the plane. When she looked back once again she felt he looked a lot like Peter. She wondered if they could be kin or something? She waved and went into the plane. Gina thought a lot about Delano and how good they felt together. She wondered if Peter would let her come back again?

Peter was standing at the gate waiting for Gina when she got off the plane. Gina smiled at the expression of relief on his face when he saw her. He ran and picked her up into his arms and smothered her with kisses. "I've missed you so much" he whispered in between kisses. Gina told him she missed him too and they hurried through the terminal to the car. Out in the car he pulled Gina to him and asked her did Delano explain why he wanted her to come to New York. Gina looked at him and she knew he knew why and he asked her there. Gina wondered why hadn't he hadn't warned her and she began to think she couldn't trust Peter. Peter explained that Delano was his associate and he had no ideal at the time Paul was one of his boys. He had explained to Delano when he had come to town that you only took revenge for the brutal way they killed Miguel. Delano had warned him about telling her the truth he wanted to find out just how loyal you were. "He tells me you saved his hide from two comrades who were trying to set him up with the Feds. He was very grateful when I talked to him on the telephone."

Gina listened to him talk and she wondered if Delano had told him she would not let him have sex with her. She had no idea he had talked to Peter he never mention it. Back at the house Gina found the place flooded with roses and carnations. She laughed when she read the card "Welcome home baby I missed you.... Love Peter" she turned to kiss him and he was gone into the bedroom. Gina walked in and there he was laying in bed waiting for her. Gina jumped on the bed and started smothering him with kisses. "I am so horny that I could simply eat you up" she said between kisses. Peter slowly removed her dress and started making love to her.

Gina started biting his nipples and slowly working her way down but as she made love to Peter she notice that he had some scratches on his back and they had healed but she knew something else that she hadn't put them there. Peter moaned in ecstasy as she ran her tongue around him and back up to his lips and kissed him passionately. He stopped and looked at her then kissed her again as he penetrated her warm and wet body. He screamed out in passion as he started stroking her and Gina dug her nails into his flesh. "I've missed you baby" she whispered as she felt his body stiffen and him climax. Peter pulled her into his arms and held her tightly as they drifted off to sleep.

The next morning she awoke to breakfast in bed Gina smiled and asked why all the special treatment "I just thought I would show the woman I love I appreciate her." Gina laughed and sat the tray to the side and pulled him down to her and kissed him passionately "then make love to me that's what I missed the most" she whispered as he returned her kisses. Afterwards while they were in the shower Gina asked him while he was lathering her back did Delano mention he had tried to make love to her. Peter didn't say anything he turned her around and kissed her and smiled lifting her up into his arms. "I think he understands now whose woman you are" he said as she screamed and fell against the shower wall.

Later when they were back in the bedroom Peter looked as she showed him the gifts Delano had gotten her and smiled when he saw the red dress. "I bet you stopped traffic in that" he said as she held it up suddenly his face didn't look pleased. Gina dropped the dress and threw her arms around him "Peter I can't be brought or bribed so don't let the gifts bother you." Peter looked at her and smiled Gina was one of a kind she had beauty and charm and was deadly and dangerous all in one. He heard Delano last words to him that if she could be gotten he would get her from him. Delano had been his friend for a long time and had always gotten what he wanted. Peter had a strange look on his face and Gina once again knew he was up to something and that it had to do with Delano. Peter talked to her about the business and the way he had changed things around for their protection.

"I open an account for you downtown at Comerica. I put a safe deposit box in both of our names and you have to go down and sign some papers today." Gina looked at him he was the first man to open an account for her and she felt honored that he trusted her so much. After they left the bank they went by the club and Gina was surprise to see he had hired some dancers. His permit had come through for the adult entertainment license. Gina decided to give him a surprise she went and talked to the DJ and he put on a record. Peter was talking to the barmaid about the shipment of liquor when he turned and saw her up on stage.

Gina started swaying and grinding her hips to the music and the men in the bar gathered around the stage. Peter had no idea Gina could stage dance and he sat down and watched her as she grabbed hole to the pole and twirled around it to the floor. The men started shouting and Peter noticed they were aroused when she finished dancing she walked over and sat on his lap and kissed him. "Well did I please you?" She asked as he took a towel and wiped the sweat off her. "Come here" he said as he took her back into the office and locked the door. "I didn't know you danced Gina you are full of surprises" he pulled her to him and passionately kissed her and then laid her down on the sofa and made love to her.

He reached over on the table after they were finished and picked up a joint and lit it. Gina walked over to him and took the joint and gave him a shotgun of smoke and he cough then slapped her on the behind. "Get dress we have a meeting downtown in about twenty minutes." Peter went back out front to finish taking care of the business of the club before they left. When Gina came out of the office two men walked up and handed her some money. Gina smiled and told them thanks and they asked when would she be dancing again Peter walked up to them and winked then put his arms around Gina. "This is my woman gentlemen and she dances only when I can stand it." They all laughed and Peter pulled Gina close to him he was not about to let anyone get to close to her he had enough competition with Delano on her ass. Gina didn't say anything but it was something about his voice and the way he said it that let her know that he was joking with the men. Was she his lady?

Gina looked over at Peter in the car and smiled and he didn't say anything at all. "Peter I don't trust you and I think I better put my guard back up" she thought as she looked out the window and then reached over and turned on the radio. She knew a lot about herself and the one thing Gina trusted was her feeling about people she knew if she doubted Peter there had to be a reason and she wanted to find out what it was. She had learned early in her life to follow her mind when it came to uneasy feelings. She looked over at Peter and he smiled and then blew at a car which cut him off. Gina wondered what was going on and swore she would find out she wasn't about to let Peter burn her.

When she saw Patrick he told her he couldn't be sure but he could have sworn he saw Peter with another woman when she was out of town. Gina looked at him and asked what was he talking about. He told her he was on a stakeout at the airport and he could have sworn he saw Peter and a woman with a hat on. He couldn't recognize the woman because of the hat. Gina told him not to let Peter know that and he laughed "I don't talk to Peter only you." Patrick told her like always he would keep an eye on her back. "Gina I don't trust Peter and if I find out he's trying to set you up you know I will eliminate him I won't let anyone hurt you." Gina smiled and reached over and kissed Patrick and told him that was why he was her only friend. Friendship meant a lot to Gina especially since she had so few people in her life. A hit woman had to be more careful than a man for she could be easily destroyed if recognized.

It was three weeks before Gina danced again at the club. Peter had been having a really bad week with the police raiding his numbers spot and having to get his boys out of jail. He looked like he had lost his best friend. Gina thought it would cheer him up if business at the club picked up but it didn't. He was busy trying to figure out how he was going to get the money replaced that he had lost and make his turn in account. Delano was furious that he hadn't picked up the money that morning like he was suppose to. Peter told Gina he had been stuck at the club and by the time he got to the shop the police raid squad was there and he was left holding the bag.

Lately the police seem to be cracking down on the number runners and spots and Peter said he felt like getting out of it before he couldn't. Gina looked at Peter while he talked but she knew he was lying to her and she wondered what he had been doing that was so important that he would not pick up the money. She looked at Peter and smiled and then she once again got that feeling that he could not be trusted. He took her over to the house then told her he would see her at the club later and took off. Gina watched him round the curb and wondered where he had been earlier if he wasn't picking up the money. The police had picked up over two hundred thousand and she knew that he had to make it good.

Gina came into the club and Peter and Delano were in the back office talking they were so loud that Gina didn't bother to knock on the door. She had brought this costume and she knew that it would set the men off. She went and talked to the DJ and told him what she had up. The dancer which was on stage wasn't really stirring up the men and the barmaid said they weren't buying drinks they were nursing them. Gina hoped her plan would work she went backstage to the dressing room and got ready. She heard the music her signal from the DJ that Peter and Delano were out front and she heard the DJ announce her.

"Gentlemen tonight we are going to get the tiger and the tail. Get your money ready men and prepare for a feast" he started the music and Peter looked at him and raised his eyebrow.

Gina stuck her leg out first and then did a flip out onto the stage. The men stood up and started clapping as she jumped up on the pole and twirled down to the floor. She crawled over to the customer sitting by the stage and slowly stood up swaying her hips and motioning him to come closer. Suddenly she popped the strap on her bra revealing her full breasts and the men started coming up to the stage to tip her. Gina bumped and grind then turned and shook her behind to the music. She grabbed the pole and twirled around and did a split to the floor and crawl to another customer.

The place was jumping men offering to buy her drinks and wanting her to do private dances for them. When Gina walked off the stage to go to the dressing room she felt someone grab her and turned it was Delano he asked for a private dance. She looked at Peter and he smiled and nodded and she told him she would be right out. Peter came into the dressing room while she was changing he stood watching her and smiling. "Well young lady I see that you can still upset my customers" he pulled her to him and kissed her. "But did I make a smile come to your face?" She asked as she returned his kisses.

Peter told her smile wasn't all she had made happen but if she could get Delano off his back she would see how grateful he was tonight when they went home. Gina winked and went out the door and back into the club. Delano had ordered a bottle of champagne and she sat down and took the glass from him. He smiled and told her he didn't know she could dance and he was waiting for his own private dance. Gina grabbed the bottle of champagne and then poured it over her breasts and he smiled and she told him to follow her to the VIP room.

The costume she had on was sheer and the champagne made it see through. You could see every inch of her once inside the room Delano pulled her to him and she smiled "these are the rules I can touch you but you can't touch me agreed? Delano laughed and sat down on the chair and shook his head in agreement. Gina walked over to the music system and turned it up and then turned and poured the bottle of champagne over her and Delano lit a joint and offered it to her. She took it and after a few draws she turned and gave him a shotgun of smoke. She then reached into his pocket where he kept the case with the cocaine and pulled it out and took a few hits.

Delano sat there watching her she was beautiful and she floated down the pole like an angel. She walked over and started dancing in front of him and he reached for her and she shook her finger at him then sat down on his lap. He was so hard it felt like it was going to bust through the zipper. She began to slowly grind and dance on top of him and when she grabbed his shoulders he couldn't help but grab her ass and stroke with her before he knew it he had climax and Gina did a backwards flip and stood up. She reached over and kissed him on the cheek and whispered "lay off Peter and I might consider you having more."

Delano pulled her to him and kissed her then told her to quit fucking with his mind. Gina laughed and turned to leave the room "Is that what I'm doing?" She winked and went downstairs to Peter who was sitting at the bar. She whispered in his ear "he got off like a firecracker and he didn't even touch gold." Peter laughed and pulled her to him and told her to do a few dances for the customers. When Delano came downstairs he looked at Peter and then at Gina dancing for one of the customers. He signaled Peter to come to him and told him he had to go get cleaned up and that he would meet him down at Ted's Restaurant after the club closed "do me a favor bring Gina with you."

Peter turned and winked at Gina as she danced for customer after customer making each man feel like he was the only one in the room. She was good he hadn't seen the club so alive since it had opened. Gina had did just what he wanted he had taken Delano's mind off of him for a moment, but Peter knew that business was something that Delano didn't let go of easily.

Peter told her she was upsetting the other dancers and she laughed and went and changed into her street clothes. One of the girls named Renee walked up to her and bump Gina into the locker. Gina turned and looked at her then smiled "Renee you don't even want to go there with me okay?" she strapped her gun to her thigh and Renee looked and backed off. Gina was just about to walk out the door when she turned and knocked Renee down to the floor "next time you push me it'll be your last."

Gina opened the dressing room door and walked out. Peter was standing in the hallway and asked what had happen Gina turned and told him she had to help someone understand she wasn't a toy. Peter shook his head and laughed and then told Gail the barmaid to make sure the place was tight he was leaving.

Jeff the bouncer told him he would lock up and meet him in the morning and Peter told Doc to pick up the money and pick up the tip out for him. "Make sure Renee doesn't get a break tonight" he opened the door for Gina and she went out and he squeezed her behind. "Damn I'm glad this is mine" he winked and she ran to the car and jumped on the hood "take me I'm yours." Peter laughed and told her to get into the car before they got a ticket. He turned and told her he had forgotten something inside the club and he would be right back out. Peter went into the club and looked around then went into the dressing room and closed the door. When he came out Renee was sitting on the bench with her head in her hands. Peter told Doc that he had taken care of Renee and to get the tip out from the rest of the girls and then left the club.

They were on their way down to Ted's to meet Delano when Peter asked what had happen up in the VIP room. Gina told him about the dance and the fact Delano got off. Peter didn't say anything at first then she reached over and stroked his cheek and told him to stop the car. She climbed over on his lap and started kissing him and whispered "he can only think about it baby you can feel it." Peter kissed her passionately and then told her to get back over in the passenger seat before they both got arrested for indecent conduct in public. Gina laughed and climbed back over and grabbed his hand and put into her panties and he fingered her all the way to the restaurant.

When he parked the car he pulled her to him and kissed her and told her he loved her. Gina opened the door and got out and straighten her dress and gave her hair a quick fluff. "Come on let's go see how Delano is acting now" they both laughed and went inside the restaurant.

They had finished eating and Peter's beeper went off and he got up to go make a call. Delano looked over at Gina and smiled then bowed his head. "What's this I know you're not shy?" Gina reached across the table and took his hand into hers. "Did I please you tonight?" Delano took her hand away and told her she knew very well she had pleased him. The only thing, which would make him happier, was if she would let him truly make love to her. Gina told him that anything was possible but right now she was with Peter and she only dealt with one man at a time. "Peter's a lucky man. I didn't realize how lucky until tonight. Will you come visit me in New York soon?" Gina looked at him and said she would but she didn't know when.

Delano looked at her like he wanted to tell her something but Peter came back to the table and reached down and kissed her and told her he had to go take care of something.

He asked Delano to make sure she got home okay for him and turned and left. They didn't talk much on the way to the house but once there Gina invited him in for a drink. "Not this time baby, Gina you know I care about you do me a favor don't tease me so hard it hurts." Gina looked over at Delano and could tell he was telling the truth. "Maybe it was for me to see that you really cared" Gina paused and looked at Delano she reached over and pulled him to her and kissed him passionately on the lips. "Good night Delano" she whispered as she got out of the car and went into the house. Delano watched her go inside and shook his head then drove off.

When Peter got in she was in the bed and he hurried and took off his clothes and climbed inside with her. She woke up and smiled at the hard on and turned and climbed on top of him and started grinding as he held on to her buttocks and screamed in ecstasy and climaxed. He pulled her down on his chest and whispered "I love you" as they drifted off to sleep. Gina wondered why she didn't believe him and what was it that he had been doing. He had been gone for nearly six hours and she knew all the business he had was usually over by then. What was Peter up to she had to find out and soon.

Delano came into the hotel room and sat down on the bed and took off his jacket. He sat there thinking about Gina and how she made him feel inside when she danced for him. Strange he never use to care whether a woman was in his life or not now suddenly he was filled with this desire to have Gina by his side. He respected the fact she was loyal to her man and she didn't sleep around. It was a rare luxury to find a woman now days that was faithful and let their real feelings show through. He got up and walked over to the bar and poured himself a drink and slowly sipped it. She had asked him to back off Peter and the fact he was considering it made him know that she had affected his life in more ways than one.

Peter and he had been friends since college and he respected him for his business flair and how he handled the money end of his business. Peter had been making some costly mistakes lately and Delano felt sure that it was time to move him on to another project before something happen. They had hustled the streets and the drug world for over fifteen years and Delano was thinking of closing down shop and possibly going into the export business. Money wasn't an issue with him he had nearly a quarter of a million in his checking account and he was well off when it came to securities and bonds yet the drug money and number money had been his personal baby and he had profited from it.

He sat down and thought of Gina's full lips and the sweet hourglass figure she had and smiled. He realized the danger, he was in by falling for her yet he couldn't help himself. Gina was the kind of woman a man wanted and dreamed about. She was good with a gun in fact she was the best he had seen come man or woman. She was beautiful and yet there was something about her that gave off a quality of sincerity, which seem to draw him closer each time he was with her.

Peter would never let her go for him to even think he could compete for her was ridiculous and yet he found himself doing exactly that. He was trying to take Gina from him and Peter had warned him that he would fight for her.

Delano remembered the last time they had fought and he didn't welcome the thought of coming up against Peter especially over Gina. He thought back to when she was dancing in the VIP room for him. The way she looked at him and held on to his shoulders as she rode him to a climax. Just the thought of it excited him she looked so sincere when she was dancing for him. The fire between them was real and he knew she felt something for him but was it enough that she would leave Peter and come and be with him? Or was it?

Peter had warned him that if he took Gina from him their friendship and business arrangement would end. He would have nothing to do with him and Delano didn't like the thought of losing his friendship yet he couldn't no matter what he did get Gina off his mind. He finished the drink and lit a joint and sat there smoking it and laughed when he thought of Gina giving him the shotgun and the way her lips felt on his cheek. He got up and went to take a shower and decided that he would let fate pick the cards for him. Somehow Delano knew before it was over he would have Gina in his arms. He had known Peter too long and he knew something was up with him. Gina was a good woman and she was valuable but Peter had been treating her short and Delano knew when it came to Peter that meant trouble.

Delano was about to go back to New York when he got the phone call there was trouble down at the club. He hurried and got in the car and drove over to see what was going on. When he got there the police were just coming out of the club. He looked in the back seats of the cars and they had no one he noticed Gina's car in the parking lot and pulled up next to it. Where was Peter was he inside the club where was his car? Delano waited till the last cop car pulled off then got out and went inside to find out what had happen. Gina was sitting in the back booth her head was down on the table and she was crying. Delano walked up to her and pulled her up into his arms and looked at her. She had a bruise on her face and he asked what had happen and told the barmaid to bring some ice for her face.

Gina explained they came to search the place and that Peter had just left to take the money to the deposit box. He had only been gone a few minutes when the police came in with warrants to search the place. She had gotten smart with one of the cops and he had slapped her. Delano listened and got angry as she explained how they had ram shack the office looking for evidence of drugs or lottery tickets. She told him they were very sure that drugs were in the bar and had searched and nearly destroyed the place. Delano told the barmaid to put a rush on the towel with ice in it and he put it on her cheek and told her to sit down. He walked behind the bar and made Gina's drink in a tall glass and brought it to her. After she had drank it and settled down he asked where was Peter it didn't take that long to make a drop off. Gina explained he had to take care of some other business before he was to come back to the club and take her to lunch.

Delano walked over to the phone and put 911 in Peter's pager and waited for him to call back. Peter was back to the club in twenty minutes he came in and looked at the mess the police had made and then looked at Gina. His face said it all when he saw the bruise on her cheek. "What the hell happen?" He asked as he took her into his arms and she laid her head on his shoulder. "Gina what did I tell you if the police come in you were to let them search baby, there is nothing here that can hurt me." He looked at her swollen cheek and then looked at Delano he nodded for him to go into the office and told Gina to sit still until he came out.

Delano and him were arguing over why he left Gina her at the club alone and unprotected. "Gina's my woman and she can take care of herself!" Peter shouted at Delano "you're fucking out of line checking me about her." Peter walked over to the bar and poured himself a drink and downed it. Delano looked at him and then opened the office door and went outside and looked at Gina. She looked hurt and he pulled her up into his arms and kissed her on the forehead. "From this point on you're never to be without protection do you understand?" He looked into Gina's eyes and she shook her head yes and then went into the office with Peter. Delano had given her what she needed...security and a peace. She found she was beginning to depend on. What was it about him that made her so secure? Questions but no answers.

He was pouring himself another drink and looked up at her. "Come here baby" he said as he held out his arms and she came over and leaned her head on his chest and whispered "I'm sorry I fucked up didn't I?" Gina looked at Peter and she didn't think he really cared about her having a bruise face. Peter looked at her and smiled "No baby you didn't fuck up I did I left you alone and Delano is right. I just got angry that I didn't think about it first that's all."

He kissed her and then told her to go get cleaned up and they would go get something to eat. Gina told him she didn't want to go anywhere with her face all bruised up but Peter insisted she not worry about it and told her to go get ready. He called a couple of contractor friends and told them he needed the bar back together and ready for operation by tonight. He had a large crowd coming in and he wasn't about to lose any money over the bullshit. Gina stood in the restroom mirror and looked at her face it really wasn't as bad as it felt. She thought of how the officer had hit her like a man, she hadn't thought he would touch her. Why hadn't Patrick warned her they would be coming in to raid the place? She put on some make up and then went back out front Peter and Delano were talking and she walked up to Peter and kissed him and told him she would be back in a few minutes.

"Where the hell you going Gina?" Peter looked at her and grabbed her arm and pulled her back to him. "I need to go find Patrick and find out what happen here today." Peter looked at Delano and he told him to leave her alone she knew what she was doing. Delano took Gina to the side and asked who was Patrick and she told him and he told her they were going with her. He told her he could not leave her unprotected and that he didn't trust Peter to take care of her anymore. Gina looked at him as he

47

talked to her about Patrick and she listen to him question Peter about where he really was. Gina knew Delano was right about everything as they went to the car to get inside she took Delano's hand and said thank you.

She sat in the back seat as they got inside Delano looked at her and told her to think about what he said to her. Once again he told her it might put Patrick in danger if they were watching him they might have figured out that Patrick was the one warning them of the raids. Was Delano right could Patrick be in danger? She thought back to how long she had been friends with him. Way before he had become a police officer they had been running buddies. Patrick fell in love with her when she was with Miguel and they had pledged to watch each other's back till death. She knew nothing would stop him from helping her stay out of trouble and suddenly she was worried about him. She asked Peter to pull over at a phone and she got out and dialed his pager and waited for him to call her. An hour went by before she got a call back from him. Peter pulled the car over and Gina went to the payphone and called the number. "Gina are you all right? I heard about the raid but it was too late for me to do anything." Gina explained that the officer named Daniels had hit her because she was mouthing off at him. "He hit you? Where are you? I'll be there in ten minutes." Gina told him where she was and he told her to stay put until he got there. "Peter's with me Patrick and his friend Delano are you sure you want to be seen with us?" Patrick told her he would be there in a few minutes for them to go to Belle Isle and wait for him at the water fountain.

When Patrick pulled up Gina got out of the car and walked over to him. He looked at her face and then took her into his arms and kissed her. "Damn baby Daniels will be sorry he touched you. I am so sorry I didn't get a chance to warn you about them coming forgive me?" He looked at Gina and she smiled "I thought something had happen to you or maybe Delano was right that they were on to you about warning us" she laid her head on his shoulder and he whispered something in her ear and she reached up and kissed him.

Peter and Delano watched Gina talking to Patrick and neither one of them said anything for a while. "How long has she known him Peter?" Delano asked as he lit a cigarette and blew out the smoke. "All her life they are extremely close as you can see." Peter sat there watching Patrick then watched as he got back into his car and drove off. Gina came back to the car and got in and looked over at Peter and then Delano. "What did he say Gina?" Peter asked as he reached into the glove department and lifted up the hidden tray and took out a joint and lit it. "He was on another case when he found out about the raid. It was too late for him to do anything about getting in touch with me. He said that Daniels would regret hitting me he's very angry about the fact he struck me."

Delano listen to them talking and then told Peter to go to the restaurant he was hungry. Gina passed the joint back to him and looked into his eyes "Patrick is my friend Delano he has been my protector since I was nineteen. He would never betray me. He will get Daniels for hitting me trust me Daniels will pay for it." Delano nodded his head and then asked her what he had whispered to her. "You're dipping now aren't you?" She winked at him and smiled "I think your true colors are shining through." Delano laughed and told Peter to hurry up and get him to the restaurant before his mouth got him into trouble.

Peter laughed and they headed out of the park when they turned on Jefferson Street to head down to Fishbone's Restaurant they saw Patrick had pulled someone over and had them spread against the car. Gina watched him as he searched the guy and then noticed that there was another man with him. Where had his partner been when he had come to talk to her? Peter and Delano had the same thought as she did and no one said anything the rest of the way to the restaurant. When Peter went to use the phone Delano looked at him and Gina asked what was the matter. Delano looked at her then smiled "Gina I will never let anyone hurt you now I have fallen in love with you. I'm laying it on the line now do you hear me the choice is yours to make. I don't think Peter has your back baby do you understand me? Gina looked at him she saw Peter coming back and she smiled and told him she felt the same way.

Delano looked at her and he reached over and took her hand into his "Gina I'm going to send my own boy to watch over you." Peter walked up to the table and hit his hand and told him to let her go. Delano looked at him but he didn't let Gina hand go until he was ready.

When he got back to the hotel Delano called his best friend Thomas and told him to come to the house right away but to let his woman know that he was leaving town. "Do what you have to I have a special favor to ask you to do for me I need your help Thomas." He had told Thomas about Gina and said if anything happen to Gina then he should make sure the same happen to him. She was to be watched twenty four hours a day. Delano meant it there would be no room for a slip up. He wanted him on a plane as soon as they had a chance to talk that he was leaving for the airport now and would be back in New York before night.

Delano asked Gina to take him to the airport and Peter told her to come to the club after she had dropped him off. He admitted that he felt safer knowing Gina had a bodyguard now and reached inside the car and kissed her then went into the club. Delano had a private plane waiting for him over at City Airport. He told Gina that she was to keep the bodyguard and that he would miss her. Gina looked at him and smiled "Delano you are letting your feelings for me show through. Peter is angry about the fact we are getting to be friends I think he feels threaten."

Delano looked over at her as the car pulled into the airport parking lot "does he have a reason to feel threaten Gina?" He turned and looked at her and Gina smiled "no, but I can't deny there is something between us." Delano smiled and reached over and kissed her on the lips and got out of the car and headed to the plane. Then he ran back to her and pulled her up into his arms and looked her in the eye. "Gina listen to me I'm sending my best friend here baby to watch over you, but there is something you should know about him. He knows Peter very well and he's coming here to find out what the fuck is up baby. I know Peter is up to something and I can't figure it out. I am trusting you to believe in me honey, because I love you for real and for some reason I think he's using you. Do you trust me Gina?

Gina looked at him and then said yes she trusted him and then she reached up and kissed him for real and he looked into her eyes and ran and got on the plane. It felt strange having someone driving her around now. Delano had told Peter to get a limo and to make sure it had bullet proof windows. Gina felt they were fussing over her too much but she wouldn't fight them on the issue. She looked at her watch she had promised to meet Patrick at Elias Brothers at five. She told the driver to take her there she was in the mood for dessert. "What's your name by the way?" She asked him as he looked in the rearview mirror at her.

"I'm Thomas" he said as he drove down the street. "Thomas I won't be in there but a few minutes how does this work do you come inside with me?" Thomas told her that he was her shallow wherever she went he had to be around her in case something jumped off. "Do you report back to Peter or Delano?" Gina asked him he waited a few minutes then said Delano.

When they pulled up in front of Elias Brothers Patrick was standing by the car smoking a cigarette. He smiled when she walked over to him and asked who her shallow was. She told him she had a bodyguard now he was working for Delano and it was for her protection. Patrick looked at him then smiled and took her inside and they got a booth towards the back by the restroom. "Listen to me Gina they are going to raid the club again only this time they plan of trying to get Peter with the money. The Feds are going after him for tax invasion that's all I've been able to find out right now. I don't think you have anything to worry about though because I didn't see your name anywhere in the computer or in the files."

Gina looked over at Patrick he looked worried "what's the matter Patrick I know that look." He told her that he felt Daniels was on to him and that he was going to have to find a way to keep in touch without them meeting in public anymore after today. He handed her a cell phone and told her that from now on they would communicate by cell unless he told her otherwise.

"Are you sure you're okay? I don't want anything to happen to you." Gina looked at Patrick and he reached over and stroked her cheek and smiled "It's nice to know that you're still my girl baby." Gina looked at him he hadn't call her his girl in a long time. Patrick told her to get up and leave before him and to pick up two Strawberry Pies and have the waitress but it on his tab.

Gina smiled he still remembered she liked the Strawberry pies from Elias Brothers. She thought back to the time they had the pie fight and she had beamed him in the eye with the tray. He must have been thinking the same thing because he pulled her down to him and kissed her. "I got to go pick my partner up he's waiting for me down at Foot Locker's, Gina be careful baby tell Peter I said I will let him know what I can find out as soon as possible, Gina I think you should know that I did see Peter with a woman. I checked the tapes baby and I couldn't make out her face but I know it wasn't you because you were out of town."

Gina smiled and headed to the door then ran back and threw her arms around him and kissed him. "I love you" she whispered as she turned and walked up to the counter and picked up the two pies and left. Patrick watched the bodyguard get up and follow her back to the car and open the door for her. He liked Delano's style he knew that Peter had another woman and he didn't want to hurt Gina and tell her the whole truth. He wished he could but he knew her she loved hard and got hurt just as hard and he couldn't stand to be the one to put her in that kind of pain. Was Delano going to be good for Gina? Was this what she had been waiting on all this time? Gina needed someone to love her, She needed more than that she needed the protection of the angels.

It would have surprised the men to learn that Gina had so much faith in God and she was regretting ever beginning this life she had chosen. She felt that it was all coming to an end now she wanted to know when and would she survive it?

Chapter Three

Gina sat there holding the pies in her lap then she looked up at Thomas and asked him did he have to report everything she did back to Delano. Thomas looked in the rearview mirror and smiled "not everything but damn near" he looked at her as she turned and looked out of the window. "I want to go home and shower and change before you take me to the club" she said as she cracked the window and let the air blow her hair. Thomas looked in the rearview mirror at her she was really beautiful he understood why Delano wanted her watched.

Nearly three weeks went by before the police and Feds came and raided the club again. This time Patrick had gotten a chance to warn Gina ahead of time and they were able to get everything out of the club into the safe house before they arrived. The Feds were pressing Peter and he didn't feel comfortable with Gina around him he wanted to keep her clean and out of harm's way. He agreed to let her go stay with Delano in New York for a few weeks until he could reroute his money and reset up his business. He stood at the airport and looked at her and smiled "Delano is happy you're coming I'm quite sure he'll take good care of you. Gina be careful don't fall in love with him he's trouble and that's with a capitol T."

Gina looked at him if he knew that Delano and she were developing feelings for each other then why send her to him? She couldn't figure Peter at times she told him she would be careful and then went to get on the plane. Gina had a worried look on her face and Thomas asked her could he help with anything. She looked at him and told him that if she asked him something would he answer her truthfully and he looked at her and told him she could ask him anything and he would always answer the truth. "If I have to lie I won't say anything at all" Gina what is bothering you so much. Is it Peter or Delano?" Gina looked at him and then said Peter she thought he was not telling the truth about something and she thought it had something to do with her and that scared her. Thomas looked at her and didn't say anything for a while then he turned and looked her in the eye. "If I were you I would put my trust in Delano have I answered the question which I know you are thinking Gina?" She looked at him and smiled then she went and got in line to board the plane.

Thomas was two seats behind her on the plane and he smiled when she turned to see where he was. Thomas and she had developed a friendship over the last couple of weeks and she trusted him. When they arrived in New York Delano met the plane with a limo and told Thomas to get in the front. He whispered something to him and he nodded and then when they got to the house he left with the chauffeur to do whatever Delano had asked him. Gina walked inside and looked around she liked Delano's place it had real class but there was something about the living room which sent chills up her spine when she came into it. She noticed a picture on the mantel over the fireplace and walked over and picked it up.

Delano walked up behind her and smiled "It's my father Ricardo he's dead now he was shot in a drive by a few years ago." Delano took the picture and put it back on the mantel. Gina once again looked at the picture she swore she thought the man looked like Peter but how could that be? She went to turn and felt a chill again and she went and picked up her jacket and put it on. Delano asked her did she want to do anything special tonight. Gina told him she didn't know much about New York and would love to go clubbing if it was all right with him. Delano laughed he said it had been a while since he actually went club hopping but he thought it was a good idea.

"I need to leave for a while but when I come back we'll kick out a few steps." He reached over and kissed Gina on the cheek and smiled "I'm happy you're here Gina I hope we can become friends while you are here with me." Gina looked at him as he put his coat on and smiled "I thought we were friends Delano don't you mean lovers." Delano turned and looked at her and laughed and told her to look in the guest bedroom he had left something special there for her. Gina went up to the bedroom and looked at the box on the bed. She laughed when she saw he had left her gun and holster sitting next to it. Gina didn't feel whole without her gun on her thigh and she wondered how he knew.

Gina grew up in Brightmoor it's a rough area of Detroit where bullets fly and young boys die every minute. She learned early in life to protect herself and she didn't let anyone take her for granted. Most of her family was dead now except for a few cousins and she had lost track of them over the years. Gina hadn't thought much of family she had been abused and knew that her life was shit. She had gotten angry one night at her father's friend when he touched her and went into his closet and picked up the gun and came out into the room and shot him. She remembered him lying on the floor in the blood and how happy she felt that he would not ever touch her again. She had taken the gun and walked out of the house and when she came back two days later they told her someone had killed him. Gina figured she didn't need to tell them it was her, but she was sure that the police thought she might have done it she had to be very careful from then on. She sat down and picked up the box and open it and laughed it was a pale blue mini dress with a jacket. Gina held it up to her and smiled as she went to go take a shower and prepare for their evening out.

When Delano walked into the house Gina was walking down the staircase he stopped and looked at her. Thomas smiled when he came in the door and saw her and nodded in approval. "Damn girl I don't think I'm going to have enough protection for your fine ass tonight." They laughed and he told her he would be ready in a few minutes. He handed Gina a gold case and told her to sit back and relax while he got ready. Gina went and sat by the fireplace and opened the case and took a few hits of the cocaine and then offered it to Thomas. He told her he had to keep his head clear tonight that Delano wouldn't approve of it. "You really look breath taking tonight I don't think I have ever seen you look more beautiful." Gina smiled and thanked Thomas and then lit the joint and smoked it while she was waiting for Delano.

Thomas turned to go out in the hall when he suddenly turned back and asked Gina had she called Peter. "No I don't want to talk to him yet why should I?" Thomas looked at her and said no "go and find out what you know already is true Gina." He winked and then turned and walked out of the room and Gina wondered how he knew that she was thinking of changing men and picking Delano. Delano had gone and put on a matching blue suit and she had to admit he looked fine. He had let his hair hang down and she found herself suddenly turned on and embarrassed. "What's the matter?" He asked as he took her hand and they headed for the limo.

"Nothing let's just say I am enjoying your company okay?" She turned and looked at him and he smiled. Gina was floating and she looked beautiful as she danced on the floor with him. She flirted and played the whole evening as they went from club to club dancing and having fun. "Let's go salsa!" She said as she ran to the limo and threw her arms around Thomas and gave him a kiss on the cheek. Delano looked at her so relaxed and beautiful and wanted to tell her never to leave him again. He wanted her so bad that it hurt to think she might leave him again. The thought of it must have shown through on his face because Gina walked back and grabbed his hand and pulled him towards the limo.

Delano told Thomas to take them to the club and told Gina they were going to stop and get something to eat afterwards. The club was packed and Thomas found a spot at the bar while they went out on the dance floor. The drummer remembered Gina and smiled and started kicking out a beat on the drum. Gina smiled and started dancing in front of him moving her hips from side to side to the beat. Delano smiled as they danced and watched the men watching her. She was alive with the music as she moved across the floor and swayed her hips. She surprised him when she flipped over and landed in his arms with her legs wrapped around his waist. She laid her neck back and her hair fell gently across her shoulders towards the floor and he held on to her as he twirled her around.

"Are you having fun teasing me tonight?" Delano looked at her and smiled and Gina kissed him "more fun than you'll ever know." She got down and took his hand and told him she was ready to go eat. Gina looked at Delano and she knew she wanted him and that there was no way she could control the feelings she had inside of her. She felt something inside of her each time she touched him and she knew that tonight if he wanted her she could not resist him. Delano took her to an exclusive restaurant and the head waiter smiled when he saw him and escorted him to his table. "Mr. Delano, are you having your regular tonight?" He asked as he signaled the waiter to come to him. Delano told him to bring the best bottle of champagne they had he was celebrating something special. Gina smiled "what are we celebrating?" She asked as she took a sip of the water and looked over at him. "Us Gina. I know that you feel what I feel now and it's no way that I can let you go, you know that don't you?"

Delano quit talking as the waiter brought the champagne and opened it. Gina laughed and sat back and watched him he seem different tonight more confident and secure about her. Gina wondered if he was right as she toasted the glass and winked at him. By the time they got back to the house Gina was on cloud nine. It wasn't the wine or the drugs that was doing it she felt something inside of her and she liked the feeling. Gina knew she was falling for Delano and she knew that he felt the same way she could feel him inside of her heart. She paraded around the room laughing and teasing Delano until he finally pulled her to him and kissed her.

Gina stood still and looked at him she wasn't sure what to do she didn't know she had so strong sexual feelings for Delano until that last kiss. She looked at him and ran upstairs to her bedroom and closed the door. "Damn!" She thought why the hell had she agreed to come here with Delano? Hadn't she realized that she would want him if they spent time together? She looked in the mirror and stared at her reflection then took off her clothes and ran and got into the shower. She hadn't heard Delano come into the room he looked around at the clothes laying on the floor and then took off his clothes and went into the bathroom. When he open the shower stall Gina jumped and fell back against the wall.

"No more playing Gina I want you" he reached over and pulled her to him and kissed her. Gina fought him at first but gave in to his kisses and found herself passionately kissing him and searching his mouth with her tongue. Delano had her pressed against the shower wall he reached down started touching her and Gina moaned and relaxed as he began to make love to her. She screamed out in pleasure as he brought her to a climax and then turned her around and started kissing her back. Delano was biting and sucking on her neck and Gina was feeling new emotions as he worked his way to a climax again. When they had finished she opened her eyes and looked at Delano tears were running down her face.

"What's the matter I didn't please you?" He looked concern as he stroked her hair back out of her face. "I didn't mean for it to happen how am I to face Peter now" she fell back into the water and Delano pulled her to him and kissed her forehead "Come here don't cry baby it had to happen sooner or later. We feel something for each other you know that by how we made love to each other." Delano looked into her eyes and kissed her and told her to get out of the shower and come into the bedroom he wanted to talk to her.

When Gina came into the bedroom Delano was sitting on the bed smoking a cigarette. He looked up at her and then back at the floor he didn't say anything for a few minutes. "Gina I'm sorry I feel like I shouldn't have touched you now. Baby I couldn't help myself I wanted you so bad I couldn't help myself." He looked at her and she sat down next to him and stroked his hair. "It's not your fault it's mine for teasing you and losing control." She reached over and picked up the tray and sniffed the cocaine then sat the tray down and walked over to the counter and picked up the brush and started brushing her hair.

Delano walked up behind her and turned her around and looked at her she was so beautiful and he could feel the pain she was in now and he couldn't stand it. "I'll talk to you in the morning go to sleep now" he kissed her on the forehead and picked up his clothes from off the floor and left the room. Gina stood looking at her reflection in the mirror it was the first time she had ever cheated on her man before. She climbed into bed and pulled the covers up over her and tried to go to sleep she couldn't she wanted Delano. Gina got out of bed and walked over to the door and opened it. Delano was coming down the hall towards her room. They didn't speak she ran into his arms and he picked her up and carried back into the bedroom and made love to her.

The next morning when Gina woke up Delano was gone he had left a note for her to call Peter and told her that if she wanted to know the truth he really loved her. And that he would not let her leave him, but she would have to face Peter and let him know the truth about them. He told her he would stand with her because from that day on they were one. Gina looked at the note and held it up to her heart and she felt a chill go straight through her. Gina froze she didn't know how she would be able to keep it from Peter. She smoked two joints and drunk a glass of brandy then picked up the phone and called Peter. He asked how she was and she said fine then the phone went quiet. "Gina I don't want to know about it so don't tell me do you understand?" Gina said yes and then got quiet again he told her he was having a lot of problems and that she might have to stay with Delano longer than he expected.

"Gina, promise me something, when I call for you to come home you'll not think about it, but get on a plane and head back to me." Gina didn't say anything she listened as he talked and wondered how in the hell would she be able to face him. "Gina I love you, and it doesn't matter whatever you do, I will still love you. I can't stand the fact that Delano is falling in love with you. I only pray I can get things straighten out here before he steals you from me." Peter laughed and told her he missed that wicked sense of humor of hers and her body next to him at night. Gina could only think of Delano she listened to Peter talking but she hardly heard him her mind kept thinking of Delano's words. They talked for a while longer then she hung up and went and sat down by the fire.

Thomas came into the room and asked her if she was okay. She looked up at him and started crying and he walked over and put his arms around her. "Gina trust me when I say this to you, Delano really cares for you he has never had a woman here in this house other than my sister and she's dead. He's my partner and my friend and I consider you my friend now" he pulled her chin up and looked into her eyes "relax baby and just enjoy the time you have with him. He's going to send you back to Peter I know him he won't take you like that from him." Gina looked at Thomas there was something about his voice that made her understand that all this was planned in some kind of way. She looked at him and smiled and he laughed "see there's that million dollar smile of yours" he kissed her on the forehead and went back out into the lobby and sat down and picked up the paper and started reading it.

Delano came back about a half an hour later with a dozen of red roses and some white orchids. He handed them to her and asked had she had breakfast yet "the maid and cook will be here in a few minutes I'll have them prepare something special for us." He looked over at her and then asked had she called Peter and was everything all right. "He said I might have to stay here longer than he had planned and that he would call you later." She looked at Delano as he stood by the fire poking it with the poker and stirring up the flame. "Gina I wanted..." Before he could say anything else Gina walked up to him and put her finger to his lips. "Don't say anything okay I don't want to regret what we did." Gina reached up and kissed him on the lips and he laughed and told her to go to the kitchen and get a bottle of champagne and bring it to him. "Look inside the back on the second shelf and bring me the strawberries too." Gina went to do what he said and as she walked past Thomas he smiled and winked at her.

When she came back into the room the maid and the cook were both coming in. Delano gave them instructions and told them to bring the breakfast up to his room. He grabbed Gina by the arm and picked up the champagne and she grabbed the strawberries and they rushed up the stairs. "Hey what's the rush" she asked as they got upstairs and he popped the cork on the champagne. He poured both of them a glass full and then took a couple of strawberries and placed them in her mouth and told her to sip the champagne while she chewed them. "Hum..." Gina liked the flavor the strawberries brought out of the wine. Delano laughed and told her to come look at something he open the doors to the balcony. It was beautiful he had the balcony full of flowers and statues and there was a small table and two chairs.

"Come on we'll have breakfast out here today" He grabbed Gina's hand and pulled her to him and poured the champagne down her throat slowly then put a strawberry in his mouth and kissed her as she bit off a piece. The butler brought the tray in and sat the food down and asked would there be anything else he wanted before he returned downstairs. Delano told him to bring up another bottle of champagne and some more strawberries. Gina laughed Delano was definitely different from Peter she wondered why Peter had let her come here with him? Delano picked Gina up and carried her to his bed and laid her down and began to place strawberries all over her. She started laughing as he nibbled and ate each one off her then he poured champagne over her and started licking and sucking up the wine off her body. She was lost in a wave of emotions and uncontrollable feelings as he began to make love to her.

Later that day they went to Central Park and he took her sightseeing and shopping. When they got back to the house the butler told him that Peter had been calling. Delano went to the phone and called him and after a few minutes hung up. He didn't say anything and Gina knew something was wrong she walked up to him and asked what was the matter.

Delano turned and smiled and said nothing "hey go put on the dress I brought you I want to see you in it." Gina said okay and ran up the stairs to change she knew that Delano was not telling her something and wondered what he was protecting her from? Thomas walked up to Delano and laid his hand on his shoulder "what did he say?" Delano told him Peter had threatened him "he told me if I hurt Gina it would be the end of our relationship but I swear I heard a woman laughing in the back ground." Thomas looked at him and then he laughed and went back into the hallway and Delano came and looked at him. "You know don't you that I'm in love with her" he asked as he lit a cigarette.

Thomas looked at his friend and smiled "don't let it bother you I think she's feeling the same thing. Let nature take its course don't rush it. If it was meant to be nothing can keep the two of you apart not even Peter." Delano smiled and went back into the living room and sat by the fire but the look on his face was concern. Peter had meant what he said he would not let him have Gina one of them would die before he let it happen. Delano hadn't noticed Gina coming into the room he was lost in thought. She walked over and stood in front of him and he smiled. "You look beautiful how about going to the ballet tonight with me?" Gina told him she had never been she wasn't sure she would like it.

Delano laughed "you'll love it let me go get ready the show starts in about an hour and we can stop afterwards and get a bite to eat before coming in."

He stood to leave the room and Gina looked at him. "Is everything all right with Peter, Delano?" He looked at her and smiled "yes he's quite his old self these days. Peter is just fine trust me."

She sat down and picked up a joint and lit it and blew out the smoke she felt someone staring at her and turned and Thomas was standing in the doorway. He smiled and told her she looked beautiful "Gina do me a favor" Gina looked at him and told him she would if she could "Gina be careful Delano is not as strong as you think he is not when it comes to love and affairs of the heart. I don't want to see him get hurt. Promise me you'll be careful with him." Gina looked at Thomas she didn't see Delano as a weak man in anything but she promise she would be careful not to hurt him. Thomas didn't leave the room and she asked him again was there something else. Thomas smiled and walked over to her and pulled her to him and kissed her on the forehead. "I'll say this much since you been around things sure are different around here." Gina laughed "I hope that's good because the last thing I want is to cause trouble." Thomas winked and went back out front and started talking to the maid about putting fresh flowers in the rooms upstairs.

It had been a while since Thomas had seen Delano so happy not since his sister had been killed four years ago in a drive by. He wondered if he should tell Gina but changed his mind and went to find Delano and see if there was anything special he wanted him to do before they left. Delano was sitting on the bed when Thomas walked in "what up? I know that look Delano talk to me." Delano looked at Thomas and shook his head "maybe I should send her back tonight before I can't let her go." Thomas talked to him about what he was feeling and then walked over to the door "Delano she was my sister I know how much you loved her and what you went through when you lost her. Don't confuse the two women they are nothing alike Gina loves life and she brings joy to your heart. Trust me my friend Gina is the best medicine in the world for you right now." Delano smiled he knew that Gina was what he had planned for with the angels. He asked for their help and his reply had been Gina.

Delano looked at Thomas and smiled and told him to let Gina know he'll be right down. He walked over to the dresser and looked at his reflection he never thought he would have feelings like this for a woman again. He didn't know how he was going to be able to let Gina go back to Detroit. Peter would not give her up and the more he stayed with her the more he felt himself falling in love with her. Then Delano thought about the voice of the woman laughing in the background. He knew he had not been mistaken and he wondered if Peter was up to his old games again. Gina would get hurt if he was and Delano knew if he hurt Gina that he would kill him. He thought of the promise he had made his father about Peter and he picked up a bottle of cologne and then he put some on and then went downstairs.

Gina was in the living room dancing and didn't see him watching her. "I like the way you shake it up" he said as he entered the room and Gina turned and smiled. "You look very handsome tonight do you really think I'll like the ballet?" Delano walked up to her and kissed her on the forehead then smiled and picked up the fur jacket and put it around her shoulders. "I think you'll love it come on let's get out of here before I want to take you upstairs."

Delano was right Gina loved the ballet she sat in amazement as she watched the dancers perform. Delano smiled as he watched her open her mind to something new she was like a child so open and willing to learn and experience life. When they left the theatre he asked her what she wanted to eat. Gina smiled and said she felt like some soul food and he told her he had the perfect place. He took her to a restaurant in Harlem that he hadn't been to in quite a while. When he told Thomas where they were going he smiled and said "don't forget I'm out here starving man."

When Delano walked in with Gina everyone got quiet and looked at them. Gina didn't understand why everyone was looking at them just then the owner came from the back and threw his arms around Delano. "Delano it's been so long since you come here. I am so happy to see you're getting out again." The man looked at Gina and smiled "I'm Dave and welcome to my home away from home" he extended his hand to Gina and kissed hers. Gina smiled and then followed him and Delano back to a booth in the back.

It wasn't like the expensive restaurants he had taken her before. This place was simple down to earth there were pictures on the walls of famous people who had eaten there. Gina smiled when she saw the picture of him and Delano she wondered who the woman was with him. Delano saw her looking at the picture but didn't remark on it. The owner came out with two plates of food Gina smiled when she saw the Ham hocks and greens, there was fried corn and okra and corn bread and candied yams. Gina sat there and ate all of it and then laid back on the seat and rubbed her stomach. Delano laughed he liked seeing her happy "how about some dessert Dave serves the best banana pudding in the state." Gina told him she didn't think she could fit another bite in her stomach but could she get some for later. He got up and went over and talked to Dave and she watched him laughing and joking with him.

When they came out of the restaurant Delano handed Thomas a plate of food and winked "thought I forgot didn't you?" Thomas laughed and told him thanks and asked where they were headed. Delano told him to just cruise for a while he would let him know in a minute. Gina loved New York and the people it was always something going on and yet there were spots that were so quiet and private. She looked over at Delano and smiled she hadn't felt this comfortable around him since they had met. She wanted to know more about him and why he seemed so different and quiet at times.

Delano picked up her hand and kissed it gently and asked if she would mind very much if they just went home and sat by the fire. Gina smiled and told him she loved it and he told Thomas to head home. After they were inside the house Delano told Thomas he could take off and that he would see him in the morning. Thomas looked at Gina and smiled then told them to have a good night. Thomas called Delano out into the hallway and told him to relax and enjoy Gina and not to let the shit about Peter ruin their time together. "I have a feeling that Gina is turning to you Delano that is what you want isn't it?" he looked at Delano and then walked to the door and open it. "Have a good night my friend I'll see you in the morning."

Gina sat down in front of the fireplace on the floor and looked at the flames. Delano came and sat by her and laid his head in her lap and she gently stroked his hair. "Delano who was the woman in the picture at the restaurant? The two of you looked so happy." Delano didn't say anything she looked at the expression on his face and knew it was the wrong subject to bring up. He looked up at her with tears in his eyes and said her name was Dianna; she was Thomas sister and my fiancé. She was shot two weeks before we were to be married by a rival of mine."

Gina put her finger to his lips and told him to hush she could tell it was hurting him to talk about her. He turned and buried his head in her lap and wept. Gina held him close and let him get it out of his system then she reached down and turned his face up to hers and gently kissed him on the lips. "I'm sorry I should have never asked you about her I didn't know." Delano looked at her and smiled then reached up and kissed her "Gina I know its seems crazy but I think I should send you back to Peter before I find myself unable to." Gina looked at him she showed no emotion at all she didn't want to go back not right now she was just beginning to enjoy herself and there was something about Delano which made her want to know more about him. "I'll go back if that's what you want but I would like to stay" she looked down at him and stroked his hair.

"Do you realize I'm falling in love with you?" Gina looked at him and smiled "Let's just say we're getting to know each other right now. Delano I don't want to hurt you I do love Peter but I can't help the way I feel about you. Something is happening between us and I just want to make sure before I make a decision as to what I am going to do. Will you give me time to figure things out?" She looked into his eyes and he smiled and pulled her close and kissed her passionately. "Gina I swear I don't know what to do about us I haven't felt like this in so long." Gina reached down and started unbuttoning his shirt and started stroking his chest "Delano make love to me I want you" she reached down and started kissing him as she removed his clothes. Delano took off her clothes and looked at her she seem to glow in the light of the fire. He stood and picked her up into his arms and went back into the study to the Jacuzzi and sat her inside and climbed in with her. "Come here" he said as he pulled her over on top of him. Gina smiled and grabbed hold to his shoulders and he started caressing her breasts. He gently kissed Gina laid her back in the water and she let him make love to her as the water beat against their bodies. She sat up and grabbed his shoulders right as he climax "Gina" he whispered "Gina my precious Gina I can't let you go." Gina looked at him and she knew that she could not leave him she didn't know how they would do it but somehow they had to stay together.

After Delano had drifted off to sleep Gina slipped out of bed and went downstairs and sat in front of the fire. What was happening to her? Didn't she love Peter wasn't it their plan to stay together and now all of a sudden she was feeling all these emotions for Delano. She felt like he was right maybe she should go back to Detroit before anything else happen between them. She hadn't realized she was crying until she felt Delano standing beside her. He sat down and pulled her close and leaned his head on hers and kissed her forehead. "Baby we're in trouble somebody's going to get hurt no matter what we do." Gina looked at him she felt so confused inside and she wanted to run away but something kept her there.

Delano promised he would not touch her again until she was sure what she wanted. Each day they spent time exploring New York and at night she climbed into bed with him and he held her tightly in his arms. They talked about everything and Gina had never been so happy in her entire life. Delano told her he wanted to do something special for her and asked was it anything she wanted. Gina looked him in the eyes and told him she wanted to be his.

Delano pulled her to him and kissed her "Gina if I tell you something I heard will you think about it? Gina looked at him and said yes "Gina the other night when Peter called I swear I heard a woman laughing in the background. I know Peter better than you do and I want you to know that he can't always be trusted. Gina I don't want to let him hurt you I'm afraid I'll kill him."

Gina looked at him and told him she knew something about Peter she should tell him. Patrick had seen him with a woman the last time she was here and that they were very friendly, and she had seen scratches on his back but she hadn't told him she had seen them. Delano looked at her and told her that from that moment on she was his woman and that he was going to come to Detroit but it had to be done his way. He needed to check something out before he came to her.

"I'm sending Thomas to watch over you baby because I know Peter and he is up to something." Delano made love to Gina that night and for the first time in a long time she felt truly loved. The rest of the week she stayed close by his side until it was time for her to go back to Detroit and Peter. Delano told her not to worry because if Thomas as much as thought he was spitting wrong he would deal with him. "Baby I promise I'll bring you back home with me everything will be alright trust me okay?" He looked into Gina's eyes and she told him she would trust him and for him not to leave her there without him too long.

Peter called and told Gina to come home and Delano took her to the airport. "I'm sending Thomas back with you he can handle Peter if he gets out of line. I'll miss you because I can't stand being without you now" he reached over and kissed her and Gina threw her arms around him and hugged him tightly. "It'll be all right baby go to Peter and if you need me call me. I won't be coming to Detroit for a while I have a lot of business here I need to take care of." Delano started to walk away and Gina ran after him and turned him around and passionately kissed him. "Gina get on the plane before I change my mind. Please baby just get on the plane." He turned and walked quickly out of the terminal to his car.

Gina sat there staring out at the clouds she didn't know how she would react to Peter. Thomas sat next to her on the plane he had been quiet up until he saw her crying and then he reached over and pulled her to him. "Gina there is something you should know I might be wrong in telling you but I feel you need to know. Delano is sending you back to Peter because he threaten to kill him if he didn't he didn't want you to leave. I have been friends with both of them for years and when my sister got killed I thought Delano would lose his mind. Gina you make him happy and I think he makes you happy, if I'm right you will have to find a way to leave Peter and he will try to hurt you because he can't stand to lose to Delano. I have a feeling someone is going to get hurt and I have to make sure it isn't you."

Gina looked at Thomas and smiled "Thomas I don't know what I am feeling for Peter right now. I won't let Peter hurt Delano something will work out it has too." She laid her head on his shoulder and whispered "Thomas I think I want to go back to Delano." Thomas told her she could not go back he had made him promise to make sure she went to Detroit, and not come back until he came to get her. Thomas held her all the way back to Detroit and Gina cried the whole time.

Peter knew right away something was wrong he looked at Thomas and then told Gina to get into the car. "Why did he send you back with her?" Thomas told him to relax that he was there to watch over her. "I can take care of Gina all by myself I don't want you here." He walked around to get into the car and Thomas stopped him and turned him around "Delano wants her watched and you'll not pressure her Peter. Don't make me check you man you know I will if I have to." Peter looked at him and rolled his eyes there had been a time when he and Thomas had been best friends. Peter had fallen in love with Thomas woman and had taken her from him but after a few months she left him and went back to New York. Thomas had never forgiven him for breaking them up.

When Delano fell in love with Thomas sister Dianna he had tried to take her from Delano. Peter knew that Delano had fallen for his plan and he couldn't let Gina see the joy in his face. He looked at Gina and then turned on the radio he knew it was too late Gina was different she hadn't even tried to kiss him. Suddenly he pulled over to the side of the expressway and pulled her to him and kissed her. "Fuck Gina! I'll kill that bitch for what he's done." Gina turned and snapped at him "you listen to me Peter whether I stay with you or leave is up to me. No one makes my mind up but me, so you can drop that fucking threat in the toilet because if anything happens to my Delano I swear you'll lose me all together along with your life. Peter if you touch him you're touching me and so help me as I sit here I telling you that it will be the end of you." She turned and looked out the window then glance back to make sure Thomas was behind them she rolled window down and held out her hand with the thumb down. Thomas speeded up the car and got on the side of Peter and blew the horn and Peter turned and he looked at him and then Thomas let him get back in front of him. For the first time since she had been with Peter she was afraid of him. When they pulled up in front of the house Peter got out and slammed the door. Gina went to get out and then froze she wasn't sure she wanted to go into the house with Peter. He was so angry and bitter at her for defending Delano and threatening him.

Peter walked over to the door and opened it and Gina got out and started walking towards the house. When Thomas got out of the car Peter turned and told him it wasn't necessary for him to go inside he could go and get a hotel room. Thomas looked at Gina and he could tell she was scared. "Come on man its late I don't want to look for a room I'll camp out on the sofa." Peter said fuck it and went inside the house and Gina turned and looked at Thomas then went inside after him. Thomas had seen Peter's temper before and he knew he had a problem with beating his women up especially those he could not control. Gina had been lucky so far that he hadn't hit her and he was worried that Peter was flipping out, because Peter now knew that Gina was Delano's woman.

Gina told Peter she was going to take a shower and she would see him in the bedroom. Peter walked over to the bar and poured himself a drink and then looked at Thomas. "What the fuck is going on? "Gina's different and I know damn well it has something to do with Delano." What he do tell her about me?" Peter was angry he was yelling at Thomas and arguing with him about the fact Delano was taking Gina from him. "Shit man I love her and he's not going to take her." Thomas looked over at him and shook his head "Listen to me Peter you and Delano have been through a lot. Gina has no ideal about you and him she thinks that all this is her fault. What will you do if Gina decides she wants to be with Delano? Peter you know it's her choice."

He looked over at Peter who was now standing at the bar staring out into space. "I know I have always tried to take Delano's women but this time I am in love and I am not willing to let go of her. Thomas does Delano love Gina?" Thomas told him he wasn't sure what Delano was feeling but that they were close. "Shit man if she finds out that I am the reason your sister got killed I think she'll go to him." Thomas looked at him he still had bad feeling about what happen in New York that weekend. Dianna was dating Peter and they traded off one weekend at a party and she fell in love with Delano. Peter started a fight with one of Delano's rivals and shot up his house and in retaliation they shot up Delano's place. Dianna didn't stand a chance she was shot through the head. Delano nearly went out of his mind he really loved Dianna and they had planned on getting married. Peter was jealous and wanted to hurt him but he didn't mean for Dianna to get killed or did he? Thomas had never been certain. By the time everything cleared and the truth came out Delano wanted to kill Peter but he couldn't once he saw what Dianna's death had done to him. They both had suffered and lost too much with her death. Peter had gone back to Detroit and open up shop and Delano stayed in New York.

Thomas looked at him now suffering and he couldn't help but wonder if he was suffering over Gina or the fact that Gina might be in love with Delano. Thomas told Peter that Delano had put Gina on the plane and had promise her he wouldn't pressure her "Are you willing to do the same for her Peter? Do you love her enough to let her decide who she wants to be with?" Peter looked at him then poured another drink and down it. "Peter I know you threaten to kill Delano he told me what you said. I won't let the two of you kill each other and I telling you now that I won't let you hurt Gina." Peter looked at him he knew Thomas meant what he said and he didn't feel like carrying the conversation any further. "I'm going to be with my woman I'll see you in the morning."

As Peter walked by Thomas stood up and warned him again that he had better not hurt Gina. Gina was just coming out of the shower when he walked into the room and sat down on the bed. "Come here Gina we need to talk." Gina walked over and sat down next to him "Peter I'm tired and confused I really don't feel up to talking. Peter why did you let me go to New York you knew Delano had feelings for me and that I liked him. Why did you let me go there?" Peter looked at her and shook his head and then pulled her to him "it doesn't matter now you're home and in time I think I can make you forget about Delano. Gina do you still love me?" Gina told him she loved him but she didn't know if she was in love with him. "Please Peter let's not talk tonight I really am not in any shape to talk about this, I don't want you to get angry you're frightening me with how you're looking at me." Peter pulled her to him and kissed her and Gina return his kiss but the fire wasn't there. "Gina make love to me tonight." Gina looked at him it was the first time in ages that she didn't want to make love. She climbed on top of him and went through the motions but her heart wasn't in it.

When Peter went to sleep she got up and went into the shower and scrubbed her skin so hard she turned red. She then went into the living room Thomas was watching television and asked her was she all right. "Thomas I want to go back to New York but I'm afraid of what will happen when I tell Peter." Thomas looked at her he realize she was hurting inside and he wanted to help "Gina follow your heart baby, I won't let Peter hurt you or Delano he knows that. Gina has Peter ever hit you before?" Thomas looked at Gina and she seemed surprise that he asked her the question. "No he's never had why did you ask me that?" Thomas told Gina that Peter had a bad temper that he use to beat up on women and especially those he couldn't control anymore.

"He's never done anything but showed me love Thomas but tonight in the car coming here I felt like he could have hurt me." Thomas walked over and hugged her and told her to go back to bed and get some rest. "Thomas has Peter ever kill a woman before?" Thomas looked at her then turned and walked over to the bar and poured himself a drink "Gina my sister is dead because of Peter and that crazy temper of his." He took the drink and down it and poured himself another one and walked over to the sofa and sat down. "Go to bed Gina I don't feel like talking right now." Gina walked over to him and kissed him and told him she would see him in the morning. When she climbed into bed with Peter she and looked at him.

Strange he was the reason for the pain Delano had in his heart and she now knew that he was dangerous. She didn't know Peter at all and she wondered whether he would kill her. Gina reached for her gun and put it under her pillow she could feel trouble coming and she wasn't sure this time if she could handle it. The next morning Gina called Patrick and told him she needed to see him that it was important. They met at Elmo's Restaurant Gina looked across the booth at him. Patrick reached over and took her hand and asked her what was the matter. Gina told him she needed him to find out about someone who had gotten killed in New York a few years back. She wasn't sure of when the girl had gotten shot up but it was in a gang hit on a house own by Delano on Lexington Avenue.

Patrick looked at her then told her he knew all about it Delano best friend sister had been shot through the head. Delano had almost gone crazy he found out that the reason his sister got killed was because of some shit Peter had started with one of the gangs there. Peter had fronted off one of the dealers and had slept with his woman it was some game they played with each other him and Delano when they were younger and Peter took the game too far." Patrick looked at Gina and he saw she was worried "Gina Peter is a dangerous man I thought you knew how dangerous he was. You mean he never told you why he came to Detroit?" Gina looked at him and shook her head "no he's never told me any of this shit. You're telling me that they played a game with women and that something went wrong and Peter got someone killed. I just don't understand it why Delano didn't tell me?"

Patrick told her that Delano was a major drug dealer at one time and that he fell in love with a friend's sister and that they were to be married. Peter had slept with the girl and some fight happen between them and Delano had won. Peter went and slept with Gomate's woman and all hell broke loose. Gomate's thought that Delano had Peter do it and he wanted justice so he ordered the hit on the house and Dianna was sitting in the living room when they shot the place up. "Why the hell are they still friends then I don't understand this kind of shit." Patrick said it had something to do with a pack they made in college or something. Delano took the heat and Peter came to Detroit and the Feds have been trying to pull him down now for years but he keeps out smarting them. "Gina you realize that Peter was known for beating his women to a pulp. I thought you knew all this about him what are you going to do now?"

Patrick looked at Gina and he could tell she was scared he hadn't seen her like that in a long time. "Gina are you in trouble?" Gina told him that she wanted to leave Peter and go be with Delano but Delano had made her come back to Peter and had sent Thomas to watch over her. Patrick lit a cigarette and then blew out the smoke "Thomas was Dianna's brother and he stopped Delano from killing Peter. It was just a boyish prank gone wrong Gina. It's the kind of thing rich kids do." Gina looked at him "what is it you're not telling me Patrick I need to know everything now." Patrick told her that their father's had all been in business together and they were bad little rich boys getting away with murder up until Dianna death. The family's split up the business and Peter came to Detroit and started up here. Dianna was one beautiful woman from what I hear she was madly in love with Delano. Some people say that Peter deliberately did it so that Delano would suffer. He doesn't like losing Gina he has a habit of getting rid of things before he loses them." Gina didn't say anything she was trying to soak it all in.

Were Delano and Peter playing a game with her? Patrick told her to be careful that he didn't want to lose her and that Peter had been on the warpath since she had been away. "What do you mean?" Patrick told her he had shot up three drug houses and that they knew he was behind it only they couldn't find anyone to confirm it. "Gina walk away if you can Thomas is there to protect you Delano has never let Thomas leave his side he's been his bodyguard for over ten years. Delano must be worried that Peter is going to hurt you." Gina stood up and put her jacket on and walked to the door of the restaurant then went back to the table.

"Patrick I need you to find out something for me find out whether or not Peter has ordered a hit on Delano. If he is as crazy as you say I think he might have done something foolish this morning. I heard him on the phone talking to someone about taking care of something that was in his way." Patrick looked worried "Gina be careful. Don't let Peter know I told you anything you're safe from his temper as long as he thinks he has you in the dark." Gina promised she would be safe then turned and left the restaurant. She went to the club and Peter was there Thomas came in and sat down at the bar. Peter asked where she had been. "I had an errand to run I was planning on surprising you but it didn't work out." Gina walked over to Thomas and then turned and looked at Peter. He looked at her and she smiled "I feel like dancing is it okay?" Peter smiled and told her to go get change the lunch crowd would be coming in soon. Gina signaled for Thomas to come with her and as they walked to the dressing room he and asked what was the matter. "Check on Delano. Tell him he might be in trouble please Thomas do it now." Thomas looked at her then went to the phone booth. When she came out on the stage he was gone. Peter was talking to some customers and smiled when he saw her and winked.

Gina started dancing but all the while she kept her eye on Peter. More than ever now she needed to pay attention to him and what he was doing.

Thomas came back after a couple of hours and told her that Delano was okay and he already knew what was up and for her not to worry. "Gina he told me to tell you he loved you and for you to do what you had to stay safe. He was coming to town to settle the matter between him and Peter once and for all." Gina looked at Thomas and saw Peter walking over "honest Thomas I think that the dress will be fine for the show." Peter walked up and pulled Gina to him and kissed her and she pulled away and looked at him. Thomas went and sat down and started watching the other dancers. Thomas was worried Delano had told him that one of his contacts had heard that Peter was looking for a special hit man. Gina was safe as long as Peter didn't realize that she knew he was dangerous.

Gina had fell in love with the charming side of Peter the one he seldom let people see. Thomas had seen him in action and he worried about what his friend was planning in his head. Thomas loved Peter but he would kill him if he turned back to his old ways. He liked Gina she was real people fresh and true and so open to life. She trusted from the heart and with Peter that was a dangerous thing to do.

They had all been born back in the sixties their families had moved to New York and started selling drugs. They became rich very fast but Peter's father had died suddenly and left Peter in the care of Ricardo, Delano's father. Delano's father was a stockbroker and invested the money he made into stock and securities. He brought a lot of real estate and sold it for twice its value. He had a nose for business and he sent Delano and Peter to a boarding school in England so they could learn and get acquainted with the rich and their customs. He wanted his son to follow in his footsteps and had made Delano promise on his deathbed to take care of the business and told him to stop selling drugs and to use his mind to make money like he did. He had promised Peter's father, his best friend, that he would see to it that Peter had the best on his death bed. When Peter's father had jumped in front of him and taken a bullet meant for him. Ricardo took Peter and began to care and protect him as his own. He made Delano promise to look out for Peter and to never hurt him up to now Delano had kept his word.

Peter was a cruel and vindictive young man in college. He had so much hate in him he would go after virgins and deflower them and then toss them aside. He had a temper that often would explode when a woman was trying to get away from him. Peter had nearly chocked a young girl to death because she didn't want any part of him. He liked fooling women and destroying them and he had cost Dianna her life only because of his stupidity. Delano had tried to kill him but he heard the words of his father on his death bed saying he was to protect him and keep in out of harm's way. It was the hardest thing Delano had ever done ...

let Peter live. He told him to go back to Detroit and gave him a hundred thousand dollars to set up business there. Delano watched him and when he got out of line he pulled him back to safety. Thomas had befriended both of the men in college but the bond between him and Delano had grown stronger than with Peter. He and Delano had become a team and Peter hated Thomas for coming in between their friendship. When Thomas found out why the house had been hit he went after Peter and they fought and Delano pulled Thomas up and had a gun pointed at Peter's head. He told him he would kill him if he ever hurt another woman or caused a death such as Dianna. Peter had laughed and told them he would start anew and that he had never meant for Dianna to get killed. Dianna was not supposed to be there that night she was suppose to be gone to a ballet show but she hadn't felt well and had stayed at her Delano's and was waiting for him to come home. Delano had been having problems with some of the men trying to take his territory and they had been in a truce for over two weeks before the shooting. Peter had dated Dianna back in college and she told him he was not the man she wanted to spend her life with and chose to be with Delano. Peter had become furious and when he heard of the engagement he went out on a drinking binge and turned up at a party Gomate was having for his crew. Gomate and Peter were friends at one time so he never thought Peter would do anything to hurt him.

Peter had been drinking pretty hard and he took Gomate's girl, Trina, into an alley and pushed her into a car and had beaten and raped her. Trina had bleed to death by the time Gomate found her he had his boys found out who was behind her death. His boys found out Peter worked for Delano and assumed that Delano was paying him back for wrecking one of his houses and killing one of his best boys. The hit was ordered on Delano and when the boys came they shot over one hundred rounds into the house and Dianna had gotten shot in the head. It made all the papers and news circuits that a grizzly killing had taken the life of a young girl and the aftermath was the killing of a beautiful twenty-two year old graduate student.

When Peter sobered up the next day he had blood all over his clothes and he showered and changed and came to the house as always when he saw the bullet holes and found out that Dianna had died he went crazy. Thomas sat there watching him now at the club and he knew that Peter was up to something. Peter wanted Gina and he was going to try to get rid of Delano. Thomas was worried he wasn't there to protect his friend but Delano had made him promise to keep an eye on Peter and make sure he didn't hurt Gina. He had given his word that he would protect her even if it meant his life. Delano didn't want anyone to know he was coming to town he was coming to take Gina back to New York with him. If he were right Peter would have him killed before he could get there and he didn't want anything to happen to Gina.

Delano had hired three bodyguards and he felt he was safe for now his only concern he told Thomas was with Gina. Thomas looked up at the stage at Gina dancing she was really good she could stir a crowd of men up and have them dropping the money faster than any dancer he had ever seen. He watched Peter watching her it was something about his eyes that let Thomas know that Peter was up to something. When Gina walked off stage Peter grabbed her and said something which caused her to jerk away her arm and run into the dressing room. Gina sat down on the bench and laid her head in her lap. None of this made any sense to her she had thought she had fallen in love with a man who was kind and gentle. He had never showed any anger towards her until recently and she was afraid she would shoot him. Gina realized now that she had been used.

Peter needed her for getting rid of trouble but even worst she felt he needed her to get rid of Delano. Gina had been raised in a rough area and had fallen in love with a hit man. He taught her everything he knew and had taken her on jobs with him. She was good she never left a trace of her other than the scent of lavender. The police had no idea she was a hit woman she learned that from Patrick. When she had gotten with Peter she had just left a bad relationship with a guy who promise her the world and gave her nothing. She had been struggling to survive in a world where crime was her friend she thought he loved her and she had been true to him. Twice she had saved his life and now she felt he was going to hurt her and it frighten her.

Gina would not let a man hit her it was her only weakness she would kill before she let anyone beat her again. Why hadn't she seen through Peter? As she thought back now over their relationship it all became clear why he had chose her for his mate. It had nothing to do with love it was all some kind of game he was playing. He wanted her before someone else got her and he thought giving her riches would make her his. Gina didn't think much of material things she knew from way back that material things didn't last they wear out and soon disappear. She got up and put on her clothes and went back out front to the bar. When she came out Peter pulled her to him and looked at her.

Gina wasn't afraid of him she was hurt and disappointed that he was not the man she had thought him to be. Peter went to kiss her and she turned her cheek and he raised his hand to hit her and Thomas caught it and smiled. "Now Peter what the hell do you think you're doing?" Peter laughed and told him to fuck off that if he wanted to knock the hell out of his woman he would and not even he could stop him. "Don't try me Peter I swear I'll kill you this time."

Peter looked at Thomas and then pushed past him and went and started talking to one of the customers. Gina looked at Thomas she thanked him but told him she could handle Peter she was not afraid of him. "Gina if something happens to you Delano will go crazy. Please be careful." Gina told him not to worry but to continue to watch her back. She walked up to Peter and put her arms around him and started laughing with the customer. Peter seem to settle down as the night went on Gina had calmed him down and was doing something Thomas could tell. Gina was smart as well as beautiful and he knew she was in control of things now. She no longer cared what Peter wanted but she would stay there until Delano came for her. She watched him laughing and a chill went up her spine. She looked over at the bar at Thomas and smiled then went back up on the stage and started dancing. Thomas watched Peter he knew that he was up to something and he also knew that he wanted to hurt Gina. He had to be careful not to lose track of him because if something happen to Gina he knew Delano would go crazy.

Patrick called Gina the next day and told her to come to Belle Isle and to hurry it was important he couldn't talk on the phone and he only had a few minutes. Gina met him at the fountain and he pulled her to him "Listen to me Peter isn't after Delano I found out that he's looking for someone to hit you." Gina looked at him she had been right Peter had decided to have her killed. Patrick warned her that the hit man was in town and that he had gray hair. He got him from out west that his contact had told him that he was an expert target and that he used a scope. "Where is Thomas at? Gina pointed to the side of the road and he told her to get into his police car and that he would drive her over to him. Peter got out and talked to Thomas he told him what he had found out and told him to take care of Gina he had been looking for the guy but hadn't been able to find him. The only thing they knew was that he was in Detroit now and that he had been paid a hundred thousand to eliminate a problem. Gina started weeping she couldn't believe in her heart that someone she had loved and cherish would order a hit on her. Thomas told him the car was bullet proof and that he was going to give Gina a bulletproof vest to wear.

Gina looked at them talking and then Patrick rushed over to the side of the car and reached in and kissed her. "I have always loved you baby girl don't take any chances stay close to Thomas." Gina told him she would and then they left the island and headed back towards the house. Gina was half way there then told Thomas to stop the car he pulled over to the side and she looked at him. "Where did your sister get killed at?" In the house where Delano and her had planned on living in right?" Thomas told her yes and asked what was she thinking. "He's going to take me the same way. He wants to hurt Delano and what better way than to have the woman he is in love with die the same way as the first one. Peter has a warp way of thinking he always would make me go and wait to do a hit. He likes the element of surprise I told him I was going home and would be waiting for him there. He showed no emotion this morning he simply kissed me good bye and smiled. It was something about the smile Thomas I know I'm right the killer is waiting for me at the house."

Thomas sat there for a while then picked up his cell phone and called Delano and told him what Gina thought and he said to take her to the airport and wait in the bar until he got there. He should be landing in town in about twenty minutes. He asked to speak to Gina and Thomas handed her the phone "Gina listen to me I think you're right and I want you to go the airport. There is too much security there and he can't hurt you inside the terminal. Whatever you do don't let Peter know where you are baby I'm on my way. Do you believe I love you?" Gina told him yes and that she thought she was in love with him. "I can take care of myself Delano I am not afraid of Peter."

Delano told her it wasn't Peter that he was worried about and that he needed her safe for his plan to work. "Gina I know you don't like having anyone tell you what to do but this time baby I need you to listen to me. Let me and Thomas handle this one give me your word right now baby so I can have peace in my soul and do what I must do to save you." Gina looked over at Thomas and then she told Delano she would do what he wanted "Delano please come and get me I love you and I want to be by your side." Gina handed the phone back to Thomas and turned and looked out the window. Thomas listen to what Delano wanted him to do and then put the phone down. He turned and looked at Gina and then touched her hand and smiled "Gina don't worry Delano won't get hurt and neither will you do you trust us? Gina looked at him and she felt lightheaded and she told him to stop the car and she opened the door and leaned out and threw up. Thomas looked at her and she didn't look right Gina told him she was okay, and to do what Delano had asked him to do with her. Thomas told her he needed to talk to Patrick and she called him on the cell phone and handed the phone to Thomas. Thomas told Patrick he needed to meet with him and that he had to be sure no one knew they were talking. He told him what they expected to do and that it all had to be timed just right. Patrick told him he would meet him over at the fountain at Belle Isle and that he hoped that what they were planning would work he didn't want anything to happen to Gina. Thomas told him that Gina would be safe that Delano was seeing to that right now and that he would explain it to him later when they met.

Once Delano got to the airport he brought a plane ticket for Mexico and told Gina to get on the plane and to go to the address once she arrived. The men are expecting you and you are to stay there until I come for you." He took Gina into his arms and kissed her passionately then took her to the boarding line. "Gina I love you no matter what happens remember that you made me feel whole and that I do so much love you." He kissed her again and she boarded the plane and sat at the window and watched him and Thomas hurry and get into a limo and drive off.

Delano had a plan he hoped it would work and that Peter would be taken off guard. Thomas and he pulled up into the lot of the club and Peter was just coming out of the door and saw them. He seemed shock to see them and then walked up and greeted them. "Hey why didn't you tell me you were coming? Gina and I could have planned something special for you." Delano walked up on Peter and looked him in the eye. "Go back inside the club and be careful not to make a false move Peter. Where is Gina?" Delano asked him and Peter said she had gone shopping and he thought Thomas was with her.

Thomas said he had lost her at the shopping center and then he had gotten a call to pick up Delano and when they went back to where he had left Gina she was gone." Peter looked at them and smiled "what's all the concern Gina's a big girl she can take care of herself pretty damn well." He had a smirk on his face and Delano reached over and pulled him to him and looked him in the eyes. "I asked you where the hell was Gina and you're giving me bullshit." He pushed Peter back against the wall and Thomas pulled his gun and pointed it at him.

Peter looked at Delano and laughed it's too late now he thought for him to do anything about it. He had told the hit man to clip her as she went inside the house if he couldn't have her no one would. Delano looked at him and told him to tell him what the fuck he had done. "Whatever I've done it's too late for you or your boy here to do anything about it now." Peter reached over and picked up a bottle of brandy and down it. Delano looked at Thomas and then back at Peter "you didn't have her killed tell me you didn't have her killed!" He shouted as he went and grabbed Peter.

Peter was pretty high he said he did what he had to do and that he didn't want to talk about it. Delano slugged him and knocked him to the floor and went and stood over him. "Peter get the fuck up right now and tell me what the hell you have done." Peter was so drunk that he couldn't talk and Delano knocked him back down to the floor. Then he and Thomas left the club and Delano put plan two into action. He had a woman who looked a lot like Gina from the back go to the house and act like she was opening the door. The woman had agreed to do it she had been on schedule to go to court on a case that she knew she was going to get life for. Delano had promise to take care of her son and raise him out of the world of crime and she had agreed to be Gina and take whatever happen as justice for what she had done.

Delano and Thomas headed out to the house in Livonia and prayed the plan would work. When they got to the house the police had the place surrounded Patrick had figured it out and had got the killer but not before he had shot the woman in the head. Her face had been totally blown off and Patrick was in tears he was kneeling over the woman holding her. Thomas walked up and the police grabbed him and Patrick told them to let them through. Delano told Patrick to come inside the house he had something he couldn't say out in the open to him. "Listen to me Patrick that's not Gina out there on the porch. Do you hear me that's not Gina but we can't let Peter know it's not her. We have to make sure he thinks she is dead or else he'll order another contract on her life." Patrick pulled him in the bathroom and told him to explain what the fuck was going on he turned on the water and listen as Delano told him what they had done. Patrick asked him where Gina was and he said that only he and Thomas knew and that he would not tell him. "Patrick I love Gina and I am going to marry her. I cannot let this plan fail we must act like we have lost the love of our life and mean it. Do you understand? Delano had never felt this form of fear before; his desperate need was to have Patrick understand and accept what he had done.

Patrick told him that he appreciated him telling him the truth and that he had his back as well as Gina's. When he came out of the bathroom he was no longer crying but angry. Peter pulled up in the car and jumped out and ran and picked the woman up into his arms. "Gina oh God they shot Gina!" He was putting on a really good act. The police were comforting him and brought him inside the house and sat him down. Delano walked up to Peter and hit him so hard that he flew over the chair and landed against the wall. Thomas looked at him with hatred and Patrick swore he would get him for what he had done. "What do you mean I just got here it could have been me lying there?" He went over to the bar and grabbed a bottle of whiskey and started downing it.

Delano fell into the chair and Peter looked at him He thought he had won the battle. The plan had worked he was sure it was Gina lying out there on the ground. Patrick hugged Delano and Thomas then walked outside to finish the investigation he had to make sure that no one noticed that the woman didn't have on a charm bracelet. Gina never took it off it had been a gift to her from her mother before she died. Peter was drunk and hadn't noticed the bracelet wasn't on her wrist yet. The paramedics were zipping up the body bag and Delano screamed out in pain. Peter stood there watching him and for a brief minute smiled then went back to crying.

Patrick went and brought a bracelet similar to the one Gina wore and place it on the table with the articles that they had taken off of her. The plan had worked at least for now they had to get the woman in the ground and pray Peter accepted the death. Delano and Thomas took a room at the Courtyard Hotel and stayed there inside the room for three days until the day of the funeral. When Delano showed up he looked grief stricken and Peter watched him walk up to the casket and lean on it. The look on his face was enough for Patrick to shoot him he was now looking into something that he felt would be the end of all the shit between the two men. He had to make sure that Gina was safe she would be too far for him to protect now. The shooter had not talked and was in custody of the Feds.

Patrick walked up to Peter and put his arms around him "We've lost our girl Peter we've lost Gina" he hugged him and then went and sat down and wept tears of relief that the plan had worked. Delano had set a plan in motion he wanted Peter to pay for what he had tried to do. Peter would not ever get the chance to ever hurt Gina again Delano looked at Thomas and then bowed his head and cried tears of relief.

Chapter Four

It had been a month now since they had buried the woman who was supposed to be Gina. Patrick was not on speaking terms with Peter he told him he held him responsible. Delano and Thomas had gone back to New York and Peter felt very cocky about pulling it off. He laughed as he saw Delano and Thomas plane take off and had gone out partying that night. Delano had him being watched every minute of the day he wanted to know if he as much coughed. The young boy's name was Diamond and he had kept his word to his mother. He sent the boy to England to one of the top boarding schools and had set up a trust fund for him to be given to him on his twenty first birthday.

He couldn't go to Mexico to be with Gina yet she was being taken care of by one of his friends from college named Pedro. When he called him to check on her Pedro said she was sad and that she was very uncomfortable around them. "The only thing she does my friend is go to the chapel and light candles and pray. I listen once to her man she praying about the lives she has taken and she is telling God to make it right for what is to come." Pedro told him that Gina knew something that no one else knew for he had heard her with the priest and he told her that she would get her wish and that he and God now knew the truth and he would never tell anyone.   Pedro asked did he have any idea what she was doing. Delano told him to put her on the phone and Gina listened as he told her what they had done and how it had worked so far. "Gina I can't come to you yet not until I know you are no longer in any danger. I love you baby and I want you to do me a favor I want you to find something to do that will keep you happy until I can come be by your side." Gina listened then she told him there was something she thought she had better tell him. "Delano … I'm pregnant. I'm three months so I can't be certain if it's yours or Peter's."

Delano didn't say anything for a long time then he told her that she was to consider the baby his and that he would find a way to come and see her. "Gina I love you the news about the baby makes me happy do you understand me?" Gina smiled and told him she loved him too and the hardest thing she had ever had to do was to stay away from him. "Gina until we are certain Peter won't hurt you again Pedro's is the safest place for you. Don't worry I'll be with you soon and baby I know it's real what is between us. Take care of our child for I know in my heart its mine and yours, he comes from the love of our hearts baby don't doubt that I love you ever." They spoke a few more minutes then he told her to give Pedro back the phone.

He told Pedro to make sure his wife knew Gina was pregnant and to take care of her and his child until he could come and be with her. Pedro told him not to worry she was safe and that he would keep a close eye on both of them. Gina placed her hands on her stomach and asked Maria Pedro's wife if she would walk with her to the chapel. She hadn't been to confession in quite some time and she needed to right things for her child. "What do you mean right things?" Maria asked her and then handed her a cup of tea and pointed for her to sit to the table. "I think I need to talk to a priest that's all, I feel strange about everything and I need guidance that's all." Maria shook her head and told her she would take her to the chapel in the morning.

When Delano hung up the phone Thomas was walking in the room he ran up to him and hugged him and Thomas asked what was going on. "I'm going to be a father! Gina's pregnant!" Thomas smiled he was happy for him then suddenly he looked scared. "What's the matter Thomas?" Thomas told him he wasn't sure Peter was right in the head. Patrick had taken the bracelet off of the woman's wrist and Peter kept looking at it. The heart he had given her was not on the bracelet and he had been searching the ground looking for it. Delano looked at him "do you think he suspects anything?" Thomas told him he was being watched like a hawk but he just didn't know what Peter was thinking.

Delano said he would find out and called Peter and told him to come to New York they were having a business meeting and all the heads had to be there. He notified all of his employees and then called Patrick and told him what was up. Patrick told him that the heart was one of a kind and that he didn't remember what the hell the damn thing looked like. "Do you think he's figured it out yet?" Delano told him he didn't know. Then he told him that Gina was pregnant and that he had to keep her and his child safe.

Patrick told him that the Feds were planning on picking Peter up for tax fraud and drug trafficking but that they were working on catching him in the act itself. They didn't want him to get away this time he told him that the only thing he remembered about the heart was that Gina told him some jeweler in Lincoln Park had made it special for Peter. Delano told him Peter was coming to New York for a meeting and he was going to find out what was in Peter's mind and let him know then. Patrick told him he and a friend would be checking with every jeweler in Lincoln Park and he would find the one that made the charm and let him know about it. Delano hung up the phone and looked up to the heavens "dear God I have never asked you for anything but I am asking you now help me show me what to do."

Delano went and laid down on the sofa and buried his head into the pillow and started crying. "Dear God that loved and cared for the lives of my parents. You know how much they loved you and cherish you I am asking in their name that you protect my Gina and my child. I do not know how I know, but I know that the child is mine. I swear on the grave of my ancestors that I shall raise the child to love you and do your will if you do me this favor. I swear I will do right by this child and Gina and whatever is to come in the future. Please hear me God as I pray this day. Please dad and mother come and ask God for help I am afraid that I am going to lose my child." Delano buried his head in the pillow and started crying and begging God to help him and not let this hate of Peter's destroy them.

Thomas stood out in the hallway listening to his friend begging God for help and he knew that Peter had better be careful because Delano was truly asking God this time for help. Delano had changed, his love for Gina was pure and he knew that Gina loved him the same way. He felt a chill go through the house and he reached for his coat and put it on. When he looked back in the room he could have swore he saw someone standing over Delano. He rubbed his eyes and looked again and there was nothing but the chill and quiet in the room.

Delano lay sleeping on the sofa and his face was glowing like fire. Thomas looked and then went back and sat in the chair. He reached in his pocket and pulled out his gun and sat it on the table. He didn't think he would tell Delano what he had saw but he stood ready for whatever was to come now and he knew that it was something that no man was ready for.

Gina was not use to the hot heat of the Mexican sun. Pedro and Maria his wife had four children and stayed in a mansion on the top of a hillside. There were trees all around the place and flowers that Gina had never seen before. Gina could not explain it but she smelled roses and there were none around she had walked the place and could find none. Gina wondered why she could smell roses and what did it mean. Maria told her not to worry so much and had Pedro send one of the staff to get some roses from the florist. She told Gina that she should relax and try to stay calm and that maybe she should write Delano a letter. Gina smiled at her but told her she couldn't write him because of what was going on right now she turned and went outside.

Pedro's place had a river which flowed around their property, and Pedro raised horses and pigs. There were chickens and a goat and three dogs which seem to patrol the place like guards if anyone as much as came within a mile of the place or the children the dogs would point and stand ready to protect and destroy. Gina had asked Pedro who had trained the dogs and he told her he had when he was a child. The dogs were the puppies of his dogs from youth and that he had along with their parents trained them to protect the grounds where his family was.

"Gina they will watch over you now and that is why when you go to the chapel I no longer come with you." Gina was beginning to show and Maria took special care to keep her out of the hot sun during the day she mixed up special oil and had her rub down her entire body with it before she walked to the chapel. Gina asked her what was in the oil and she said holy water and oil from the priest. "He says it's for the purification of the child inside of you Gina. I believe a child can be pure from sins of our lives." Gina looked at Maria she hoped with all her heart she was right for she needed more than anything for the sins of her life to be righted.

Maria would walk with her in the evening alongside the river and talk about her life with Pedro. Pedro had saved her life and she had married him in return. She had grown to love him over the years and he had built this place for her after he had married her over the exact spot where his family house had stood. Maria said that Pedro and she had been blessed and that they knew now that she was special and that she should not worry so much for it was not good for the child she carried. Pedro had made her happier than she had ever been in her life.

Maria knew Dianna and Delano very well she told Gina of the love they had shared and how hurt he had been when he came to them to heal his heart. "It is a special honor for us to have you here with us Gina and we shall protect you and guard the child as Delano has asked us." Gina sat down on a rock and stared out at the water she wished she knew for sure whether it was his baby or not. The doctor had said he would do a blood test and let her know the results. She still couldn't believe that she was pregnant and that Peter had hired someone to kill her. Maria told her he could do worst that if he found out she was alive he would order another hit on her and the baby would not matter. "Peter has a cold heart and he doesn't care like Delano for life or love." Gina could not believe that she had been so wrong about him. Maria told her that it would not be the first time a woman was blinded by what she thought to be love. She spoke from experience and she told Gina that Delano loved her and he was hurting not being with her it was necessary for her to be patient. "Let's go for a swim the exercise will be good for the baby and the water is so wonderful here at night." Maria took off her dress and dived into the river and began swimming. "Come Gina, come feel the precious water and let your baby be blessed by the movement of God hands."

Gina smiled and took off her dress and looked at her stomach that now was forming and jumped into the water she touched it and smiled and then started swimming. Maria was right the water was so warm and yet it was cool as they swim back and forth. As they walked back to the mansion Gina asked Maria how did she know she was in love with Pedro when did it happen. Maria laughed "it is a funny story I was out trying to feed the chickens and I fell in the pig pit and couldn't stand up. I yelled for Pedro to come help me but when he saw me there all muddy he started laughing and I got angry and started throwing the mud at him. He came to get me out and he fell in and then we both sat there laughing and crying and I knew I loved him. From that day to this we have spent each day with each other and have shared our love with our children and our friends."

Gina smiled it was a good love story and she knew in her heart that Delano and her would make it if they got through this. Maria told her she would teach her to make a special dish that she knew Delano favored and she could surprise him when he came and cook it for him. Gina said it would make her happy to be able to please him. "Is it natural to be so hungry?" Maria laughed and told her she had many more months to go and that she would see many changes in the days as they came. When they came back to the house Pedro was smiling he asked where they had taken off to. Maria smiled and kissed him "see Gina even now he is still jealous and I am now a big fat woman with puffy cheeks." Pedro picked her up into his arms and kissed her "this is not fat Gina it is the love of my heart and nothing will please me more than to see my friend Delano and you happy like we are."

Gina smiled and told them she was going inside to get something to eat. Pedro told her to wait he had some ribs cooking on the grill out back and that they would be ready in a few minutes. "I make my special sauce for them and you see the baby will like it very much." Gina laughed as they walked around back to the patio as she turned the corner the wind blew the smell of the ribs towards her. Gina said she hoped he had cooked enough because she was starved.

Delano watched Peter all through the meeting he was drinking heavy and his thoughts were very confused. He kept saying he had lost something that he had to find and Delano asked him what was so important that he would help him look for it. Peter told him he didn't want his help that he would find the damn thing his self even if he had to dig the damn grave up and see if they had buried it with her. Delano told him he was talking out of grief and for him to concentrate on the business. That he was losing money and making foolish mistakes Peter looked at him then told him to fuck off and leave him alone.

One night when Peter was drunk and talking to himself he mention the jeweler and Delano had Thomas find him and make another heart exactly like the one he had made for Peter. He told him it had to be exactly the same and he wanted to see it when it was finished.

The heart had a knife in it and it open and had the inscription inside Love Peter. Delano wondered how he could have ordered the hit on Gina if he thought he loved her. What did the knife in the heart mean? He had never seen anything like it before and wondered why he would give Gina a heart with a knife engraved through it. He had Thomas fly out and put the heart in the grass close to the area where he searched every day.

When Thomas came back Peter asked where the hell he had been all day. "Damn Peter I do have a woman though I don't seem to see her much lately." Peter turned and looked at him then smiled "lucky for you Delano don't like your kind of women huh?" Thomas looked at him and rolled his eyes "Delano loved my sister and if I were you I wouldn't say anything else." Peter laughed and told Delano he was going back to Detroit he had things to do there. Once they were sure he was on the plane he called the guards and told them to let him know when Peter found the damn heart and what his reaction was. It took Peter two days to find it after he got back he was on his knees searching the grass when he saw something sparkling.

Thomas had put a lot of dirt on it and had made sure the lash was broken so when Peter found it he figured it had fell off when she hit the ground. He picked it up and started laughing and picked up the bottle of liquor and started drinking it. When the guards reported that he had given the bracelet to one of the girls that danced at the bar, Delano asked which one. The guard told him a girl named Renee was wearing it and that she was with Peter now and they were getting drunk and fucking up like crazy. Delano told them to keep a close eye on them and not to let them out of their sight. Peter was on a drunken crazy he was fucking up he left the club unattended and had started gambling and losing money like running water.

He wondered what he should do he had gave his father his word he would protect Peter but he didn't feel like even seeing him much less protecting him. Delano was missing Gina so much that he had to go see her. He planned a trip to Mexico and told no one other than Thomas where he was going he was only to be gone two days. When the limo pulled up at the mansion and Delano got out Gina was in the back feeding the chickens.

Pedro saw him and ran and hugged him and Gina heard the children screaming Uncle Delano is here! Gina dropped the pan and went running around the side of the mansion. When she saw him she ran into his arms and he started kissing her. He picked her up and carried her into the house and then stood her on the floor and looked at her. She looked radiant the sun had lighten her hair and skin now was golden brown. He looked at her stomach and smiled then picked her up and carried her to the bedroom and locked the door.

They tore each other's clothes off and attack each other with such a fury that no one could deny the love they felt for each other had they seen them that night. Delano laid Gina on the bed and rubbed her stomach and asked did it hurt her when he made love to her. Gina pulled him down on her and just as he laid down the baby kicked and Gina and Delano looked at each other. "Did you feel that?" She said "your child knows you are here with us." Delano gently began to make love to Her it had been so long and she was so hot and wet. As they made love the baby kicked and it seem to make it more special than ever. Afterwards they laid in each other's arms and he told her about the charm and how Peter had given it to Renee.

Gina looked at him then shook her head and started crying he pulled her to him and asked what was wrong. "How could I have been so stupid how could I have been so blind." Delano kissed her and wiped away her tears "you're not stupid baby you thought he loved you and you loved him. I know you did Gina and I know that you are not over him yet. Listen to me I will not let anyone ever hurt you again I love you and this child, our child will have a happy life." Gina laid her head on his chest and listen to his heart beat "Delano were you playing a game for me with Peter I have to know the truth." He turned her to him and told her that he was not playing with Peter that he truly had fallen in love with her.

Gina looked into his eyes and she could tell he was telling her the truth she laid on his chest and drifted off to sleep.

The only time Delano left Gina side was when she and Maria went down to the river to swim. Even then he sat on the rocks and watched her he never thought he could be so in love with anyone in his life. Pedro came and sat by him and asked how were things back in New York and with Peter. "Bad. Peter is drowning his self in liquor and hanging in a really bad crowd now. I fear I won't be able to keep my promise to my father much longer Pedro." Pedro listened to him talk and could feel the pain in his voice. "Listen my friend we have known each other for a long time and I have never questioned what you chose to do. This time I warn you to be careful if Peter finds out you tricked him he will not stop until she is dead. Gina is too far along in the pregnancy now; if she starts to worry about you it will not be good for the baby."

Delano laid his head in his hands and shook his head. "I don't know what to do Pedro I have always kept my word when it came to my father. I feel I cannot break my vow to him but if I as much as think Peter is going to hurt Gina I swear I will kill him myself." Pedro placed his hand on his shoulder and looked out at the women swimming "they are beautiful in the light of the moon we are lucky men my friend." Delano looked at Gina and smiled he felt blessed and he didn't see how anything could stop the hope he had in his heart for her now. "I have to leave in the morning the limo will be picking me up and I don't want to upset Gina. I hear she's planning on fixing me something to eat tonight and I want the evening to be perfect for her." Pedro smiled and told him to come back to the house and to make sure he looked surprise because he wasn't suppose to know about the meal he asked who told him and he said the children had but had sworn him to a secret promise. "Don't tell them I told you Pedro they tell me many things about my Gina and I feel now that the child she is carrying is blessed."

Pedro said those little barn snatchers are always creeping around. Delano laughed and they walked back slowly and talked of the trouble with Peter and how he should handle him.

When Gina brought the plate to the table Delano smiled "Damn Maria you didn't have to make such a good meal on my behalf." Gina hit him on the head and told him she had made it and he had better like it because it took her nearly two weeks to learn to cook the pork the right way. Delano took a mouth full and smile it was perfect and he pulled her to him and kissed her. "It's good baby almost as good if not better as Maria's." Gina smiled and turned and went back toward the kitchen "I have another surprise too!" She went into the kitchen and came out with a cake. "I made it all by myself and I even made the icing Maria did not help me this time I tried to do it all by myself." Delano pulled her down into his lap and held her as she fed him and then had her cut a large chunk of the cake. When he bit into it his face turn green and he started choking and laughing at the same time.

Gina started crying "you don't like it after all the work I did to make it. I wouldn't even let Maria help me." Delano said taste it baby and she took a bite and then spit it out. "Maria I mixed up the damn salt and sugar again!" Everyone started laughing and Delano pulled her into his arms and kissed her. "I love the thought and the effort you put into it honey but I swear I am no saint I can't eat that pile of salt." Gina kissed him and he picked her up and winked at Pedro and took her upstairs. After they had made love Delano told Gina he was leaving in the morning to go back to New York. She looked sad and he told her not to worry he would come back as soon as he could.

When the limo came, Gina would not go down and say good bye. She said her heart could not stand the sight of him leaving. Maria sat by her side and held her hand and they prayed that the danger and confusion would be over soon and that they would be back in each other's arms before long. Gina reached over and pulled Maria to her and kissed her. She then jumped up and ran down the stairs, she got to the door right as the limo started off "Delano! Delano! She screamed out and ran to the limo he jumped out and ran to her and kissed her "what precious what is it?" Gina kissed him again and told him to think of her and their child that she loved him and nothing would ever change that. Delano touched Gina stomach and told the baby to watch over his mother for him and the child kicked the spot where his hand laid.

Delano was smiling when he got back in the limo he stuck his head out the window and blew a kiss to her "I love you Gina." Gina stood there and watched the limo disappear over the hill and she went back into the house and sat to the table. Pedro came into the room and placed his hand on her shoulder "He'll be back soon trust me he will not stay away long." Gina looked up at him and smiled "maybe by then I'll be able to cook the damn cake right." They both laughed and Pedro went out to tend to the animals and milk the goat. Gina sat to the table and she laid her head down and she talked to the baby about how much she missed Delano already. The baby kicked and Gina touched her stomach and got up and went and oiled her body down and then walked down to the chapel.

The dogs followed her and sat outside the chapel door and would let no one come near while she was in there. The town people knew that someone from Pedro's house was in there praying and they did not go in. Pedro was a very rich and wise man he took care of the people in the small town and they loved him and protected him. Any strangers coming into the town were reported to him and the people watched over Gina like bodyguards and reported to him of everything they saw her do when he was not around her.

All the way back to New York Delano thought of Gina and the way the baby felt when it kicked him. He was going to be a father in three months and he felt like screaming it to the whole world. He wondered if Pedro was right that Peter would straighten up. He hoped so he would not let anything now happen to his family. When he got back to New York Thomas met him at the gate his face said it all. "What's wrong?" He asked Thomas shook his head and told him to prepare for bad news Peter had been in an accident and was in serious condition. Delano stopped and looked at him "what happen how did it happen?" Thomas went on to explain that Peter and Renee had been drinking heavy all day and that they were racing down the freeway and the car went out of control. Renee had died instantly but Peter was in serious condition. "He's been asking for you I told him you had gone out of town on business and would be back today."

Delano went and got into the limo and told the driver to head to the hospital. "Thomas if I don't tell someone I'll bust Gina looks so beautiful and when we were making love the baby kicked me man. It was wonderful. I swear man I have never been so happy in my life." Thomas looked at him and smiled he was happy for him. Thomas had prayed God would send him someone to love when his sister had gotten killed. Delano was such a strange man and he had been through so much in his lifetime and had changed and grown over the years. The thought of him being a father made him happy and to know it was Gina made him happier. "Hey that means I'm going to be an uncle!" Thomas said after a few minutes and he and Delano smiled all the way to the hospital.

Delano had an ideal he would see if he could get Peter's blood type. He told Thomas that he needed to know if it was Peter's baby or his and that it would take a lot of pressure off of Gina if she knew who's baby it really was. Thomas told him he had become very friendly with one of the nurses and that he was sure she would give him the information and for him to quit worrying. Delano looked out the window and prayed God would let the child be his. Peter was pretty beaten up he had both legs broken and his arm was broken and he had fractured his jaw. The doctors said they didn't know if he could endure the time it took to heal his liver was in really bad shape and he needed surgery but they couldn't do anything until he got a little stronger. Peter looked up at Delano and started crying "man I got to tell you something

I don't want to die with it on my conscience. I had Gina killed Delano I couldn't stand the fact she was in love with you and I wanted to hurt you. Please I know you won't forgive me I have taken both of the women you loved away but I swear I wish I could bring Gina back to you. Delano I was wrong I know it now I should have been happy for her and you but instead I was a fool. You've been my best friend and my protector for so long I swear I am sorry Delano… God knows I am. I need you to forgive me please man say you'll forgive me."

Delano looked at Peter and then at Thomas he didn't know what to say "Peter it's alright listen to me just get better man that's all." He sat down in the chair next to Peter and looked at him. He wanted to tell him that Gina was alive but he couldn't if Peter lived and the baby was his then he would cause trouble for him and Gina. He sat there praying God would do the right thing and make it right for him. For two days it seemed like Peter was going to get better then he suddenly went into a coma. Thomas managed to get his blood type Peter was B positive and Delano was type O. He called Gina and gave her the information and told her that Peter was in a coma. Gina didn't say anything she sat down on the bed and listen to Delano talking. "Gina are you all right baby?" Gina told him she was fine and that she let him know what the tests revealed. "Delano if it's Peter's baby what will we do?" Delano told her it didn't matter whose baby it was he loved her and his child and that was how it would always be."

Gina hung up the phone and went down the road to the chapel and lit a candle for Peter she knelt down and told God she still loved him and that she was sorry she had caused so much trouble. She asked him to help her and Delano have happiness, and if at all possible help Peter to find peace and let them be happy. "Dear God I am not worthy to ask you anything I am just a sinner and yet you have given me this chance to do this miracle and have this child. Am I worthy of such an honor? She looked up at the cross and then cried and the baby kicked and kicked and she got up and as she went to stand she felt a strange feeling come over her and she suddenly wasn't sad but happy. She put her hand on her stomach and the baby kicked and she told him she would behave and not cry anymore and He quiet down. As Gina left the chapel she felt a strange feeling come over her and then a total peace within her spirit.

When she got back to the mansion Maria looked at her and told her she should not have been out in the hot sun. "Come inside let me fix you something cool to drink." Maria didn't like the way Gina looked she called the doctor and he told her to bring her to the hospital at once. Gina was nervous and concern about the baby she wanted to talk to Delano and Pedro told her to relax he was getting in touch with him now. The doctor took one look at her and rushed her into emergency surgery she was going into early contractions and they feared she was going to lose the baby. Gina was praying and pleading with God so hard they had to give her some medicine so she could relax. Delano was beside himself and he ran out of the hospital and hired a private plane to take him to Mexico.

He felt his heart beating at a rapid pace and he feared the worst. "God please don't take our child I know I am not worthy to ask but this is my plea from my heart, don't let anything happen to my child please." Thomas had made the trip with him he could not let Delano go through this alone. His friend told him if there were any change in Peter she would contact him right away. When they arrived at the hospital Delano found Pedro and Maria standing in the chapel. The baby was still in danger but the doctor had taken some blood from the baby and the baby had type O blood. There was no doubt about it the baby belonged to Delano.

Delano fell to his knees and started weeping "God help me! God please help us!" He pleaded "I have to face Gina God you have got to help me!" Pedro and Thomas picked him off the floor and took him over to the bench and sat him down. Maria came and sat by Delano and took his hand and looked at him. "Delano I want you to listen to me Gina is frightened and she doesn't know yet that it is your baby. I believe that everything is going to be fine but you have to convince Gina to relax and not get upset. Once she finds out that the baby is yours her fear will increase and that will cause the baby to come to early. She has only two months left Delano and the baby is two small but even if it comes early there are good doctors here and they are ready to help the baby. Delano look at me. Gina and you are in love and this child is your lovechild it will be all right do you believe me?"

Delano looked at Maria and threw his arms around her "Maria I don't know if I can do this." Maria took his face into her hands and kissed him "you go see your woman and make her believe in this miracle from God." Delano stood then asked for a priest and when he came he talked to him and told him he wanted to marry Gina. The doctor told him she couldn't be moved but that they could do the ceremony in the room from the bed. The arrangements were made and Delano went and brought a ring and then came back to the hospital. When he walked into the room with the priest and Pedro and Maria and Thomas Gina feared the worst. Delano told her to relax and to listen to him. "Gina marry me, you're carrying my baby honey and I want you to marry me before my child is born."

Gina looked at him and smiled "what are you talking about?" He explained that the tests had come back and the baby was his and hers they were both type O blood and that Peter was not. Gina's face lighten up and she smiled "oh my darling I am so sorry I couldn't even do this right." Delano reached down and kissed her and told her never to say that again. "You are the light of my life and I want you to be my wife." He put his hand on her stomach and leaned down close to it and whispered "listen to me son I want you to hold on. Daddy is here and he will not leave your mother alone again." The baby kicked hard and his footprint could be seen on Gina's stomach. Delano smiled and told the priest to marry them for it was not only his wish but also the wish of his son.

The priest blessed the baby with holy oil and then proceeded with the vows after they were married the baby began to come. "Gina listen to me the baby will be fine he is my son and he knows I love you and him trust me and relax and bring him home safe. I will be here waiting I will not leave you alone again." Gina looked at him as they wheeled her into the surgery room. Delano yelled for them to stop and he touched the baby's stomach and said "if you wish to come home now do so but you must live for if you die you take both me and your mother with you." The baby kicked hard and Gina screamed out in pain and fainted and they rushed her inside the labor room. An hour later the doctor emerged from the room and came into the hallway and walked up to Delano and told him that his son was doing fine and Gina was now resting. The baby would be in an incubator because he was only four pounds and six ounces but that he was strong and moving and causing much trouble in the labor room. Never had they had such a time with such a small baby. Delano fell to his knees when he heard the news and thanked God. He prayed that God would keep his son safe and protect his wife.

Thomas was called to the phone and when he came back he told Delano Peter had come out of the coma and was asking for him. Thomas told him he would have to go back and that he would he would attend to Peter. "You stay here with your family my friend my nephew needs you more now than ever. I am very proud to be able to help you right now." Delano hugged him then went to check on Gina when she opened her eyes he was laying on her stomach. She smiled and reached down and stroked his hair and he woke up. "Hey beautiful how are you feeling?" Gina told him she was tired and asked how was their son doing. "The little man is a handful he's crying and causing much noise for someone so small." Gina laughed and then drifted back off to sleep. Delano went to the nursery and they let him come inside and sit by his son. Delano talked to him and told him to eat and get strong that he had much to live for and that he was very proud to be his father.

All the while Delano talked the baby never cried he listen to him. The nurses said it was a miracle that the baby knew his father's voice. Delano stayed in the hospital and didn't leave Gina's side until she was up and back to herself. The baby was named Ricardo Antonio Delano and he was growing with each passing day. Three weeks after his birth he was allowed to come home at five pounds and nine ounces. Delano was so proud he had brought a small house not far from Pedro's place and had it fixed up for Gina and the baby. He had the place filled with flowers and gifts for both Gina and his son. Gina glowed with pride at her two men.

She was sitting feeding the baby when she asked Delano when would he be going back to the states to check on Peter. He looked at her and told her he had planned on going the end of the week. "Delano I am going to go with you I believe God is leading me to do this." Delano looked at her he said he was scared about Peter's reaction but Gina said she was not afraid anymore. God had heard her prayers and she would not let Peter ruin their life or their son's the matter will be settled. Delano told her he would do as she wished but that he would not let her out of his sight.

Peter was doing much better when Thomas picked them up at the airport he told Delano he was not sure Gina should be there. Delano told him that it was her decision and that he would stand by his wife. Thomas took Ricardo into his arms and smiled he was a proud uncle and he thought that the baby looked like Delano. They had to get special permission to bring the baby up to Peter's room and the doctor was on standby for any problems that might happen. Delano went in first and Peter was sitting up in the bed and was happy to see him. Delano told him there was something he needed to know and that they had wanted him to prepare himself for a shock. Peter looked puzzled but told him he was ready. Delano walked over to the door and opened it and Gina walked inside the room holding the baby in her arms.

Peter looked as though he had seen a ghost he said nothing but looked at her every move. Gina spoke "Peter I am no ghost.

I have come here today to end this mess between you and my husband." Peter looked at Delano and he shook his head "Peter, this is Delano and my child, Ricardo, and I want you to take him into your arms and hold him." Peter was crying he could not believe Gina was alive much less that she was holding a child of Delano's. "How I saw you dead I know you are dead I have the fucking charm I put on you." Peter was frightened and his pressure was going up as he talked he was angry and Gina knew that he was hiding something. Gina walked over to him and held out the baby and laid him in between Peter's broken arms and reached over and kissed him on the forehead. "I am no ghost Peter thanks to my husband, Thomas and Patrick I was able to survive the hit you planned for me. I have forgiven you in my heart and I want you to be an uncle to our child. You see I didn't know I was pregnant and you would have killed not only me but also my child. Peter I am sorry I do not love you the way you wanted. I am in love with you though and you hold a special place in my heart for it was because of you I met and fell in love with my husband. Peter God is giving you a chance to live and I am forgiving you and asking you to straighten your life out. Time is precious and if you hear me I know you will do as I say."

Peter looked at the baby in his arms and smiled he looked just like Delano and he was smiling at him. Peter bowed his head and thanked God that Gina had not died. He looked at Delano and smiled "well I see now why you were under so much control you my friend are full of surprises." Delano walked up to him and picked up his son "I did what I had to do to keep my woman safe Peter and keep my promise to my father and yours." Peter was crying he told them he would never forget what God had done for them. Gina took the baby and then left the room and Delano told Peter that if he ever again did anything to hurt Gina or his family that he would kill him his self. Peter looked at him and told him he no longer had to worry about him and Delano and Thomas turned and left the room.

In the limo on the way back to the house Delano asked Gina how did she know Peter would accept their marriage? Gina smiled and told him God had told her it was okay to go home. Delano reached over and kissed her and then kissed his son on the forehead. The child was growing in an incredible rate and even the doctors were amazed at how much he was growing. It was not normal for such a thing to happen and the doctors told him to watch the child carefully and make sure that they did keep the appointment for him. Delano accepted the fact that Gina trusted Peter now but he didn't he learned long ago that Peter could not be trusted. He felt the fact that Peter had accepted Gina being alive too quickly and had not questioned where she was had to be part of the wicked plan he had to bring him down. He decided to keep a close eye on Peter and who came to visit him.

Thomas agreed with him that something was up only he too could not figure what. Peter couldn't walk yet and the fact he was confined to the hospital made it easier to keep tabs on him. Thomas friend had joined in with them and she kept a record of who came and went and she found reasons to be in the room while his visitors were there. It took a month but they found out the plan Peter was planning on taking the baby away from them. When Delano first heard what Peter was planning on doing he went and got Gina's gun and headed for the door. It was Gina who stopped him she called him back into the room and told him she had come up with the perfect way to get rid of Peter and him keep his promise to his father.

Gina had Delano explain the will and the reason his father had made him promise to take care of Peter. It was a long story but the short of it was that if Delano had no heir all of the money would go to Peter along with the money. He had not meant for Dianne to be killed he had intended on Delano being killed. Everyone had thought Peter was sorry about Dianne death but when he had ordered the hit on Gina he slipped. Gina had figured out the whole thing revolved around the charm that he had given her. She asked Delano what did the knife in the heart mean. He said he didn't know that it had puzzled him too. Gina looked at him and Thomas and laughed "you two are so silly didn't it ever occurring to you Delano that it was a strange thing for your father to ask you to do. To protect Peter and not let harm come to him why didn't you ever question your father as to why he asked you to do it." Delano said it was something that just wasn't done what his father asked for was always granted and he had never ever not done what his father asked of him.

Gina said that while she was in the chapel in Mexico a man had come in one day and he had the heart with a knife on his arm. Gina was surprise to see it and had asked the man what kind of tattoo was it. He said it was the sign of a traitor that his wife had cheated on him and that it was a reminder to him not to fall for fake love again. Delano looked at Gina then turned and went to the will and took it out of the safe and sat down and read it. He had never read the will before it was something he couldn't face. He had simply taken over his father's businesses and continued on with the promises he had made. Gina told him the heart with a knife was an old symbol from Greek times that meant you had been knife in the heart.

"The man said that his wife had cheated on him and that he had gotten the tattoo as a reminder not to go back to her. Don't you get it Delano when he gave me that charm I hadn't met you yet. I didn't know you even existed I wondered why he would let me come to New York and be with you. I am fully capable of taking care of myself and he knew I had Patrick watching over me." Delano was listening to her and still reading the will he didn't understand why Peter was to inherit half of the money in the company or why Peter was to be given control if something happen to him.

Gina shook her head "I knew you didn't know so why I was in Mexico I did some investigating of my own. I called Patrick from the chapel and told him what I thought and to research for me through the files of the Feds and find out about your father and Peter's father. It was a strange thing Patrick told me that they had been raised in the same town in Italy and had come to America with only one woman but two boys. One boy stayed with the woman and the man named Peter and the other boy was given to your father Ricardo. Delano stood up and went up to Gina and turned her around and looked her in the eyes "what the hell is it you're trying to tell me?"

"Peter is your brother Delano he has known all this time that you are his brother and that you didn't know it. Patrick figured it out and he has the proof he will be here in a few minutes to show you. I had to be sure before I came back to America that I would be safe and my baby our baby would not be hurt. Doesn't the will make a provision for children something about the first born child. Delano went back to the will he had tears running down his eyes why hadn't he read the damn thing earlier. The boy to have the first child was to inherit everything and become heir to a saving account in Italy. His father had told him in the event of Peter's death he was to go and open the deposit box and read the letter inside. Delano sat down in the chair and finished reading the will and then threw it down on the table he had the truth right there in his hands all these years and had never read it.

"Delano, Peter knew you trusted your father and it's a long story wait until Patrick gets here and he will explain it better." The doorbell rung and Patrick came in and had a thick file with him. He kissed Gina on the cheek and looked at the baby and smiled. "Delano I have very little time I must return this file back before anyone is aware I have taken it. Sit down my friend it will not be easy for you to understand at first. Your father and a man by the name of Peter fell in love with a woman who was living in Italy. She was born into a family of great wealth and was to inherit a great deal of money at the death of her parents. She married the man named Peter Silano and then something happen and she found out that he had lied to her and that the only reason he had married her was for the money. She met your father Ricardo who was a known drug transporter and fell in love with him. They have all these pictures of them making love in this file and there are notes saying that she got pregnant with twins. One of the twins died and you Ricardo lived she named you after the man she loved and Peter was not aware of it. He thought you were his son until she got pregnant again and this time gave birth to Peter. He looked at the two boys growing up and noticed that you looked nothing like him." Patrick took out the picture of Peter Silano and Delano looked nothing like Peter. They were trying to catch your father and put him in jail so he came up with a plan. He went to Peter and told him that you and Peter were his children and that he would give him great wealth and protect his son's and bring him to America if he did as he said. Peter Silano agreed on one term that your mother had to stay with him and not ever see him again. Your father made an arrangement and they sealed it with this tattoo on their left shoulders. Peter was a smart man he came to America and then turned your father into the police. You were only five then and so you didn't know what was going on. When your father got out of jail he had planned on killing Peter but something went wrong and instead of Peter dyeing your mother was killed at least that is what he was made to think." He took out the picture of Delano's mother and showed it to him. Delano remembered her she was the woman in the picture on the mantel with his father but much younger.

Patrick told him that after your mother was killed, and he told Peter who you were and told him to never tell you. There is another will in a safe deposit box and it tells of the truth of how the two of you are brothers and that if either one of you destroys the other the first born child was to receive all of the inheritance. Delano sat back in the chair and looked at the file and pictures and it all made sense to him now. Why his father never wanted him and Peter to depart friends and why he made him promise to take care of him. It had been the dying wish of the woman he loved and had accidentally killed.

The Feds knew that the bullet that had killed his mother had not come from his father's gun but from Peter's. He had killed his wife for cheating on him and not leaving the money to him. She had left all of the money to you and your father with the point of your father protecting Peter and keeping him safe from Silano. Delano looked at all of it and shook his head he was at war with his brother. Peter was his brother it was almost more than his heart could bare.

"Jesus I did the same thing my father did I fell in love with you Gina, Peter's woman." Gina walked over to him and told him to prepare for a shock the night that Peter gave me the charm he told me it was a gift from his father and that he could not lose it. He had given the charm to Renee because she was his wife. "What the hell are you saying?" Delano stood up and Patrick showed him the marriage license. Peter married Renee ten days before he met Gina and they had came up with this plan only it all had to be up to you and Gina. They were not sure the two of you would fall in love so they help it along. "This is all to fucking much you're telling me that my brother arranged for me to fall in love with Gina then have us killed so that he could get the fucking money. How much damn money are we talking about anyway?"

Patrick handed him the last piece of paper and he read it and fell back in the chair. "You're telling me that in an account in England and there is seventeen million dollars to go to the first heir." Patrick told him he had checked and the money was there that it had grown with the interest and that Peter knew about it. Renee died and she was pregnant he didn't tell you that part he thought Gina was dead and he had planned on getting another woman and marrying her and having a baby before you and claiming the money. Gina looked at Delano she had never seen him so mad and she knew that Peter was in for a world of hurt. Patrick told him that the fact that Gina had the baby the money went to his son and showed him the photo of the file that of the will in the deposit box. Delano shook his head and laid it down on the desk.

All this time he had thought Peter to be his friend, and he was not only his brother but also his enemy. Patrick told him he had to get the file back to his friend but he hoped in some way he had help. "Delano take care of your son and Gina they are in great danger as long as Peter is alive. Gina you must tell him the rest for I must go now." Delano waited until Patrick had left and then walked over to Gina and pulled her to him. "Gina what have I done to you I have placed you in greater danger than I could have ever imagine. What the hell are we going to do baby? He's going to try to kill our child."

Gina looked at him and smiled "do you really think I would let anyone hurt our child. I am a Detroit girl baby I know just how to deal with Peter and stop this shit." Delano looked at Gina he had never heard her talk the way she was doing now. She walked over to the table and pulled out the envelope she had gotten from Patrick. "I did some research on my own and I found a flaw in the arrangement between your father and Peter's. You see they both loved your mother and they felt horrible about her death. At least your father did he left this for you in the deposit box. I took the birth certificate and showed it to the bank president and he allowed me to open the box because I am the boy's mother. I took this out and left the other stuff there for you to go through. Remember when I told you I had to take the baby to the doctor and you spent the night with Peter, that was the night I did it I met with the bank president and flew back here before you knew I was gone."

Delano looked at her in amazement as she talked and then handed him the envelope. "Open it you'll be surprise at what it contains" Gina went and picked up her son and kissed him then went and stood by Delano as he read the letter.

"If you are reading this letter my son then I know that your father kept his word and that I can now tell you the truth. I am sorry that I have put you through this but in order to keep you alive I had to pretend to be dead. Your father and I arranged for someone to take my place and it was she who was killed not I. Your father knew if Peter knew I was still alive he would have me killed and you so he protected us both my love. I went to England have been living here in Norwest Castle waiting for the day that

I can hold you in my arms again. You my love were my greatest treasure for you lived after all the stress Peter put me through. Your father loved me and I made him promise to give me up and take you and raise you. I knew that Peter was an evil man and that he would try to kill you if he thought his son could not get the money so I came up with a plan. It worked if you are reading this letter for I am still alive my love and waiting to see you and feel you in my arms. Your father came to me the month before his death and told me that he had let you think your brother was your friend. I do not think he should have done it that way because it meant that Peter would raise him and he would inherit all of the hate that he had in his heart.

Peter Silano was a cruel and evil man and he wanted to kill his own child. That is why he never told him that he had me killed. I was shot but when I got to the hospital the doctors and my father your grandfather brought me to where I am now. Your father found a woman and put her in my grave and Peter being the fool he was never looked inside the coffin. When your father told me that Peter had died and that his son was exactly like him I knew I had to do something. I had your father come and see me and he brought me all the pictures and photos of you. All these years he has made sure that I knew how you were and what you were doing along with your brother. I made him promise to make you keep an eye on your brother and in return for him doing that for me I left all that I had to you my love. You see Peter will not inherit one dime of the money for he is like his father a cruel and evil man and I knew he would try to kill you and your children if he knew about the real money. You see there were two wills one that you have and the one that is in the state office. I knew you could not hurt Peter but my son I can I want you to know that I am coming to America and will meet you in the hospital by his bedside. I met your darling wife and she is worthy of your love and I am a proud grandmother. I made her promise not to give you this until everything was in effect. I helped her get the files she needed to prove to you who I am. Delano my love I have been with you now for two months and you didn't know it was I. I hope you will come to the hospital tonight for I am taking my son back to England to live with me and I promise you that he will not hurt your child and my grandson. Come Delano and see me and you will understand everything my love. I am waiting to hold you...

Delano looked up at Gina and then took his son into his arms and told Thomas to bring the car around to the front of the building. "Gina she says she has been with me for two months I don't understand how. I would recognized her I know her from the picture on the mantel. I haven't seen her." Gina reached over and kissed him and told him to come to the hospital and he would understand it all. All the way to the hospital he held his son in his arms. Gina sat there watching them and smiling she could not believe it herself at first. He had protected her the same way his father had done his mother.

It was all so strange and yet so beautiful she could not wait for him to see who his mother was and for her to get her wish to hold him in her arms again.

When they got out of the car at the hospital there were police everywhere Gina told him not to worry that it was all right the police were there to protect not only him but his son and his mother. Delano took Gina's hand and walked into the hospital and to the elevator up to Peter's room. He stopped at the door and the policeman open the door and he saw the woman and then he understood. He let go of Gina's hand and went and walked into the room. She turned around and took off the wig and Delano ran into her arms and she hugged him. Peter sat on the bed silent and looked at Delano he had all kinds of fire in his eyes but there was nothing he could do.

Thomas came into the room and laughed he couldn't believe it at first. It's the nanny he had hired to watch over his son. Without knowing it he had hired his own mother to watch her grandchild. Delano's mother told everyone to sit down and she would help them understand what had happen. "Peter you are very much like your father and for that reason I choose now to take you home with me back to England. You will never be able to walk again and will need help in caring for you. When your father died Delano he sent me a letter telling me what he had tried to do on his death bed. I disagreed with him but to come back to America I had to get clearance from the government. A young man by the name of Patrick figured out who I was and came to see me in England at my castle and told me what was going on here in with my two sons. Peter I am ashamed of you for you to want to take your own brothers life is horrible, but to try to kill his child my grandchild I will not forgive you. Peter for the crimes you have done to your brother and his wife I remove all rights to the heritage you were to receive and give them to the child of your brother. I will leave enough money for you in the event of my death to be taken care of but as of tonight you are no longer a citizen of the United States. You were brought here illegally and I now will take you back to my home and for your crimes you will be punished by God. Your father thought he had killed me Peter and he raised you to hate and for that I will never forgive him. You see Peter you are not the child of Peter but of Ricardo. I found out I was carrying Ricardo's child again and so that your father would not kill you I told him it was his child. You and Ricardo are true brothers and were conceived by the same man the only man that I ever loved. He loved you so much Peter that he let another man take you and raise you and he provided for you and took care of you until the day of his death. Peter you are angry at me but I feel you will in time out grow that hate and come to love your brother and his wife and son. I intend on helping you my love, for I have love you more than life; you see for you to live I had to give you up to a man that I didn't love. The heart with the knife was tattoo on your father's shoulder by me to remind your father that he had hurt me. He lied to you all those years by letting you think that Ricardo was the enemy when he alone was the only enemy of us all. Peter I am your mother and I will not let you destroy yourself. I intend on getting you the best doctors and doing everything I can to help you walk again. I have an escort waiting to take us back home tonight and I wanted to end this nightmare and make it right. Gina I thank you for loving my sons enough to pursue the reason for the madness. Peter, Gina loved you and you were a fool to let her go but I see the love she has in her heart not only for you but also for your brother. She was like me in love with two men but only loving one for the heart can only endure one love. Gina sought out the truth to help you find peace that is how much she wanted to help you and your brother. When she found out the truth I made her promise to let me deal with my sons my way and she agreed. My darling son look at me" she stood at the bed and waited for him to look up.

Peter looked at his mother and he was so mad that his face was red with fire. His mother walked over to him and looked at him "because of your evil ways look at what has happen to you my precious sweet child. She reached over and kissed him on the forehead and then turned and looked at Delano he still could not believe she was alive and standing in front of him.

He thought back to the day he had hired her He liked the smile and the warm way she talked to him the wig had fooled him that with time and she now stood before talking to him and it seemed like a dream. It all seem like a dream to him and he didn't know how to take it he wanted to scream he was so happy but how could she be so sure that Peter would do what she wanted him to. It was as though his mother was reading his thoughts she turned and walked over to him and took him into her arms and hugged him so tightly as the tears ran down her face. "You look so much like your father he was a kind a loving man who had more heart than anyone will ever know. He gave up his sons so they could live and he gave me up so I could live and now we will leave here tonight and go home. I will expect you to come see me son in a few months I will be turning sixty nine and I will host a huge party and introduce you to my world and my friends. I am proud that you took after your father he raised you right."

Delano kissed her and then walked over to Peter and took him into his arms and kissed him. "Peter I know you hate me but I do not hate you I feel a little confused finding out you are my brother. I wish you had told me sooner maybe all of this could have been avoided."

Peter didn't answer him and his mother walked over and took his hand in hers. "Peter forgive me if you must hate someone it should be me but trust me when I say this if we had to do it all over again to save your life I would do just the same thing. Peter your father loved you he wept so hard the night he gave you to Peter that I feared he would not be able to raised Ricardo and I know that all of this is hard for you to accept. But Peter the man who raised you wanted to kill you and your father could not let that happen. So he did what he had to do to protect you. Look at me Peter I am the heart with the knife in it. I was the one who got hurt Peter never loved me he only wanted the money and the power I had behind me. He made Ricardo do something that nearly destroyed him he loved you and on the day you were born he told God to help him do this thing and that he would let you go to Peter. It was the hardest thing he could ever have done to give me and you up at the same time nearly killed him. Peter you have been wrong to hate your father and brother. Look at all that you have done. You son killed your father and tried to kill your brother and even worst your nephew. Do you understand the evil that has been done here and that God has protected you against yourself Peter and has kept my prayers. I asked him to let me see you and your brother reunited and I asked him to let me see my grandchild born and brought into this world. Peter I am your mother and this is your real brother and you are blood and nothing you do from this day will ever change that."

Peter bowed his head and suddenly he was crying "Peter I will not be fooled by your wit or your fake charm you are going home now with me." Bridget looked at him and then warned him that she would remove the curse that Peter had placed on him. That she had gone to Italy and had taken a vow on the grave of his grandparents that the wrongs would be righted, and the curse would be removed before her death. She told the men at the door it was now time for them to leave and to prepare the way. She turned and looked at Delano and told him that the child Gina held was blessed and that in time he would understand all. "Until that day Delano you must keep that child safe and he will let you know when it is time to stop watching him."

Delano looked at his mother he did not understand but he gave his word to her that he would do as she said. He walked up to Peter and looked him in the eye "I loved you as a brother even though I thought you were my friend I don't know how you could have betrayed me so Peter. I love you brother of mine even more now, but here me when I say to you that I will let nothing come between my family and me. I will fight the battle for us to become one again and you will accept my wife and child. Peter I am sorry your wife died along with your son and in my heart I know that God will make it right." Delano stood aside and he let the men begin to wheel Peter's bed out of the room. Delano walked behind the men as the wheeled him down to the elevator and out to the ambulance.

Thomas drove behind in the limo to the airport and Delano got out of the limo and told Gina to stay inside with his son for the windows were bullet proof and inside the car they were safe. He walked over to his mother and he stood at the gate and kissed her and watch them board the plane. The ride back to the house was silent only the baby made noise and Gina looked over at Delano as he stared out the window. Delano came into the house and went upstairs he said nothing Gina looked at Thomas and asked him was he all right. "He'll be fine Gina give him time it's been quite a bit to take in one day. Gina may I be frank even I am surprise to find out that you knew his mother was alive and that you didn't tell him. What concerns me is why you didn't, do you mind telling me?"

He looked over at Gina and she sat down holding the baby in her arms and looked at Thomas and told him to sit down.

"Thomas when I found out about the games the three of you played with women while you were young it hurt. I thought I had been a game and that I had been used as a fool. When I found out I was pregnant it was more than my heart could bare and then I went to this darling chapel not far from Maria and Pedro's home. It was there that the priest talked to me about finding out my own true feelings and then following them to the truth. I decided to find out what Patrick could find out about Delano and Peter and it was very important to me because of the child I had in my womb. I guess you could say I wanted to know if Delano had used me to hurt Peter. I was shock when I talked to Patrick and he came and met me at the chapel and told me that he had uncovered something which even he could not believe. I listen to him talk about a woman who was deported back to England because of a lie she had told. He decided to investigate the woman instead of Delano's father and he learned of how she had come here with two boys and two men. He was very interested in her and so he kept prying his friend to find out more and that is when he found the file. Her parents were of great statue and held high positions in England. They were ashamed and defaced when she became pregnant with an American man's child. They were shocked to find out that the men were gangsters and that she chose to go to America to be with them and the children. Through the years the government had been watching her and the men and had tons of pictures of them doing things together. What surprise Patrick and even myself was the fact that most of the pictures were of her and Ricardo. Very few of the pictures were of her and Peter's father. Patrick decided to go to England and investigate it further he had a friend there who helped him researched. When he found the picture of the woman in the society paper and it was the one in the photo even Patrick was taken back. He went to see her and it took a while before she broke down and told him who she was, and why she could not come back to America like he wanted. She agreed to come only if the government would allow her and so she called the Feds and asked for permission to come and bring her son home. The Feds were more than happy to get rid of Peter and they allowed her to come here for him. When I was at the chapel lighting my candle for Delano she appeared one day. When she told me who she was and what she wanted to do to help me I thought I would faint. She is a beautiful woman and I found myself feeling her hurt and compassion for the boys she gave up to the men she loved. When she told me the truth it was to help me. She promise me that if I stood by her that everything would be all right. She told me she had not seen Delano and held him in her arms since he was five years old, and that it would pleasure her to see him and give her greater joy to hold him in her arms. I was the one who told her to come and try out for the nanny's position. We had no idea that Delano would hire her on the spot to come and care for the child. Not telling him the truth has been the hardest thing I have ever had to do. But she warned me until she could reveal herself and take Peter back with her that I had to keep quiet. Peter never loved me Thomas he had only used me but it backfired on him. I fell in love with Delano and that is why I had to know the truth for myself. I needed to know that they hadn't done this to me on purpose. That I was in love with a man that love me back I didn't want to be hurt again not with a child to raise. Thomas I fear now that Delano will never forgive me or trust me again for not telling him the truth sooner. It is a price I am willing to pay for I thought I was doing the right thing he needed to know his mother was alive and she needed to hold her son in her arms. It wasn't until I got sick that I realized that if the baby or I died that it would have been all in vain. I thank God for hearing my prayers and forgiving me and giving me a chance to prove I am grateful for the love he has shown me in letting our son live."

Gina kissed Ricardo on the forehead and looked up at Thomas. He reached over and kissed her and told her that never had Delano ever played for her that Delano had truly fallen in love with her. He watched his friend grieve over his sister for years and when he had saw him developing feelings for her he too was afraid that Delano would get hurt. That was the reason he was sent to Detroit to watch over Gina it was to make sure that she was not in it with Peter. Thomas told Gina he had become aware of her love for his friend and that he knew in his heart that I was not in the game that Peter was playing. They knew Peter was up to something but he had even fooled them when he didn't tell them about the truth. To know that your brother is trying to kill you is a hard thing to shallow yet I tonight watch Delano as he learned the truth and I know that he loves Peter even more now that he knows he is his brother. He has always treated him like a brother always coming to his rescue and protecting him from himself. I feel great sorrow for Peter for he has a lot to try to forget and heal over." Thomas looked at Gina and asked how did it feel to hold a multimillion heir in her arms. Gina looked at him and said to her he was only her son the son of a man that she loved more than the breath she breathes.

Delano walked into the room and placed his hands on Thomas shoulders and looked down at her. He had been standing there all the while listening to them and he had tears in his eyes. "Thomas take my son upstairs I need to talk to my wife." Thomas took Ricardo and turned to go upstairs and Delano reached over and kissed the baby on the forehead and smiled then sat down next to Gina. Gina feared the worst now and she sat there with her legs crossed swinging them at such a rate that Delano reached over and laid his hand on her knee. "Gina I listened as you told Thomas how it all came about. I feel I have underestimated my wife. I never thought you would hold anything back from me and to tell you the truth when you and Patrick told me all this tonight I was beside myself. To find out that I had done the exact same thing my father had done was a shock. I don't think I ever realized how much he loved my mother and me until today. The truth of the matter is that he loved Peter more for he gave him to a man that he despised. I understand him now that he loved Peter and he knew that if his father found out that it was his child he would have killed him. Peter has not yet figured out how much our father loved him but I have. My father was a very strange and strong man I didn't realize how strong until tonight. I am very proud on you Gina for if not for you I would not have learned the truth until it would have been too late. I loved you from the first moment I saw you I cannot explain it better than that. But it was when you danced for me that I realize that I truly was in love with you. I had you come here to New York to tell you but you took my heart by your devotion to Peter. I was jealous of him for I knew he didn't love you and that he was playing some kind of game. I had no idea what it was and I felt Thomas could find out for me but even he couldn't figure it out. To learn of what he has done to us and why hurts in a way that I cannot explain. Gina I never tried to use you I truly love you darling and the fact that you have given me my mother back along with a son is more than my heart can stand. I truly feel blessed darling and I can't tell you how much it means to me that you loved me so much that you chose to help bring her back into my life. I feel strange, I liked her from the moment I met her that day and hired her. I can't tell you how many times I stood and watch her holding our son and giving him the love of a mother. This is all so unreal to me right now yet I know in my heart that the truth is the only thing that counts."

Delano reached over and pulled Gina into his arms and kissed her and she started crying "oh my darling it over it's really over." Gina and Delano sat there on the sofa and held each other and cried together over the freedom they felt inside. "Gina I must admit something to you I was shock at how you talked to me this afternoon young lady. I didn't know you had it in you like that I knew you were a gangster, but baby the way you threw your words this afternoon I know I had better watch my step around your cute ass." Gina started laughing at him and kissed him "silly man of mine I will always have your back."

Delano stood and walked over to the picture on the mantel and looked at it and smiled then turned and went and picked Gina up into his arms and carried her upstairs to the bedroom. When he went to undress her he laughed he saw Gina had on the gun on her thigh. "Well I wasn't all that sure about how Peter would accept the news and I was ready to defend my family if necessary." Delano jumped on the bed pulling her down and kissing her "I love you" he whispered between kisses "I love you back" Gina said as she let him make love to her. Later after Gina had fallen to sleep Delano stood up and went to the baby's room and found Thomas holding his son in his arms.

"Gina is something else isn't she Thomas?" Thomas looked at him and smiled as Delano took his son into his arms and carried him and put him in the little bed. Delano covered him up and stood there looking at him. "She has given me more than I can ever give her back" he said as he and Thomas went downstairs. Thomas sat down in the chair and looked over at Delano and smiled. "She has done more for you my friend than I think could be imagine; by giving back your mother. I wonder if Peter will ever accept everything which has happen and what Gina has done for him." Thomas reached over on the table and picked up the joint from out of the ashtray and lit it then blew out the smoke.

Delano walked over to the mantle and looked at the picture of his father and smiled. He picked it up and hugged it then sat it back on the mantle and turned and looked at Thomas. "Thomas Gina has given me more love and hope than any one man deserves. I feel like doing something special for her but the truth of the matter is I don't know what it could be." Delano walked over to the bar and poured himself a drink and went and sat down in the chair by the fireplace. "Thomas I wonder how my father did it. How was he able to give up his son to a man he knew would teach him to hate him and me. All the years he watched him destroying his son and he had to stand by watching and doing nothing about it. I have gained a new level of honor and praise for the man. I wish only now to help my brother in some way get stronger and get pass all of this." Thomas looked over at Delano and smiled and told him that something would work out.

Delano told Thomas to go home to his family that he had kept them from him long enough. Thomas laughed and told him that lately he didn't know whether he was coming or going he had been so busy. Delano told him to take a few weeks out and go somewhere with them and enjoy them that he would be alright until he returned. Thomas stood to leave and looked back at him and for a minute he thought he saw someone standing over him. He rubbed his eyes and Delano asked him what was the matter and he said he must be tired and left to go home.

Chapter Five

The next four months Gina and Delano were running every day with the paper work which came from the will and the money being put into accounts for his care of his children and children to come. The will provided for children which were to be born in the future and it was a special part in the will about a child which Peter would have and Delano's father warned him not to tell Peter about the money or the words he had written. Delano's father had provided for his grandchildren and had made sure that not one day would they have to want anything. Delano talked to his mother everyday on the phone and they began to get to know each other in ways that made Gina's heart throb with joy and great pride as she listen to them talk.

Peter was not doing well at all his attitude was beyond reproach and even his mother had just about had it with him. Delano told her once he had taken care of everything that had to be done with the will that he would come and talk to Peter. "Mamma I know I can help him but its means me really forgiving him for what he's done to me and Gina." Delano talked to his mother for a few hours then he hung up the phone. Gina was coming down the staircase with Ricardo he was growing bigger every day and so alert and in control that Gina was just overwhelm with everything about him. He would hear Delano's voice and started moving in his direction. He would not stop crying until his father picked him up or said something to him.

If Ricardo was crying and cutting up all Delano had to do was say "son be quiet" and Ricardo would be quiet and be still. It was the most amazing thing to watch and Gina just love to see him do it. Ricardo loved his father and there was no doubt about it, yet there was something about the love they had for each other which was amazing and unreal. Gina had never seen any child respond to their parents voice the way that Ricardo did Delano's. Gina handed Ricardo to Delano and he reached up touched his father's face and smiled. "Okay son now I am going to have to put you down and get back to work." He sat the baby down on the carpet and he started playing with the blocks on the floor. Gina smiled as long as Delano was in the room she was free to be at peace with doing something for herself. Her son got into everything and some days she felt she could not keep up with him. Delano had not hired another nanny for some reason he was waiting she thought he had hope his mother would be allowed back to America and she would care for her grandchild. He had interviewed a few women but didn't feel secure with any of them. Gina had to let him do it his way for he was very protective of his son. He had the butler and maid come in and after they finished doing what he asked they left; they were not permitted to touch the baby for any reason. Gina was sitting on the sofa painting her toe nails when Ricardo crawled over to Delano and looked up at him and said "Daddy love me." Gina looked over at Delano and he looked at her. They both looked at Ricardo and he looked up at Delano again and said "Daddy love me." The child went back over to the blocks and started playing with them. It was his first words and they were of the love for his father. Delano got up and went over to Ricardo and picked him up and kissed him and smiled at his son. "Yes Ricardo, Daddy loves you very much" he kissed him and sat him down on the floor and the child went back to playing with the blocks. Gina was smiling it was the most special moment in her life and she wanted to cry. Her child's first words were of love and more important it was of the love of his father.

Delano walked over to her and kissed her and pulled her close. "Daddy love mamma too!" Gina and Delano looked at him and he was looking at them smiling. Gina and Delano had tears running from their eyes "My goodness I didn't know he could talk did you?" Delano asked Gina smiled "No honey, but I love that he is talking of our love it makes the moment more than special." Delano reached down and picked him up and kissed him and Ricardo hugged him said it again "Daddy love me." Delano kissed him and started tickling him and Ricardo reached over and started tickling Gina "mamma play" he said. They sat there that night playing and laughing with their son and listening to him talk and play with them.

Every day he talked more and more and when Delano told his mother she asked him to come home soon so she could hear him. Delano told her to wait a minute "come here son talk to grandma and tell her you love her." Ricardo crawled over to the phone and he picked it up and listen to Delano's mother talk to him he started laughing and then said " Granny love me too daddy!" he was so happy that Delano was taken off guard and he took the phone back and he told his mother he would come to England in a week. "How is Peter doing?" he asked his mother she told him she was having one hell of a time. He was angry about not being able to walk. She had found a doctor willing to do this special surgery on his back, but he wasn't sure Peter was mentally up to the surgery; and what it took for him to heal afterwards. "Of course you know that Peter has and attitude with me but Delano, trust me I am able to match my son, wit for wit. He will do as I say or I'll show him a side of me that he will wish he had never brought out."

Delano had never heard his mother talk in the way she did that night. She was getting tired of Peter's bullshit and wanted to end it and Delano suddenly realized that Peter had met his match. Gina walked up to the phone and took it and she told Bridget to hand Peter the phone. She had never called Delano mother by her first name and she had not talked to Peter since she had left the hospital that day. Delano's mother went and gave the phone to Peter he refused to take it and she told him Gina said take the damn phone and she tossed it at him. Peter picked up the phone and held it to his ear "Listen bitch! I will be to England in one week and I'm telling you that me and you Peter are going to have the talk of a lifetime. You think bitch I have changed! I am the same hoe that saved your life and took others that you might live. And you played me worst than I have ever been played and I say to you okay. I will be there and you know me hoe, I am coming to check your ass. So you better get those damn legs of yours working and pull your shit together because it will definitely be on."

Delano was shocked he couldn't believe it was Gina talking and yet he was standing there listening to her. Peter was angry and he went to yelling at Gina and she told Delano to step outside the room then she turned and said never mind stay put "listen you have wit- bitch I'll be on the next plane me and my man, and my baby to see your fucking ass. Fuck next week hoe I'm on my way." She tossed the phone to Delano and walked out the room. Ricardo said "mommy mad daddy" and looked up at him "Peter in trouble." Peter heard Ricardo and he got quiet and Delano asked was he still there. "Peter I will not be able to control Gina I know that and I can hear her upstairs man slamming things around. She's on the way I guess I'll see you in the morning or leased by tomorrow night." Peter said nothing and Delano knew he was scared "Peter I'll see you tomorrow." Delano hung up the phone just then Thomas walked into the house. "Damn man what the hell is that?" he asked hearing all the knocking around upstairs. "Its Gina man she's up there packing we're headed to England tonight. Man you should have heard her she lit off into Peter's ass man and she told him she was on her fucking way. I swear man I'm scared to go up there you didn't see or hear her man."

He reached down and handed Ricardo to Thomas and Thomas took him and told him he sure the fuck wasn't going up there. Delano walked up the staircase towards the bedroom you could hear Gina in there packing and he walked up to the door and she flashed her eyes at him and went back to packing. "Call the fucking airline and hire a private plane." Delano didn't move and she turned and said "did you hear me I said call and get a private plane!" Delano walked over to her and turned her around and pulled her to him "I'll call and get the fucking plane woman but who the hell do you think you're yelling at." Gina turned and looked at him then she laughed and said "darling husband of mine call the fucking airline now please I am ready to go." She picked up the two suitcases and the baby's bag and walked pass him.

Delano stood there looking with his mouth open. "Damn! He went downstairs and called the airport and told them he need a private plane and he needed it an hour ago. They started giving him static and Delano booked the whole 747 every seat on the plane and they were in England that next afternoon. When the limo pulled up to the castle both Gina and Delano looked in amazement. It was huge they looked like they were walking into a fairy tale. When Ricardo saw the castle he started smiling and when the limo door opened he was trying to get down on the ground.

"Home daddy" he kept hitting Delano and Delano let him get down on the ground and he stood up and started walking towards the front door. Delano and Gina stood shocked Ricardo acted like he had been there before and they were shocked. When his mother open the door she smiled at him walking "come to grandma honey you're home." Ricardo walked up and smiled then fell down and got back up "grandma love me." He reached up and she reached down and picked him up in her arms and kissed him "yes my darling grandma loves you very much." Gina walked into the mansion and turned and looked at Delano and he nodded and she turned and asked where Peter was. Delano's mother pointed to the butler and told him to take Gina to Peter.

When Gina walked into the room Peter was lying on the bed in a sitting up position. "Bitch if you think I'm gonna let you fuck me up you can forget it!" Peter was angry he as yelling at Gina and she was giving him word for word. "Bitch who the fuck you think you are. I have sat in dark rooms and kissed much ass for your dumb ass. And you try to kill me and mine just for some fucking money." Gina was angry she walked up to the bed and reached over and slapped the shit out of Peter he grabbed her and went to swing at her and she caught his hand and then looked him in the eye. "You want to tangle with me hoe then come on. What you forgot who the fuck I was or something bitch I'm not some hoe on the street anymore. I am Gina, and you can believe me when I say that the day you walk and can fight back like a man; I am going to let my man whoop your natural ass. Now bitch you want to hit me come on do it because I want a reason to fuck you up!"

Gina stood there her eyes were cold and Peter let go of her hand and for the first time in months he moved his legs. He was so mad at Gina that he turned his legs and threw them over the bed side before he knew what he was doing. Gina walked up on him "Come on you dumb mother fucker I want you to walk. Get the fuck up you traitor and face the shit ! you're laying there like some bitch, because you know you are wrong and can't face yourself." Gina was so angry she reached over and pulled him to her Peter was standing up and she was yelling at her.

Delano ran upstairs and his mother followed as they entered the room they stood in shock at what they saw. "You think you can fight me bitch you wanted to kill me hoe well here I am think on it bitch! you'll never touch this pussy again! You'll never feel my lips on your fucking dick or my arms around you! You wanted me dead hoe well come on and face me bitch; come watch this Brightmoor bitch beat your natural ass." She step back and let Peter go and he was standing on his own he reached for her "bitch I'll fucking knock your head off you ..."

Suddenly Peter realized he was standing on his own and he started crying and reached for Gina and she backed away from him. "You think I am going to let you get away because you're standing hoe hell no you owe me big time and I said come and get me bitch!" She backed away and Delano reached for her and his mother pulled him back. Peter was so mad that he walked a step and tried to get her then fell backwards on the bed. He struggled and got up and went towards her again but could not reach her because Gina kept moving backwards. "I don't give a fuck who hears me I will fuck your natural ass up. I am the same bitch that you needed when they had you cornered over on Mack and I had to come and rescue your plastic ass." Peter was yelling and telling Gina if he got his hands on her he was going to kick her ass. Gina turned around and pulled up her dress up and slapped her ass. "Here it is fucker if you think you're capable of doing it! Come the fuck on!"

Peter walked over to Gina his steps were slow and he kept falling but he finally got her leg and pulled her down to the floor. Gina and Peter were down there fighting throwing blows at each other and Delano was watching Peter get his ass beat by his wife. His mother stopped him from interfering "Delano look she's making him fight back leave her be she knows what she's doing." Peter hit Gina in the lip and it cut and started bleeding and Delano broke loose from his mother and reached over and pulled Gina up off the floor. He walked over and snatched Peter up off the floor in one movement "Bitch do you think I would let you hit her again like that. You might be my brother, but I have been needing to kick your ass for years. The shit you have put me through and now you think I will let you fuck my wife up? What the hell do you take me for you had better pull your ass in check or so help me Peter I'll beat your ass like it has never been beaten before!" Peter turned and he was walking he threw his hands up at Delano and said "Fuck you!" and Delano knocked him down on the floor.

"Bitch I don't care if you never walk again you silly fucker I will kick your ass for every day you have caused me to suffer." He hit Peter again and he fell to the floor and Peter stood up he and Delano were throwing blows at each other. Gina watched Peter get his ass kicked and by the time Delano was finished Peter was standing on his own and walking towards the bed. "Damn I give up shit man between you and Gina I feel like I been hit with a truck!" He was crying and then he stood up and started shouting and screaming "I'm walking! Damn I'm walking!" he hadn't realized it until that very second that he was up and walking. Gina walked up to Peter and pulled him to her and kissed him passionately on the lips and then slapped him so hard it echoed in the room. "You had better be able to convince me that you're sorry because if you don't not Delano, your mamma and nor anyone else will be able to keep me off your dumb ass." Peter looked at Gina and he stopped screaming and pulled her to him and hugged her. "Gina thank you I swear I'm sorry baby, please forgive me, I don't know what else to say." Just then Ricardo came into the room he looked at Peter and pointed at him "you're bad you made mommy mad" Peter looked down at the child but he said nothing. Ricardo went up to him and hit him on the legs with his fists "you make my mommy mad and I get you." Ricardo was hitting Peter so hard with his little fists that Peter had to laugh. "Damn you got my nephew ready to kick my ass to huh?" Everyone laughed and Ricardo walked over to Delano and reached up for him to be picked up into his arms. Delano reached down and picked him up "daddy get him he make mommy mad." Ricardo looked at Peter and Delano smiled and told him it was okay, that Peter, was daddy brother, and he needed to get straighten out.

Ricardo looked at Peter and he stared at him for a few minutes "daddy brother?" he asked and Delano told him yes that it was his brother. Ricardo looked at Peter in the eye and said "don't kill me I not bad" he put his arms around Delano and Peter dropped his head and fell back on the bed. Delano and Gina looked at each other they hadn't realized that he understood what was going on.

Peter asked Delano to bring him the child and Delano walked over and stood there looking at him but he did not hand Ricardo to him. Ricardo turned again and looked at Peter "don't kill me I not bad I am a good boy right daddy?" Delano kissed and hugged his son and told him yes he was a very good boy and that no one would ever kill him. Ricardo looked at Peter and then he looked at his grandmother and reached for her. She walked up and took the child from Delano and he kissed her and looked into her eyes "he kill me grandma?" he looked so sincere when he asked her she looked at Ricardo and kissed him "no darling Peter will not hurt you, not now, not ever." Ricardo looked at Peter and then reached for Delano "I'm daddy's boy I am good you are bad boy Peter you need a spanking." Everyone started laughing it was amazing they watched a child corrected Peter and Peter face said it all he was shame and hurt.

Peter looked at Ricardo and told him that he was sorry he had hurt his mommy and daddy and would he forgive him. Ricardo looked at him "you my friend Peter?" Peter looked at the child and stood up and walked to him and took him from his mother's arms. He had to sit Ricardo down for a minute on the floor. You could see he was in pain and yet he picked up Ricardo off the floor and looked him in the eye "I will never try to hurt you again little man you spank Peter good he's sorry." Ricardo reached over and kissed him on the cheek and then to everyone's amazement said "Peter walk now daddy forever" then he turned and looked at Peter and in a clear voice which shocked everyone said "Peter you lie now, but you will be my friend and I will help you get your wish."

Peter set the child down and he looked terrified of Ricardo. Delano helped him back to the bed then turned and picked up his son and looked at him. Delano turned and looked at Peter and his eyes burned with fire as well as his voice when he said "Peter my child says you lie, and I believe him! Beware of me Peter from this day forward for this child is blessed, and I know it and if you try to touch one hair on his head... I swear by the graves of our grandparents and our father that I'll kill you." Ricardo touched his father's lips with his hands and then looked at Peter and Peter bowed his head in shame.

The next morning the doctor ordered a series of tests they had no idea how Peter was enduring the pain. When Peter walked out the doctor's office he was warned that he still needed the surgery and that he would have to have time to still heal. When the doctor was alone with Delano's mother he asked what had happen that Peter got up and started walking. She turned as she walked to the door and looked at him "He got his ass kicked." It was two days before Peter came to Gina and looked at her. She was sitting on the patio getting some sun and Ricardo was playing in the grass. He loved being able to run wild and he was walking and talking better every day. "Gina I've come to explain myself if you let me, will you?" Gina looked at Peter and rolled her eyes at him.

"Gina look we've fought and the truth of the matter is I must admit that you really gave me a run for my money. I think you would have beaten the shit out of me if not for Delano and Lord knows I'm glad you didn't have that damn gun. I haven't seen you that mad in ages. Not since the time I fucked that money up remember?" Gina looked at him but she showed no emotion on her face. "Gina I had been told every day that Delano had been the reason my mother was dead. I hated him I knew he was my brother and I hated him. When my dad told me he was going to steal my birth right I wanted him dead. Especially after my father died I had no idea that it was all a lie. I don't know how to get you to understand that for twenty nine years I have hated my brother. I couldn't love you I loved Renee; that is why I gave you the heart with the knife in it. I married Renee and I didn't tell you about it I was wrong. Renee had me believing all kind of shit. I am not holding her at fault I hold my own self. We sat up one night and thought of how to get both you and Delano out of the picture. Man I got to be real with you I loved that hoe that's why I married her. Gina I do love you but you know we got a brother sister thing, and it's no getting around that. I saw how you looked at Delano and how he looked at you and man I could have killed the both of you on the spot. Renee wasn't right and neither was I Gina. Baby I know I did you wrong and what the fuck can I say not one thing that will make it right, so I come to you now and I ask you to forgive me. I swear I love that boy of yours he's one hell of a Delano and that's no shit. I have never seen a child so smart and yet Gina I have to live with it, not you; that I tried to kill you and him. Please Gina if I lose your friendship I will not be the same because I know how much you mean to me now. Thank you Gina for making me quit feeling sorry for by ass. I mean it from my heart and that's all I came out here to say to you. It's a big castle and if you don't want me around it's not hard to get lost in these walls. But Gina I swear I want to laugh with you again I want to be your boy. And you were right the fact I know my brother gets to fuck and kiss that sweet ass of yours eats at me but then that's my own fault too, so what can I say or do. Gina look at me; quit doing what you are doing to me I know you are my girl. I know it and nothing will ever change that again." He started back in the castle and Ricardo walked up to him and laughed "race Peter come race." Ricardo started running down the grass and laughing "Peter too slow mommy" he fell on the grass and rolled and laughed at Peter.

Peter finally got to him and picked him up "one of these days I'm going to win." Ricardo started laughing "no you won't I won't let you." Gina looked at her son and smiled she never answered Peter she got up and told Ricardo to come go and find grandma. Ricardo looked over at the rose garden and pointed "Grandma in the roses again." He walked over to her and jumped on her back. She turned and kissed him "my little angel will you help your grandma with her roses?" Ricardo went and dragged the garden hose over and she turned it on and he watered the roses and himself.

Delano was in the study talking on the phone when he got off he asked Gina what was Peter saying to her. Gina looked at him and said not enough for her to believe him. Delano walked over to her and looked at her "Gina what aren't you telling me? I want to know now! I know you baby, at least I know you won't lie to me so what is wrong?" Gina looked at him and she told him she knew he was sorry but that he was still full of hate and until she knew in her heart he had let that hate go she would never trust him with her son or her life again. Gina walked away and went and took a shower. She turned and Delano was getting inside with her he pulled her to him and started kissing her.

The water was beating against their skin and he pushed Gina against the shower wall and looked at her. Gina grabbed his hair and pulled him down and kissed him as she climbed up on him and he made love to her. Delano moaned as he felt her hot wet body and his join together. Gina raised her legs up and balance them on the wall of the shower and Delano grabbed hold to her behind and dug his nails into her and climax. They were coming out of the shower when they heard the little wagon that Ricardo pulled around coming down the hall. When he saw both of them wet he laughed and the reached in the wagon and handed Gina a rose. "Here mommy I wet to like you and daddy." Delano picked him up and he looked at him and smiled "what am I going to do with you little man?" Ricardo laughed and smiled and hugged him and turned and looked at Gina. "Peter not good boy mommy?" Gina looked at him she stared him in the eyes and said "not yet baby not yet."

Delano looked at her and she turned and went into the bedroom. When Delano came into the bedroom he looked at her and then went and put on a bathrobe. "Gina there is something else what is it?" he looked at her and sat down on the bed and she went and sat by him. "Delano something is wrong I feel it and if I think he's trying to hurt my child I'm telling you I'll kill him." Delano looked at her he didn't know what to say he knew Gina had slept with his brother and that they had been through a lot together. If she said something was wrong then something was. He walked out of the room and went to find Peter; he was in his room and sitting by the window looking down at Ricardo and his mother on the lawn playing. He hadn't seen Delano and Delano watched him for a while he didn't like the way Peter was looking at his son.

He walked up and Peter heard him and turned and Delano picked him up by his shirt collar and lean him out the window. He was almost about to drop him when Gina walked into the room "Put him down Delano and leave and I will come and find you and talk to you in a few minutes." Delano still was holding Peter half way out of the window and he had a look on his face that would have scared the dead. "Baby put him down, don't drop him out of the window let me talk to him." Delano looked at her he still had Peter hanging out of the window half way and his mother saw them and ran with Ricardo upstairs to them. She walked into the room and asked what the hell was going on.

"Something's wrong mom I saw it in his face when he was looking at you and Ricardo a few minutes ago. I know you bitch I will kill your ass you two face..." Delano went to drop him and his mother caught his arm and pulled Peter back into the room and broke the hold Delano had on him. She looked at Peter and then slapped him so hard that for a moment Gina thought she had broken his jaw. She went to hit him again and Gina yelled "I said for everyone to please leave the room I want to talk to Peter." When Delano turned around he noticed the gun in her hand. Gina had the trigger pulled back and she was pointing the gun at his head.

"Didn't I tell you I would kill you hoe if I thought you were lying to me, all that shit you talked was bullshit; and I am not about to risk my son's life over your stupid fucking mind." Peter looked at all of them and shouted "damn I was thinking of my own fucking child. I killed my own son Gina in that fucking car wreck! I wish I could bring him back, that's what you're feeling look at me baby I miss Renee and my son. She was carrying a boy Gina, a boy, damn baby I am not going to hurt Ricardo, you and Delano got me wrong this time." Gina did not let the gun down she looked at him and Delano walked over and took the gun slowly from her and then he and his mother left the room and left them alone.

Gina walked over to the chair and sat down she looked at him but showed nothing "Gina the day of the car wreck we had just come from the ultra sound and had found out it was a boy. We were both fucked up and I should have been thinking of what I was doing. We were going to sober up and go right it was our last fling and Gina I killed them." He dropped to his knees and started crying Gina looked at him she didn't move. Peter cried for nearly five minutes and Gina didn't move or show any emotion to him. When he got up off the floor she looked at him and then stood up and walked out the room. Peter called to her but Gina kept walking towards the stairs. "Gina you hear me come here! He shouted Gina turned and walked up to him and looked him in the eye. "You listen to me you stupid bitch! I know that you feel hate for my son and I know why, until you come straight with me Peter, don't say another fucking word or I'll blow your brains out."

Gina turned and went down the staircase and went into the parlor where Delano and his mother was. Bridget walked over to her and she looked Gina in the eye "you tell me this minute what the fuck is going on with Peter. I will not allow you or anyone to kill him he's my child. I want to know what you know Gina and I want to know right now!" Gina looked at her and started to turn and walk away and she reached over and pulled Gina to her. "I said right now and I mean it." Peter walked into the room and told his mother to let Gina go, he walked over to Gina and looked at her. They stood there like two boxers ready to fight and Delano walked over and stood behind his wife.

Peter looked at her and then backed away a little. "Does she have that damn gun on her?" His mother took the gun and showed him she had it. "Peter if you don't come clean I swear I'll shoot you myself." Peter looked at his mother and he knew she was not kidding. He looked at Delano and Gina and then walked over to the desk and picked up a cigarette from out of a gold case.

Peter lit it and then turned and looked at all of them and laughed and his mother fired the gun and shot him in the leg. "The next one will kill you I said tell me what this girl is so damn mad about and I mean right fucking now!" Peter couldn't say it he looked at Gina and knew that he couldn't say it Gina walked up to him and slapped him. "This dumb bitch hates my son because he lost his Delano and he still has thoughts of bullshit in his head. I swear I should kill your fucking ass now you stupid bitch, but my son love you. He can feel your hate for him and so can I it's not his fault your dumb ass got drunk and you and that bitch crash. It's not his fault that your child is not here to play with him. You have to let that hate go or so help me I'll take that bloody gun from your mom and kill you and bury your ass and you know I'll do it. Until I know you are right bitch don't talk to me ever again." She turned and walked out of the room and Delano walked up to him and knocked him down to the floor and started pounding on him.

Blood was everywhere and Delano kept pounding on him. When his mother shot the gun at the vase over their head it broke and fell to the floor and Delano stood up and walked over to her and took the gun and pointed it at him. He pulled back the trigger and his mother stepped in front of the gun and told Delano to leave the room and take the gun with him. Delano didn't move and she slapped him and told him to do as she told him. Delano went to find Gina and his son and slammed the door to the room as he left. Peter was bleeding and coughing up blood and his mother walked over to him and stood over his body. She looked at him and then walked to the door "you better pray you can help yourself because right this minute I feel like taking your life son. I brought you into this world, and I swear I'll be the one to take you out." She opened the door and walked out of the room and Peter passed out on the floor. Delano and Gina were in the bedroom and Ricardo was sitting on the bed. He reached up and looked into Delano eyes and then stood and hugged him "help Peter daddy, help Peter now!"

Delano looked at his son and he didn't move Gina turned and looked at him he was standing there like a grown man "help Peter now!" he shouted at them and Delano got up and went and open the room door and saw Peter lying in the puddle of blood. He was unconscious and his leg was turning blue. Delano didn't move and Ricardo hit him and yelled "help Uncle Peter now daddy!" Delano did not move and the child ran up and slapped Peter and told him "wake up Peter I'm here wake up." The child was slapping Peter so hard that his face was turning blue "Peter wake up!" Ricardo yelled and Gina walked into the room and looked at her child. Peter opened his eyes and Ricardo looked at him lying in the blood. "Peter you still bad?" Peter looked at him and sat up and took him into his arms and hugged him. His color started coming back into his face and he was kissing and hugging Ricardo so hard that Gina started towards him. Ricardo looked at Gina and shook his head "Peter my friend mommy, help him please."

Gina walked over to the phone and called the butler and told him to have a doctor come right away that there had been an accident and Peter had got shot in the leg. She then went and tried to pick up her son but Ricardo held on to Peter. "Peter my friend now daddy you and mommy say sorry." He looked at them and he didn't move Gina looked at her son and shook her head "sorry Peter" she said then turned and walked out of the room. "Say sorry daddy" Ricardo looked at him and then walked over and grabbed Delano's leg "say sorry daddy now!" He looked up at his father and Delano looked down at him and picked him up; then looked at Peter lying on the floor "Sorry Peter" then he turned and he and his son left the room and went to find Gina and his mother.

When Delano walked into his mother's bedroom her and Gina were standing by the window looking out. Ricardo looked at his grandmother and said "say sorry Peter, granny" she turned and looked at him she was angry and he knew it. "Say sorry Peter, granny!" she didn't say anything and he made Delano put him down and he walked over to his granny and hit her on the thigh "say sorry Peter! He shouted at her. He hit her again and said it over again and she picked him up and looked at him. "Sorry Peter" she said and then she went to take care of her son. Gina looked at Ricardo and he looked at her "mommy mad at me?" Gina walked over and picked him up and kissed him "no darling mommy not mad at you why do you say so?" Ricardo looked over at Delano and then at Gina "Peter my friend for real mommy he love me" Gina looked at him and then she gave him to Delano and ran out of the room and went to check on Peter.

When she came into the room he yelled "Please Gina I can't take any more I swear I love Ricardo I swear it! Gina walked over and looked at his leg and told him the bullet went straight through that he was all right and she reached over and kissed him on the cheek. He looked at her and then asked what made her believe him Gina stood up and went to the door and turned back to him "your only friend" then left the room. His mother told him that Ricardo had helped him breathe that they all had left him to die. When the doctor came and started working on Peter's leg Ricardo walked in and climbed up on the bed and put his arms around Peter "it okay Peter, I know you won't hurt me I know" he kissed him and sat there and watched the doctor repair the leg. "Peter fixed now?" he asked the doctor as he turned to leave and go "yes son Peter is fixed now."

Ricardo stood up and walked up to him and held out his little hand and the doctor reached down and shook his hand. Ricardo said thank you and went and climbed back on the bed with Peter and laid his head on his chest and drifted off to sleep. When Gina came in and saw him and Peter sleeping she closed the door and went and found Delano. "Delano its over baby lets go home. I want to go home." Delano looked at her and told her they would leave the weekend.

On the plane back to the Detroit he held his son and listen to him talk about Peter and how he loved him. "Peter and me going fishing when I get bigger" he looked at Delano and smiled "daddy you come too ok?" Delano told him he didn't know how to fish and Ricardo laugh and then looked at Gina and reached over and kissed her on the cheek. "Peter say kiss mommy for me." Gina looked at him and smiled "do you do what Peter tells you Ricardo?" Ricardo didn't say anything then he laughed and smiled "Peter tell me his son in heaven cause he stupid." Gina and Delano looked at each other they had no idea that Peter talked to their son, about his son.

"Mommy daddy not stupid cause I with him." Gina smiled and told him to be quiet and let her get some sleep she was tired. He looked at her and then laid his head on Delano and smiled.

When they arrived back in New York Thomas met them at the airport with the limo. He told them they looked tired and they said they were. When he asked how things went they told him Peter was walking and doing okay now. Ricardo looked up at Thomas and smiled, "Peter and me are going fishing you come to Thomas." Thomas looked down at the child and picked him up and told him that he would love to go fishing with them. Back at the house he asked Delano what the hell had happen and he told him. "Shit man I can't believe that Ricardo saved him. I guess that child is blessed." Delano looked at him then told him to keep an eye on Ricardo for him that he and Gina were going to lie down and get some much needed rest.

In the bedroom Gina laid on the bed and she looked pale. Delano told her the trip had just been too much for them. Gina looked at him then she smiled, "no darling, the trip is what was needed. I look at my son and I realize that because of him Peter lives. I left him to die and so did his mother and you. It was Ricardo who saved his ass and now I know that all this shit is really over. Honey come to bed" Gina pointed to the spot next to her and told him she was in need on his attention. Delano smiled he was glad to see that Gina was relaxing for the first time in months, he was happy to be home.

Chapter Six

It had been ten years since Gina and Delano had come back from England with their son. Ricardo was a child of great wonder, he was now eleven, and he acted like a man of fifty. He had wisdom and strength that even the doctors could not explain. Each year he would go and see his grandmother and sit by her side listening to her tell him of his grandfather, and the love he had for her and his sons. She told him about herself how she had to fight to live and survive in hidden places and corners, while a man who was raising her son, Peter, tried to have her killed. He listened of how their family was torn apart and would say nothing.

His relationship with Peter, was one that Gina watched but said nothing about to anyone. Ricardo talked to Peter like a son, he told him he was angry at him for trying to take his life, that until the day he died he would always watch him. The day Ricardo told Peter that he turned and faced him, looked him in the eye; and told him that he would not ever hurt him, then asked him did he believe him. Ricardo stood mute and never answered. When Ricardo was nine, he was already standing four foot ten inches. He had broad shoulders forming like his Father, and had long brown wavy hair, which he did not allow anyone to cut. He told Gina one day when he was only two that she was never to cut his hair. Gina thought he was being a little silly, but he made her promise never to have it cut. Gina told him okay but she had no idea why she had promise him such a thing. One day after Peter had asked him again whether or not he believed he would never hurt him; Ricardo turned and looked at Peter, stared him in the eye then said, "Uncle this is what I know. I know that you now love me, and that I, Ricardo, am your friend." He turned and walked to the door then looked at Peter as he opened it, "if you ever try to hurt my mother or father again, Peter… I will kill you."

Ricardo turned and walked out of the room, closed the door behind him. Peter felt a chill run through his body when the child left the room. He stood still. For the first time since he had tried to kill Gina and Delano, he felt true fear. He wondered how a child could be so strong and firm, and he knew not to ever cross Ricardo. He went to the window and looked at him walking across the yard to his mother, and wondered whether Ricardo meant what he had said. Suddenly Ricardo looked up at him and Peter at the window. Peter swore he knew he was watching him, so he backed away from the window out of sight. Yet the child continued to stare up at the window as though he could see him. Peter knew that Ricardo, not only meant it, but he would definitely do it.

It was coming summer, and the leaves were beginning to change. The flowers were beginning to bloom and everything was beginning to come to life. Ricardo got up that Saturday morning, and started packing a suitcase. Gina walked into his bedroom, and was surprise to see him packing. "Ricardo, where are you going? We haven't planned a trip anywhere?" Ricardo turned around and looked at his mother, "it's time now for me to go to Detroit, and see the place that I was conceived." She looked at him in shock. She had not been back to her hometown since his birth. "What are you talking about Ricardo? I was here when in this house, when your father got me pregnant? He turned and looked at her and said, "No you weren't, you and dad made love in a shower at that club. You never told anyone, not even Peter knows; but I know. I want to see the place now."

He turned and finished packing, and Gina ran out of the room, down the stairs to Delano. "Did you tell Ricardo about the night at the club when I was drunk? You had come back to the club for some papers that you had left on Peter's desk, and found me in a teasing mood. Remember? We made love, did you tell him?" Gina was hysterical. Delano jumped up out of the chair, reached for her pulling her to him, He could tell she was scared. "Gina, baby no! I didn't tell anyone; remember we swore to each other, that we would never speak of that day." He looked at her and Gina pulled away and walked over to the bar, then poured herself a tall glass of whiskey, and drank it down in one gulp. She turned and faced Delano "Ricardo, is upstairs packing and he knows about that night. He told me he is ready to go see the place he was conceived in. He wants to go to Detroit, Delano and I am afraid of him! How the hell did he know we made love? I swear I have never told anyone about that night!"

Gina looked at him and just as Delano was about to speak, he heard his son coming downstairs, with the suitcase dragging the steps. Ricardo walked into the room looked at them then remarked, "Why aren't you packing? I'm ready to go." He looked at Delano as he walked up to him, "are you coming Dad to Detroit with us? Or are you staying here?" Delano looked at Gina and then back at his son "Tell how you know about that night, we never have told anyone son, about it you must tell me how you know."

Ricardo told him he saw them making love in a shower in a club. His mother was drunk because she had been fighting with Peter. He knew all about the whole day, he talked as though he was in the room with them. Delano sat down on the sofa, Gina came and sat by him, they listened at their son telling them about the night he was conceived. Gina herself did not know what night she had become pregnant, and she was scared by what he was saying. Ricardo walked over to Gina and reached for her, "I can

145

see things Mommy, I have never told anyone until now. I can see my grandfather talking to granny in this house, telling her that he was going to send her away. I can see them crying, her begging him to come with her, and not make her do it alone. I can see Peter in the car when it crashed, and as Renee died, I can hear their son crying in her womb. I can see you mommy with your Father, the night that the police raided the spot where he worked, and the way he shot all of them." Ricardo walked over to the front door, turned and looked at them "I see Peter sitting in the police car with a man, I can see more than this Mother; and I am telling you I am ready. I must go now to the club, to see this place. I know you are scared of me. For I feel it. Mommy I am your son, you love me, are you afraid of me? Gina looked at him then got up and walked over pulled him to Her, hugging him with tears in her eye, She told him she was scared to death, and asked what else did he see. "Mom I know that you killed your father's friend, that the reason you had to live in the house on Chapel, was because you ended a nightmare of abuse and had chosen to free yourself. Your Mother, was a cruel and hateful woman. She hated you and your Father. I know that you had never been loved, until the day that my father and you met. He has loved you from that first day. I know that he loves me more than life, and would give his life up for me. I know these things and more Mom, and I am not afraid because grandfather, has talked to me and told me to go and look at the place I was conceived, and that all will be clear."

He looked at Delano and Gina and they said nothing. They got up and went upstairs and started packing. No one said anything. Delano turned and Ricardo was in the room, "Thomas is coming, he would be there in a few minutes." Delano looked at him and asked him what made him think that Thomas was coming. He was at the house with his wife and son. "No, Thomas has left the house, and is on his way here to take us to the airport." Delano sat down on the bed and pulled Ricardo to him and asked what was going on. Thomas opened the door downstairs and called for Delano. He told him to come upstairs to the bedroom. Thomas looked frighten. He walked over to Ricardo and looked at him. "Ricardo, you came to me in my sleep and told me to come here this morning, and take you to the airport. I woke up and was lying in bed with my wife and son. I knew what I had seen in my sleep was real. How did you do it Ricardo? I am here and I see all these suitcases, so I swear I am scared. How did you do it?" He looked at Ricardo and then at Gina and Delano. Thomas was shaking; he demanded to know how the boy had been able to come into his mind like that. Ricardo looked at them all, then stood back and raised his arms up towards the heavens. He then turned and looked at the vase on the mantel over the fireplace and said "come now!" and the vase flew into his hands. Gina screamed and fainted. Delano stood up and walked over to his son and looked at him in the eye. "Do it again! I want to see you do it again!" He was not angry or mad, He was amazed at the power his child possessed. Ricardo looked at his mother and held his hands out to her. Gina was lying on the floor and he said with his hands out in her direction "mother get up and come to me now!"

Gina stood and woke up, walked over and stood in front of her son. She was in a trance of some kind. Ricardo looked at her and said "mother wake up now! Gina opened her eyes and wondered what the hell was going on. Thomas was still standing in the room, he looked as though he had seen a ghost. "Thomas, thank you for being there for my father. I know about the night that the gang shot up this house, and the way your sister died. I know that you came into this house and that it is because of you, that my father is alive. For this Thomas, I shall bless you and your son, and he will never want for anything ever again." Thomas looked at Delano and Gina, then he asked what the hell was going on.

He walked over to the bed and Ricardo walked up to him, put his hands on his forehead and touched him as he said "look Thomas at what I know" after a few minutes, Thomas stood up and hugged him, then left the room. When he came back he had a black book in his hand, he handed it to the Ricardo. Thomas told Delano that he would be downstairs waiting to take them to the airport. Ricardo gave the book to his father, and he looked at it; he had seen the book before, but he couldn't remember where. It was dusty, and had mold on it. Delano reached for a towel from off the bed and wiped it off. It was a bible. When he opened it up a letter fell out on the floor. Gina walked over and picked it up and it burned her hand, so she dropped it. Delano reached down and picked it up, and opened it, and saw a familiar handwriting.

It was his father's bible and the letter was too him. "Delano, if you are holding this bible then I know that the vision I had last night has come true. I am writing everything down as I saw it last night as I slept. I have just put your mother into hiding son. Peter is trying to kill her, and I must let the only woman, I have ever loved, go and not ever see her again. I am doing it so that my grandson, can be born, and come into this world. Son, if you have this bible, you are now going to understand more than you have ever thought could be real. I saw a child come to me last night, and tell me what to do so that he could be born, and come and live and carry out my wishes. He told me of my life, and the love I had for Bridget. He knew that if I didn't do it just right, that he would die, along with all the hope I had for you. This child, was about five feet tall, he had long brown hair, and looked like you son. He was very wise, and very strong. He told me that he was the future, and that he was in his mother heart, and that he wanted to be with her. This child told me how to get my wife to safety, and then told me how I was going to die. Then the strangest thing happened I swear he touched me and kissed me. I felt him son, this child that was in my dreams. He touched me, and told me that he was all that I loved, and hoped for; and that he would be born because the love of my son's heart was so pure and strong, that he would not let anything other than that happen. He asked me to trust him, and write this letter and I placed it in this bible and hide it, and from the minute I did it, I knew that the vision I saw was sealed. I did it son, and I placed this bible in the fireplace, in a hidden safe, that I have never told anyone about. I told the child I would do what he asked if he would keep my wife alive for me. Son, the child whom stands before you is a part of me, and I know that whoever the woman is that gave birth to him, loves you the way I loved my wife, and that the two of you will be happy. Son, do as he says and you will be blessed, but if you don't you will encounter the pain of his mind. This child is real. I know it. I feel him and I will be with him until his death. Do as this child is telling you and go with him you and this woman, and I will see you son. Do you hear me? I will see you. I don't know how it will happen, all I know is that I need you to call your mother, tell her to come to where the child says, I will be there waiting for you and her. Son! Bring my wife to me now!

The letter fell from Delano's hand and as it hit the floor it disappeared into ashes. Gina walked over and asked him what had he read. He told her to wait a minute and went to the phone to call his mother. Ricardo told him he didn't have to call Granny, she is downstairs daddy, She is coming in the house now. Delano ran out the room and down the stairs, and there at the door was Peter and his mother, standing in some kind of a trance. Ricardo walked up to them and raised his hands and said "granny wake up now! She looked around the room and then at Peter, who was still in some kind of a trance, then looked at Ricardo and stared at him.

"You are doing this who are you?" She looked at Delano and then back at Ricardo, and he went and stood in front of the fireplace, turned and faced her "These are the words of the night that you left that grandfather told you granny. In a voice that sounded like his father, Ricardo his son spoke "my darling, this night I send you away, but I swear we will see each other before you die, and on that day we shall be together." Ricardo walked up to his grandmother and held out his hand to her, and turned and told Delano it was time to go. "Son, what is wrong with Peter? Why isn't he woke yet?" Ricardo turned and looked at him, and then at Gina, who was coming down the stairs with the suitcases.

"Mother, I need you to come and take Peter's hand, and hold it please." Gina said nothing she did what he asked. Ricardo turned and looked at his grandmother and told her to take Peter's other hand, and for Delano to come and hold his hand. Delano walked over and they and formed a cross around Peter. Ricardo held up his hands and reached out and touched Peter "demon leave my uncle now! All of a sudden a gray cloud of smoke came and flew pass Delano, and Ricardo, and up the chimney. Peter opened his eyes and looked at all of them. "What the fuck is going on! How the hell did I get here! Peter was screaming and yelling he was frightened, but no one was saying anything. Ricardo and them still had their hands around Peter, and he passed out on the floor. Ricardo let go of his father's hand, and then reached over and stroked Peter's hair. He told him to wake up and look at him. Peter opened his eyes and looked at Ricardo and he smiled and told him to get up. "Peter, I love you" he said and then he turned and told his father it was time to go. No one said anything all the way back to Detroit. Thomas did not come with them, but right before he had put them on the plane he had looked at Delano, then told him that he felt bless to have known his son. What he said to Delano was still in his mind as they got off the plane and they got into the limo.

The driver took them to the club and Delano opened the door, and felt a cold presence in the place. The club had been closed down for over ten years, no one had been inside, it was dark and musty. Ricardo told him to wait and then the child went inside, then came back out and told them to come in, that his grandfather had very little time. Gina looked at Bridget and told Delano to hug his mother before it was too late. She was crying and she knew that he didn't understand, but that she was not afraid, and that before he went inside he had to say good-by to his mother. Peter asked her what the hell was she talking about, he was shaking and looking at the both of them.

"I am telling you two men to say good-by to your mother, before it is too late." Gina went inside, and Ricardo stood at the door and told them to hurry. Peter held his mother in his arms and told her he loved her, and that he would miss her. She looked at him and told him that everything was all right, and that she knew he would be okay now. She looked at Delano and hugged him and told him that the love he held in his heart for her, and his father, had made this all come true. She looked at her grandchild and told him she was ready. Delano reached for her and kissed her and then they walked inside the club. Gina was sitting on the stage and she looked at them, and reached her hand out for Delano. He walked over to her and held his hand out to Peter, and told him to come and sit down. Ricardo climbed up on the stage and then raised his hands to the heavens and said "grandfather we are here, and now I am ready" he reached his hands out to his grandmother, and she walked over to him. Suddenly there was a bright light filling the room. A blinding light, which seem to come from the ceiling. There in the light was their father standing in a blue suit. He looked over at Bridget, and told her to come to him, and she walked over and he kissed her. She looked over at them on the stage, and out of his father's mouth came these words "son this is the day we have waited for. This day, when all of us would stand together as a family, as one unit. It is our love, and the love that is in this child, which has made all of this, come true. Young lady come to me; he reached his hands out to Gina, and she stood and walked toward the light, and the man. "I am grateful to have met you, and thank you for the love that you have inside your heart, it is because of you that I have my wife back, and my sons are safe. Thank you so much" He kissed her, then he turned to Peter and told him "Son, listen to me, I loved you more than life itself. I know you do not know me, and I feel great pain, even now, because I wish I could have told you who I was. But think of the time when we were in the park, and I pulled you to me and kissed you. Remember son, I told you one day I would come back and fill your heart's desire didn't I? Today son, I grant you the prayer you prayed when Delano and Gina beat your ass. I grant this wish to you because I know how much you love Renee and the child. Son, do not be afraid of what is to come. Delano, you stand by your brother. Now it is over, and the rest is the future, and no one can change it. He held out his hands to Bridget and looked at her and smiled "I told you I would never let you go again woman if I got my wish, and this is it. Come to me now for I have suffered without you long enough, and can wait no longer to feel you in my arms." He turned and looked at her and raised his hands to the sky and disappeared. Bridget fell to the floor as the light disappeared.

Ricardo walked over to his grandmother and reached down and kissed her. "Good by grandmother, thank you for loving me so much. I will make sure they are all right now." Delano and Peter and Gina stood there in shock, they could not believe what had happened and yet they all had witnessed it. Ricardo walked back to the room in the back, and went into the dressing room and stood on the very spot where Delano and Gina had made love, and laid down and spread his arms out, and a light came from inside of him and filled the room. He was talking to someone and they only could hear him. He was laughing and telling them that he was happy for them, and that he knew they were happy now. Gina watched her son talking to his grandparents and she said nothing. No one did. They stood there listening to him laughing, and telling his grandfather that Peter would have his son back soon.

Peter stood there listening he was frighten at all what was happening. He could hear Ricardo and he didn't understand how, since he had not been with anyone in years. Just then the door of the club open and into the room walked a young woman with blond hair and blue eyes. She looked at Peter and he looked at her and she smiled and walked up to him and said hello. "Who are you? Peter asked and she said that she was called Renee, and had been looking for him. "What do you mean you have been looking for me, I don't know you do I? No, you don't know me, but I do know you. I am Renee Wilson. I was born not far from here and I have known for a long time that I would meet you. You and I are going to get married, and have a child. Do you believe me?

Peter looked at her and then at Ricardo. Ricardo smiled and walked up to her "Hello Renee, I am Ricardo, I have been waiting for you. Renee bent down and looked at him and smiled, "I know it, and I am here, is this my husband? Ricardo reached over and took Peter's hand and put it in Renee's hand, told him to look into her eyes. Peter looked into Renee eyes and then jumped back, and let go of her hand. He said nothing but stood there looking at her. Renee walked up to him and then held out her hand, and he took it. She turned to the stage where Delano and Gina were standing and smiled and said "hello Delano, how are you?" Delano looked at her and raised his eyebrow. He knew he had seen her before and yet he couldn't remember where.

"Delano don't you remember me? Think back to the airport, the day you were going to Mexico, to see Gina." He looked at her and his eyes got big; it was the young lady who had set next to him on the plane. She smiled and then winked at him "do you remember what I told you that day Delano?" Delano looked at Gina and started laughing and sat down on the stage. "Yes, Renee I remember, you told me to have faith, that everything I wanted was about to come true."

Gina looked at him and asked him what she was talking about. "I was so worried that day. I thought I would get caught coming to see you. This girl was about sixteen then and she came and sat next to me and introduced herself to me. She told me to quit worrying that everything was going to be all right. She sat by me the whole trip and when I went say good bye she was gone." Renee walked over to Bridget lying on the floor and then smiled and reached down and kissed her. She then walked back over to Peter and took his hand and kissed him on the cheek. Peter looked so scared that Ricardo went to him and looked at him and then he took his hand. Peter looked down at the boy and he raised his other hand up and took Renee's and then smiled.

"Open the door daddy the ambulance is here." Delano went to the door and the paramedics came in and looked at the woman lying on the floor. They told Delano she was dead, and then asked him as series of questions. Delano answered them and then they took his mother out to the ambulance and drove away. Delano looked at Peter, he and Ricardo and Renee were still holding hands. Ricardo looked up at Peter and told him to look into his eyes. "Peter, this is your wife, she is the one who will take care of you, and make sure you have the son you love so much back." Peter looked at Renee and she smiled and told him that she had been waiting all this time to kiss him and then she reached over and kissed Peter and he kissed her back.

Delano looked at his son and then told him to come to him "is there anything else I should know son?" Ricardo started laughing and then he reached over and pulled Delano down to him and whispered something in his ear. Delano looked at Gina and smiled "Gina when was the last time you had a period?" Gina looked at him she had been so caught up with everything the last few months, that she hadn't considered the fact that she hadn't come on. She looked at him shook her head "what is it what did he tell you? Delano walked over to her and picked her up into his arms and twirled her around the room. "You have my daughter inside of you Gina! You're pregnant! Baby you're carrying a girl." Gina looked at Ricardo and he was laughing and pointing at her stomach, and then he walked up to her and placed his hand on her stomach. Gina stared at him. Ricardo placed his ear on the side of her belly and laughed "I can hear her singing mommy she is like you."

Delano looked at him and asked him what did that mean she was like Gina. Ricardo looked at him and said "my sister looks just like mom, and she is happy to be coming here. She will be here in time for Christmas. Mom I must get ready for her." Gina stood there shocked she could not believe that the child knew she was pregnant, she told Delano she wanted to go to the hospital right away and find out if he was telling the truth. They all went to the hospital in the limo. Peter and Renee were talking now and laughing as though they had known each other for years. It was amazing Gina had never seen Peter so happy and gay. He talked like a stranger yet she knew it was him.

The doctor ran a series of test and then came back into the room and told Gina that she was pregnant, that the baby was about five months along, and that it had a strong heart beat. Gina said nothing she walked to the limo holding Ricardo's hand. Once inside she asked him how long had he known she was pregnant. He started laughing "since the night you and daddy made love in the Jacuzzi." She looked at him and then at Delano, that night they had made love like animals in the water. She had never wanted him more and she smiled, and he took her hand and they went to the airport.

Bridget was buried next to his father, and as they stood over the grave, Ricardo walked up and held out his hands over both graves and smiled. "Goodbye grandfather. I love you, and this is your last wish come true." He knelt down and touched the ground and it lit up and a cross was made in the dirt. He turned and told his father he was tired and wanted to go home and go to sleep. Delano walked over and picked his son up and turned and told Thomas to take them home.

When they walked into the house Delano took Ricardo up to his room and laid him down on the bed. He stood there watching the child and wondered what was in store for them. He knew he was blessed and he didn't know what miracle could have given him such a child. He stood there looking at him and then walked out of the room, and down the stairs to Gina, who was standing in the living room. She looked at him and ran into his arms and kissed him, and he smiled and told her they were about to start an adventure into something that even he had no idea how to handle.

Gina looked at him and she suddenly felt lightheaded, he picked her up and carried her to the sofa and laid her down. Gina looked at him and asked him was she dreaming or did all of this really happen. Delano smiled "it's hard to believe but it really happen honey. I guess we have to prepare ourselves for whatever else is coming. I feel strange and excited about our daughter coming, yet I am concern about all this and I know you are too." He looked down at Gina and she nodded her head yes and reached out for him. "Delano I love you, and if this is all happening because we love each other, so be it." Delano laid down next to her on the sofa and rested his head on her stomach and they drifted off to sleep.

Gina opened her eyes and slowly focused on the room. Delano still was sleeping on her stomach. He was holding her tightly around her waist, his hands were actually locked behind her back. She smiled then glanced over at the mantle at the picture of his grandparents. She smiled their wish had come true finally. Delano moved and Gina looked at him then back at the picture. So much had happen and now she was carrying another child. A girl. She wondered what was in store for them. Her son…there were no words for what she felt in her heart about him. She had lived through him doing some of the most amazing things she had ever witness. Now here she had witness a miracle and it was all centered around her child. Her miracle. Or was it? Things had been so crazy and Gina felt like she was living a nightmare and would wake up any minute. She loved her son but she had to admit that the things he did scared her a little. After all, she didn't know what to even think about the fact he could do such miraculous things. She felt the baby kicking and Delano moved and squeezed her tighter. Gina looked down at him sleeping and wondered how he was really taking all of it. They really hadn't talked much about all of the strange happening. She wondered whether or not he was scared a little or if he was really handling things. She had questions but no answers and she felt the need to know more about what was in store for them. Just then the smell of roses filled the room and Gina looked up at the picture on the mantle and it was giving off a bright light. The smell was strong and sweet and Gina smiled and whispered hello as though someone was in the room with her. She now felt certain that God had heard her when she was praying in the chapel. She asked for him to forgive her and to put things right. Was this his way of doing it? Again questions but no answers. She suddenly was very hungry so she tried to move Delano over so she could get up without waking him, but he opened his eyes. "Anything the matter? He asked her giving her stomach a kiss. Gina assured him that she was fine and just hungry. She told him there was some leftover roast beef and potato salad, and some fried chicken in the fridge. Delano said he was hungry to and jumped up pulling her to him and giving her a kiss on the cheek. "Come on honey, let's feed that child of ours. They got up and rushed to the kitchen to see what they could get into it.

They were eating a roast beef sandwich when Delano asked how she was getting on with everything. "I guess okay after I have to learn to accept everything I guess everything will be alright." She looked at him for a moment in silent then she asked "Do you think that this is a blessing? All that is happening or do you think it might turn into a curse? Delano raised his eyebrow "Honey it has to be a blessing there could be no other way to explain everything that has happen. Gina agreed and they finished eating and headed upstairs to check on Ricardo. When they opened the bedroom door Ricardo was sound to sleep but he was not laying on the bed but floating in air up over the bed. Gina stared for a minute then she closed the door and her and Delano walked speechless back to their bedroom.

Chapter Seven

Peter and Renee were married in October in a chapel in Las Vegas. The night they made love Peter felt a strange feeling inside his heart. He looked at Renee and she smiled and winked at him and went to the shower. Peter came in after her and asked her did he do it was she expecting his son. She looked at him and smiled and told him that his son would be in his arms by summer and for him to relax and enjoy the time they had together because it was limited. He asked her what she was talking about and she smiled and told him that she was only here to finish the wish granted to Ricardo and that he had to trust her. As the months went by Renee got bigger and looked paler. Peter couldn't understand it since she spent so much time in the sun trying to get a tan. He decided to take her on a trip to New England for a weekend of fun but they had to come home early. Renee wasn't feeling well at all.

Peter and Renee flew home that night and he called Delano in New York and told him to put Ricardo on the phone. He had learned over the last few months that when there was a problem he didn't understand about Renee, that Ricardo usually had the answer and he was hoping that he had the answer this time and that she would be feeling better soon.

Delano asked what was the matter and he said nothing that he needed to talk to Ricardo. Ricardo came to the phone and said nothing he listened to Peter talk and then he hung up the phone. "Father, I must go to England right away, there is a problem and I must help Peter out." Delano asked him what was going on and he told him that Peter's son was on the way, but that he had not finished doing what must be done. That he must go to Peter now, and he asked Delano to come with him. Gina came into the room and looked at them she knew by the look on his face that something was wrong.

She asked where they were going and he told her to England. Gina turned and went and started packing over the last few months she had learned not to question anything that her son said only to do what he asked. She walked down the stairs and gave Delano and Ricardo a hug and told them she would see them when they got back. Ricardo smiled and walked up to her and laid his hand on her stomach and started talking in Italian to his sister. Gina didn't speak Italian and neither did Delano they watched him telling the child something and Gina felt the baby kicking and she smiled and told him to go do what he had to do. Ricardo looked up at her and smiled "Mom Gina says to tell you that she is happy you are happy today." Gina looked at him and smiled and nodded and then closed the door and went and laid down on the sofa and stroked her stomach.

"Daughter, I know you can hear me and this is my heartfelt wish; that you will come and help me get through all of this." The baby kicked hard and Gina smiled and told her she needed her so much, and that she wished she were here the baby kicked again and then quiet down and Gina went to sleep.

When she woke up she went to the phone and called Peter and asked him what was going on and he told her that he didn't know and that he was afraid for his wife and child. "Something is wrong. Gina, I know it. Ricardo told me nothing, is he on the way?" Gina was quiet for a moment then said, "Yes Peter, they are on the way. When it is over, please have Ricardo call me, and tell me what is going on." He agreed he would do it and told her that Renee had come back from the doctor only minutes ago, and that they confirmed she was over six months. Gina smiled and told him it would not be long, and he would hold his son in his arms. She hung up the phone and went and sat down in the chair by the fire and rocked back and forth. She could feel her child moving inside of her and she was smiling and sitting there holding the bible which belong to Delano's father in her hands.

It opened up to Psalms 100, and Gina read it and smiled, then got up and went and fixed something to eat; then came back and sat in the chair and started rocking again. She was sitting there singing "happy is the day that the Lord blessed me, happy is the day that the Lord blessed me. I am free and all is true, happy is the day that the Lord bless me." Gina knew that those were the words that the child inside her was singing, and she knew that whatever was wrong could be righted by Ricardo presence.

Delano and Ricardo arrived in England and went to the castle Ricardo said nothing to him but talked in Italian all the way to the castle. Once he saw the castle he looked at his father and took his hand "Father, your grandfather, has sent us to her get rid of the demon ,which still remains here, and to help me free Peter, so he can come and do his will." Delano looked at him and said he needed to know what it was he was talking about. "I am talking about your nephew, Father his name is Peter, and he is in trouble and needs my help. Father, Do you know how precious love is? The power that love can do?" Delano looked at him and smiled "Son until I met Gina and fell in love, I don't think I ever really knew what the power of love could do. I believe in you son, I know that it is nothing to worry about; but I am not a man of faith, and sometimes I must admit that I am afraid, at all the things that you can do."

Ricardo took his father's hand and smiled and as the limo pulled in front of the castle. He squeezed his hand and looked into his father's eyes, and told him that more than anything Peter, his brother, needed him to be right by his side. Peter and Renee met them at the door and Ricardo walked up to her and held out his hand and she took it, and walked into the garden to the roses that his grandmother had planted. Ricardo stood her in them and then smiled and touched her stomach. Renee looked down at him and asked him could he help her child finish the mission. Ricardo turned and saw both his father and Peter standing there, and he told them to join hands, and raise them to the sky.

Delano took his brother's hand and raised it to the sky, and then he looked at his son and turned to Peter and asked him was he ready. Peter told him as long as he stood by his side and didn't let his hand go, he thought he could take what was coming, and then he turned and told Ricardo he was ready. Ricardo smiled and raised his hands to the sky, and called out in a loud voice "open the gate and let the child breath. This is an order, open the gate and free my cousin, for I am here and demand you to release the spirit, which tries to take him now." The ground was shaking, and the walls of the castle began to move, as Ricardo talked. The roses all turned from red to gold, and Ricardo once again in a very loud voice yelled out "I call out to you and say it again, open the gates of the air!"

Renee fell to the ground and Peter and Delano ran toward them and Ricardo turned and told them to stop and not come any closer to her. He reached down and touched her stomach, and then called up to the sky again "please hear me I am here. Open the gates he cannot breathe!" Peter then understood what was happening and so did Delano. The child had the cord wrapped around his neck and it was suffocating. Peter rushed into the house and called the doctor, told him what was happening. He told Peter to not move her and that a team of doctors were on the way to help him. Peter ran out and Delano was on his knees praying ,he pulled Peter down and looked at him "listen to me Peter, raise your hands and you beg God to help him right now. Ricardo needs help. Your son can't breathe, he is taking your child and breathing for him. Please Peter, don't let my son die help him save your son."

Peter looked up at the sky and raised his hands up, and looked at the heavens and yelled in a loud voice "please help God help my son and nephew live, don't take them away. Please God help us!" Then Peter laid his entire body down on the ground and he said it again in a voice that Delano had never heard before "I am Peter, and the demon which was in me as taken my son. God and is trying to take not only him, but Renee too. I know I am a sinner, and that I have been wrong all my life. Forgive me this day for the sins of my life, and bring my son and Renee, back to do what your will is." Suddenly Ricardo started choking and Renee woke up and she started screaming out in pain.

Ricardo reached over and touched her stomach, and then raised his hands up again; and this time in a voice, which frighten all of them, he yelled "Demon you cannot have him. This is our child let him go now!" and he reached out into the garden and picked up the golden rose, and laid it on Renee's stomach, and then called out again. "Grandmother, come now and free him, before it is too late." The servants and the doctors were all standing in the yard now. They looked at what was going on but they could not move, they were frozen in place. Ricardo turned and looked at his father "Father, run and call Mother, tell her to touch her stomach, and keep her hands there until you call her back. Hurry father, we are running out of time."

Delano jumped up and ran to the phone, and told Gina what Ricardo said, and she did it and went to the rocker and kept rocking, and talking to the child in her stomach. Ricardo was yelling in a loud voice something in Italian, and suddenly, Renee started screaming and yelling for Peter. "Peter come here! Peter hurry come here! She was turning blue, and she looked at him, but he was not moving. "Demon, here me this day, let my man's feet go, or I shall cut off yours! The ground was shaking, and even the roses were moving, and the air all around became hot, and seem to burn. Peter ran to her side, and reached for her hand, and Ricardo called out again "I said to release him now!" Suddenly a gray cloud came from Renee, it was large and dark, and went up into the heavens and she passed out.

The doctors ran to her and Ricardo, fell to the ground, he was not breathing. One team worked on Renee, while the other doctors worked on Ricardo. Five minutes went by, suddenly, Ricardo open his eyes, looked at his father and held out his hand. Delano ran to him and picked him up and kissed him "I'm fine dad, honest everything is all right now." The doctors still had not been able to wake Renee, she laid there blue, they said she was dying, and that the child was dead. Surely no child that young could live through this? Ricardo walked over to them, and pushed them aside, and then called to her "Renee, listen to me, the baby is fine now, arise and go to your husband and be happy."

Renee open her eyes and stood up, she looked as though nothing had happened, the doctors checked her out, and said that she and the baby was okay. Then they all stood looking at Ricardo, he turned and looked at all of them, and raise his hands up "Remember none of this go about your business. This is over go about your day as I say." When Ricardo brought his hands down, the doctors all smiled and walked out of the garden, and the servants went back to work. Delano walked over to his son and picked him up, and looked at him and smiled, then kissed him. Peter ran to where they were standing. Threw his arms around both he and Ricardo, and thanked them. Ricardo smiled and told Renee to come and listen to something. He placed his hands on her stomach, and then held them to her ears. Renee listened and then she smiled and reached down and kissed him, then went to Peter and kissed him, and told him that she had heard his son's heart beating, and that he was fine.

Peter and Delano, looked at Ricardo, and no one said anything .They went into the castle and called Gina. Delano looked over at Peter and Renee, and smiled at them and then he walked up to Renee, and touched her stomach, The wind blew through the garden, and the smell of roses, filled the air, and Renee told both of them to go to the window and look in the garden. They went and out in the garden, stood two couples holding hands, and waving at them. Delano and Peter recognized one couple as their parents, but they did not know the other couple, and yet they knew that they were their grandparents. Both men waved and the couples disappeared into the air, and the scent of roses, became stronger within the room.

Delano went to the phone and called Gina, he told her what had happen. She asked to speak to Ricardo and he took the phone. "Hello mother, everything here is fine, but please let me talk to my sister for a moment" and Gina placed the phone on her stomach, and he spoke in Italian to his sister, and told her his cousin was fine, and that he would be home soon." The baby kicked very hard, and Gina raised the phone to her ear "Momma, I am okay. Now you can go to sleep and when you wake up we will be there." Gina asked to speak to Delano she told him to come home, that she missed him, and that she would hear all about it then, that she was tired, because the baby had drained her by helping them. Delano told her he was on the way, and he and Ricardo left the castle and went back to the states.

Once in the house, Delano asked his son was his wife and daughter okay. Ricardo looked at him and said "nothing or no one, can hurt Gina, father, she is strongest of all that are to come." Delano looked at him and then went to his wife and took her into his arms, and then laid his head on her stomach, and the baby kicked him. He smiled and whispered into her stomach, to his child, "I feel blessed to have been a part of it all, take care of yourself, for I long to see the love of your face." The child kicked him and her foot print, was on Delano's face. Gina reached up and it went into her hand, and she placed it on her heart, and smiled and they both laid down on the bed and Ricardo, climbed up on the bed with them, and they all went to sleep.

They slept for two days, no one moved from the bed. When Thomas came to the house he stood and looked at them, and all around them was a rainbow of many colors, and he closed the door, and went downstairs. When the servants came, he told them to go home, and to come back in three days, and not before. Thomas took his gun and sat it on the table, and went and called his wife and told her to pray that all was well for everyone. Then he went back to his post, and sat there reading the bible. He read Job and he smiled as he read each word. Job, was a man of great strength, who had been tested. Thomas now understood all that was going on, and he no longer had fear in his heart, but great joy for he knew the children of Delano and Peter, were blessed and that they were children of the God, that was in the bible.

Thomas looked up at the heavens and raised his hands "I am Thomas, a sinner, who has never believed in anything, other than what I could see and feel. I know you are real, and I thank you for trusting me, and giving me my son and wife. I stand here guarding your children, and will leave when they awake." Thomas sat back down and he picked up the bible, and the room filled with the smell of roses and he drifted off to sleep.

When Delano woke up Ricardo, was standing and looking at him, he smiled and touched his fingers to his mouth, and signaled his father to come with him. Once outside the room he reached up and kissed him, and told him that Gina, was still resting because Maria, was still very tired. "Gina, is a brave woman, father, for she has stood the test; and she has helped in ways she does not know yet. Father do not make love to Gina when she wakes up, but do hold her in your arms." Delano asked why he could not make love to his wife. Ricardo told him "because if you touch her before Maria is ready, you will hurt her father. I know you don't want to do that."

Ricardo looked at him and told him that the love that they had between them was holy, and precious, and that he had to trust him. "You can make love to her in three days father, and all will be well." Ricardo started to walk away, but his feet were not touching the ground. Delano looked but said nothing, he went back in the room, climbed back in bed next to his wife, laid down next to her and his child. Gina woke up and turned to him and she wanted him to make love to her, he smiled and told her to wait three days, and then he would make love to here like never before, and they closed their eyes, and went back to sleep.

During all the time they slept, Thomas slept by the door .He opened his eyes, when he heard someone trying to come in. He would pick up his gun, and tell whoever was there to go away. Thomas never opened the door, he talked threw it, and each time he peeked through the key hole, and saw no one; but the knob on the door was moving, as though someone was trying to get inside. Thomas looked at the door and warned, whoever it was that he was standing guard, and no one would enter that house until it was time. The room filled with the smell of roses, and Thomas looked at the fireplace, and it lit and the flames were white, and out from them flew a angel, and she told him that she was there, and that he had done well, and she reached down and touched his forehead and showed him many things. Thomas sat back down in the chair, and the angel went back into the fire, and it disappeared and he went back to sleep.

Gina Maria Delano, was born on Christmas day, at the midnight hour. She came into the world crying, and the nurses swore it sounded like she was singing, instead of crying. When Gina brought her home, she handed the child to Ricardo, and he held her up to the sky and said "God she is here now, help us do your will." He handed the child back to his mother, and she went and sat on the sofa, and he came and sat next to her and smiled. "She looks so beautiful doesn't she mother" Ricardo touched her on the head and made the sign of a cross, and Gina said yes, then asked him was she like him, and he smiled and said yes. She looked at Delano and shook her head and he came and sat down next to her.

The baby raised her hands, and made the sign of a cross, and Gina and Delano smiled. They had no idea what was to come, but they knew it was going to be all right. Over the next five years, they watched their children growing, and they knew they were special. Delano had made arrangements with the government, for Peter to come to the United States, only on emergencies, and they had agreed. During those five years, Delano and his son, talked of many things and they became very close. They would go to England, and fish in the pond on the land, and then take the fish and toss them back into the water. They never ate one of the fish they caught. Peter and Delano became the best of friends, and they grew stronger in love, and their families were happy, and the smell of roses, surrounded them at all times. Whenever they would leave, Gina and Maria, the girls, would stand watching and waving and smiling at them, and when they would return Maria would speak in Italian, to her brother about all.

The bond between the children was so strong, that when one would cough, the other would too. Gina watched her children growing, and she knew that something was coming, and she wondered what the children were there to do. Gina looked out at the garden and saw them talking to the roses, and she shook her head. They were strange children they talked to flowers and to their grandparents every day. Gina wouldn't go out when she saw them talking, she felt it was a holy time, and she didn't want to interrupt them.

Delano came into the house one evening, and asked where the children were, and Gina pointed to the garden and smiled. "They have been out there all day, honey, talking to your parents, I am worried for they haven't eaten since morning. I had the cook fix them something special, and he left it in the oven. Have you eaten yet?" Delano told her that he had been busy all day, and that he too had not eaten. He walked over to the garden door, and called for the children, to come into the house. When they walked in they were glowing, Delano told them to go and wash up and get ready to come and eat dinner.

Maria looked up at her father and smiled, and told him that his mother had sent him a kiss, and a hug. He smiled and asked how were they doing? She told him they were doing well, and missed them very much. Gina looked at them and smiled and went into the kitchen and started preparing their dinner. The cook had made a Beef Roast with fixing, a large salad with lemon dressing. Gina smiled she knew the children loved roast and would eat well that evening. She felt the presence of someone in the kitchen with her and turned, Maria was standing at the doorway. "Mother I love you today more than words" she said then she went and sat down at the table. Gina smiled she had been thinking she loved them too, and she took the food out to the table, and they prayed and started to eat.

Chapter Eight

Gina and Delano watched the children, Delano nor Gina knew what they were saying to each other. Gina watched her daughter begin to look more and more like her with each passing day. As summer approached, both children were laughing and saying they had to go the England to see their cousin. Ricardo was now going on eleven and he had not seen Peter or Renee, since he had saved the child's life. Gina and Delano packed and they went to the airport to go to England in time for the child's arrival. The doctors kept telling Peter the baby would not be due until July, but Ricardo had said that his cousin, was on the way, and that he would be home soon.

Delano had not questioned anything since they had come back home. He and Gina simply did as his son wanted, and they found their lives to be happy and blessed. There had been no problems and Thomas and his wife were expecting a girl. Thomas had hit the lottery and had been able to put the money he wanted, away for his son, just like Ricardo had told him. Often Thomas would come over and sit and talk with Ricardo about the future, and what was expected of him. Ricardo told Thomas for his faith and undying loyal friendship, he would be blessed all his days on earth, and live a long life. Thomas told him all he wanted was to be happy with his wife, and children.

They arrived in England, on the third of June, and went directly to the castle. Gina looked at her daughter as she neared the castle, as she pointed and started talking in Italian, to Ricardo they were both smiling and laughing. Once the limo stopped, the children climbed out of the car. Ricardo took his sister's hand and took her inside the castle. He was talking to her in Italian and Gina wondered what they were saying, when her daughter saw Renee she ran up to her. Maria looked at her then reached up and touched her stomach, Renee felt the baby kicking. She smiled and then went and sat down, and the child climbed into her lap, and hugged her. She put her head to her stomach, started talking to the baby in Italian. Renee looked at Gina and Delano, and called for Peter to come to her. Peter hurried down the stairs, and greeted his brother, and hugged Ricardo, and welcomed them home. Just as Peter reached over to touch Renee, Maria looked up at him and said "hello Peter." It was the first time the child had spoken English and Gina was shocked that her first words were to Peter. She reached her hands out to him and Peter picked her little hand up and smiled "Well you're Maria, how are you today?" Gina laughed and said "time to go get Peter?" He looked at her, and Renee's water broke, she told him to call the hospital that the baby was on the way.

As they all rushed to the hospital Ricardo and Gina kept talking to each other in Italian. Everyone wondered what they were saying, while Renee screamed out in pain, and reached for Peter. "Oh my God… it's horrible the pain of life, is so hard to take" she said and she squeezed his hand. Peter told her they would be to the hospital soon, they were only three miles away. Ricardo told Peter to move, then he and Maria held up their hands to the sky, and the baby's head began to show. "Oh my God, the baby's coming" she shouted as the baby began to push its way out. The children were talking in Italian and chanting something, as they worked with the baby head.

Peter and Delano and Gina were scared none of them knew how to deliver a baby. The limo driver was driving as fast as he could, but the baby was on the way. All of a sudden Maria reached over with her little hands and touched the baby's head, and Renee pasted out into Peter's arms. Ricardo told Peter not to worry, that Maria knew how to get her cousin out of the body. Peter looked at Delano and Gina and he closed his eyes, and prayed that God was in the limo. Ricardo looked at him and smiled and told him God was there, and so was grandmother and grandfather too. They all looked in amazement as the little girl open her hands, and into them the baby pushed his way out. Ricardo put his hand on the bloody baby, and told the baby to come home.

The baby started crying and Ricardo took the baby and placed it into Renee's hands, and told her to open her eyes now. Renee opened her eyes and there in her arms, was the baby all bloody and crying. She looked around at everyone and asked who had delivered the baby, and they pointed to Maria. She held up her little bloody hands, and took the baby's hand, and Ricardo took the other hand; and they held their hands up to the sky, and started talking in Italian again.

Ricardo smiled and looked at Delano and said to him "Dad, your father is sitting by you, turn and smile at him." Delano turned and in the reflection on the limo window, he could see his father and mother smiling. Gina stared but didn't say a word, she reached out and took Delano's hand and they prayed. When the driver got to the hospital, they rushed Renee and the baby inside to be cleaned up. When they went into the hospital room later they brought the baby inside, and Maria walked up to the bed and climbed up. The nurse went to stop her and she turned and stared at her and the nurse backed away. Maria looked at all of them then left the room quickly.

Ricardo walked over to the bed and he took the baby, and he and Maria went over to Peter and handed him his son. Peter looked at the little boy, and he opened his eyes and then closed them. Ricardo looked at Peter and then he and his sister, started walking around in a circle around Peter. Maria was singing something, and it was in English, so they were trying to hear what it was. As they walked around Peter and the child, she got louder "here is the child... here is the child. Hold him... Love him... Here is the child. Hold him... Love him...here is the child." When she quit singing she looked at Peter and smiled. "Peter, here is Peter, he is the head. Do you understand?"

Peter looked at the child and said no, he did not understand, and he looked at Ricardo. Ricardo told him to hand him Peter, and for him to go stand by his brother, and looked at them then he would understand. Ricardo held the baby up and Maria came and stood by him and then all of a sudden the room filled with a bright light, coming from the children, and the room filled with the strong smell of roses. Delano and Peter looked at each other the children were forming a triangle, and it became brighter as Ricardo began to chant. "Here we are... here we are. See us...see us.... Here we are. Here we are see us. See us and come and bless the day." Maria held up her hands to the heavens, and a glaring light beamed from them, and Gina stood watching her children, and her heart felt like it was going to burst. All of a sudden the light went away, and Ricardo took the baby to his mother, and told her to feed Peter he was hungry.

When they came home from the hospital, the ride was quiet, and they all sat looking at the children. Delano looked over at Ricardo and then asked him what were they to do now. Ricardo told him they had to take the baby to the roses, then they could go home. They went into the rose garden and stood there and Peter gave Ricardo the baby, and told him to do what he had to. Ricardo took the child, and he and his sister went to the spot where the baby had nearly died, and held the baby up to the sky. Maria began singing in a loud voice "here we are... here we are.... Come to us.... Come to us... here we are.... Here we are.... Come to us.... Come to us." The sky over them open up, and bright light shined down on the children, and seem to surround them. Ricardo was speaking in Italian, and Maria was singing louder and louder "here we are... here we are.... Come to us.... Come to us." Gina reached out and took Delano hand, and watched the children begin to rise off the ground, and seem to float in the air towards the clouds. Peter and Renee stood looking at them, and they were all shocked. The children were no longer on the ground, but in the air floating on a cloud. Above the children's head was a cross, and what looked like an angel, standing over them. The angel reached over and put her hands over the children, and said something in Italian to them, and they nodded their heads, and then began to go back down to the ground. Once the children feet touched the ground, the angel disappeared, and the light went back up into the clouds.

Ricardo walked over and handed Peter to Renee, and told her to be careful not to touch his hair yet. Renee asked Ricardo why couldn't she touch the child's hair, and he told her because it was full of the fire of life. Ricardo turned and walked over to his father and his Maria, ran up to him and said to pick her up. Delano reached down and picked up the child, then she told him to take her over to Peter. He did as his child said, and she reached down and touched the baby's hair, it went from brown to white, and Maria laughed and smiled. "See daddy, Peter is home now" she looked at him and pointed at the child. Peter and Renee looked at each other and then took the child into the house, and up to the nursery. Ricardo told his father they could leave in the morning, because Thomas needed him at home. Delano asked him was Thomas in trouble, or his family? Ricardo told him no, that nothing could touch his family, or Thomas, for they were the watchers and protected by the angels of heaven. Delano pulled his son to him, and asked him was there more to come. Ricardo turned and told him much more and they went home.

When they arrived at the airport Thomas met them, and told Delano there had been a problem, over at the factory, he needed him to come and help straighten things out. Delano went to leave with him, and Ricardo called to him and said "dad it's Tom, who has the money. Look in his locker, and you will find it okay?" Delano looked at him then at Thomas, he got into the car and they headed to the factory. Thomas told him that the safe had been broken into last night, that all of the money was gone which was inside. They had just put the payroll money in there, and he looked over at Delano, and asked him did he really think Tom had it. Delano looked at him and laughed "shit man …if you knew the half of what I have seen, you would understand that Tom had the damn money."

Tom, had worked for Delano for ten years, he found it hard to fire him, but he did. "Tom I don't want to hurt your children, by you not being there with them as they grow up, for this reason, and this reason alone, I will not press charges." Delano told him he would if he ever saw him again, or found out that he had done wrong by them. Tom had over fifty grand, in his locker along with some other things, that were from the safe. "Tom, this one thing I will do for you, I will let you have the money you have stolen, for it is only money, and it does not mean anything to me. If you use this money for any other reason than to care for your children, your breath will be taken, and you will die, and they will still live on." Tom was frighten. He didn't want to touch the money, but Delano told him to take what he had stolen, and leave his factory, and never return again, for him to take heed to the words he had spoken to him.

Thomas looked at Delano as they were driving home, and asked him did Peter have a boy. Delano looked at him and told him not only did he have a boy, but that the boy, was like his children. "Jesus help us" he said as he sat there and thought of all that had happen in the last few months. "Thomas, I have never told anyone this, but I must say something and you are my friend, so I am going to say it to you. My children can float man, in the damn air. I saw it myself, I can tell you other things too, but I don't want to frighten you away from them."

Thomas pulled the car over and told him that he was not afraid, that he had seen something when Ricardo had touch him that day. He had seen a triangle with light, he asked was that what he had seen. "Yes Thomas, I saw that and much more. Thomas, what can I do? I do not think I can send him to school with the other children, so I must hire a tutor for both of them, so that no one will come and expect anything, other than they are my children. Jesus... Thomas, I feel like its some kind of hell. I don't know what to say it is." Thomas reached over and took Delano hand, and told him to have patience, that whatever the children were, they were his and that he loved them, and that it would all work out all right. "This one thing I will say to you, I know those children are from God, and you know I was never a man of God, but today I know that he exists, and the children are here to do his will. I pray I will be here to see the glory of God don't you Delano?"

Thomas looked over at Delano, and he was crying, he touched his shoulder and told him to look at the car window, and he turned and there was his father smiling at him, and out from the window came a voice so loud that it shook the car. "Fear not the children son, love them with all your heart and soul, and trust that they are here for a purpose, and this is your father talking to you. Thomas, you have been faithful, and this is our wish for you, that all that you touch from this day forward will be blessed and that you and your family will have happiness and joy." He then disappeared, and Thomas started the car and they headed for home.

As the years went by Delano and Gina, watched the children grow, and get closer and closer. They could speak five languages, and often they would call their cousin, and talk to him over the phone in Italian. Ricardo and his sister, were growing at an unusual rate, and so was Peter's son. Ricardo told Delano that they had to go to England, to see Peter and bless the way for the new arrivals. When Delano asked him what he was talking about he told him to wait and he would soon find out, and for him not to worry, but to hurry, for the demons were mad, and they were going to try to stop it from happening. Delano hurried and went to Gina he told her they were about to go to England, and asked if she was ready to witness more miracles.

Gina looked at him and shook her head yes, and then they packed and left that very day for the castle. It was the month of June when they arrived in England, and the smell of roses were around them, and people looked and smiled at them, as they walked through the airport. When they arrived at the castle, the children open the car door, got out and then laid flat on the ground. When they stood up the castle door opened, and the children saw each other, and ran into each other's arms, and started talking in Italian, they were excited. They formed a circle and began to dance around spinning in at an incredible rate. Ricardo looked over at his father and told him and Peter to come, and to go and get Renee and Gina, and bring them to the garden. It was time.

When they all stood at the foot of the garden, the children turned and joined hands, and then smiled at each other. They began to walk around in a circle and as they walked they chanted "here we are... here we are.... Come to us... come to us.... Here we are... here we are.... Come to us.... Come to us." Maria held up her hands, as Ricardo took Peter's hands, and they held their hands up to the sky shouting in a loud voice together. "Here we are.... Here we are... Come to us ...come to us." The children chanted and as they did they began to rise up off the ground, They were floating in the air, and the clouds open up as a bright light shined down on them. They went higher into the air, much higher than Delano or Gina had ever seen them go before. They were nearly twelve feet off the ground, Gina and Renee both had their hands over their hearts.

Peter and Delano knelt down on the ground, and watch their children floating in the air, and Gina looked up at the light and seemed to be glowing along with the children as a light from heaven shined down on them. They all stood amazed at what they were witnessing. The children were laughing and talking as they floated in the air, and the light blinded Peter and Delano. Gina and Renee, were the only ones, who could see the children and what was happening. They were talking to their grandparents and they were singing to them. The kids began to descend down to the ground, when their feet touched the ground once again, the light went away and this time Ricardo hair, which was long and brown, had turned the color of gold. He picked up both of the children into his arms, and walked over to the roses, which he and his grandmother had planted, and allowed each child to take a rose. They held the roses up and they turned to gold, and he sat them down on the ground, and his hair went back to brown.

Ricardo walked over to his father and touched him, and Delano fainted, and fell to the ground. Gina screamed and asked him what had he done to his Father, and he told her to be patient, that he was talking to grandfather about them. Ricardo then touched Peter's eyes, and he could see again, and he stood up and went and grabbed Renee's hand. Peter and Renee looked over at the children at what they were doing. The children walked over and put the roses on Delano and then they formed a triangle around him, and began to sing in Italian. As the children finished singing the roses went from gold back to red, and Delano open his eyes, and got up off the ground and then turned to Gina, and started crying.

Peter and Renee rushed over and asked what had happen, and for him to tell them what he knew. Delano looked at them and then turned to the children, and told them that they were here to do something, and that he nor them or anyone else, would able to stop them. Delano looked at Gina and told her that she was going to have another child, and she shook her head, telling him she couldn't; she just couldn't do it. Delano told her it was too late, that she was already pregnant, and that she was going to have twins. Gina fainted and Peter caught her right before she hit the ground.

"What the hell is going on Delano? You tell me I need to know now; I am scared of what is happening?" Delano looked at Ricardo and he walked over to his uncle, reached out his hands to him and told him to come to him. Peter laid Gina down on the ground, then went to Ricardo. Ricardo placed his hands on each side of his head, Peter started screaming. He ran into the rose garden and fell down and started praying. Renee ran to him and tried to comfort him, but he was out of control. His son walked over and put his hands on him, Peter looked up at him and he calmed down and smiled. "My precious son,.. oh my God… my precious son." He reached over and pulled the boy to him, holding him close to his heart, as a glow on his face appeared. Renee asked what he saw she told him to tell her what he had seen. He told her he could not explain it, that it was just too much to say. He got up off the ground went over to his brother and hugged him and they smiled as they looked into each other's eyes.

As they looked at each other, the children formed a circle around them, and started walking around chanting "glory... glory... glory ...come to us. Glory...Glory... Come to us." As they chanted a light shined down on their fathers, and surrounding them, then it disappeared. Gina opened her eyes, got up off the ground then walked over to Renee and hugged her.

Gina told Renee she was hungry and they went into the castle to get something to eat. While they were busy in the kitchen, they could hear the children outside in the garden, laughing and talking to their grandparents. Renee asked Gina was she ready to have twins, she looked at her and told her she still did not believe she was going to have more children. " The truth of the matter Renee is that I hadn't planned on more children. I know Delano hadn't. This whole thing with the children has drained us, yet if this is the will of God, then let it be."

The next day Gina and Delano and the children went back to the states. Gina went to the doctor and they told her she was expecting twins. They were identical and they were boys but they said there was something blocking the screen, they could not figure what it was. It might be another child, they could not be certain right now, but they knew something else was on the screen, and they tried to show Delano what they were talking about. Delano smiled when he saw his father's hand inside of Gina's womb. His father was making sure that nothing happen to the children, they were the final part of the plan, he needed nothing to happen to them. Delano told the doctor's not to concern themselves with the shallow, then he took Gina home. Gina asked were the children okay, he said they were fine, that she had nothing to worry about, none of them did. Gina got bigger with each passing day, as she got bigger the children began to move at a rapid pace in her stomach. Anytime Ricardo came near she had to sit down, the children would be kicking so hard that she would lose her balance. "My brothers are anxious to be with me Mom, that's all. It's been a long time since we have seen each other, they are ready to come home now." Gina looked at him and shook her head, and asked when were the boys to arrive. He told her they would be here in time for his birthday, and for her not to worry so much about things. Gina told him she would try and asked where his sister was. "She has been talking to grandmother all day about something. I don't know what I can't hear them. Maria is stronger than I am mom. She can control things I cannot."

"What do you mean she can control things? Ricardo I don't understand what you are talking about." Ricardo looked at her and smiled "Mom, Maria can do things I cannot do. Just ask her to do something and she will." Gina called out "Maria come to me right now." Maria came down the stairs, looked at her and asked what was the matter. "You know what the matter is. Show me what it is you can do Maria. I must see now, so that when you do it, I won't be afraid, okay." She laughed and then went over by the fireplace and she raised her hands and started flying around the room.

Gina looked in amazement at the child, as she flew around the room, then she stopped and reached her hands out to Ricardo, and he flew to her, as she came down to the floor. Gina looked and said nothing; then she asked what else can you do, Maria? "I can talk to the dead people mother. Do you want to see me do it?" Maria was excited, she wanted Gina to see her do it. Gina was scared but she said "okay, let me see what you are talking about." Maria said "come here Grandmother and show Gina that you are okay" she opened up her hands and a glow came from them, and Gina saw Bridget standing in the light of her daughter hands.

Gina nearly fainted, she could not believe her eyes, just then Delano open the front door and Gina called for him to come into the room immediately. "Look at what our child can do" she asked him still in amazement. The child smiled and started flying around the room as Delano looked, but didn't move or say anything. Ricardo walked over to him and told him "just wait till you see what my brothers can do!" Gina looked at Delano and he looked like he was going to faint; he walked over to the sofa, and sat down next to her. "What the hell has been going on today while I was gone? Jesus, every day there is something new. I swear I don't know if my heart can stand the strain of all of this shit."

Gina looked at him and smiled "oh come on now you mean to tell me you can't take the fact that your daughter can fly? Well give me a fucking break! because I am the one carrying your sons. Lord knows that I got a feeling we are going to see the heavens open up." Delano started laughing and they shook their heads, as Maria kept flying around the room. Delano asked Ricardo could he fly too and he said only with Maria help. "Dad do you want to know what Peter can do?" Delano said "okay what can Peter do."

"Peter can bring the dead people to life." Ricardo started talking to Maria and she nodded and said Peter could do more. "Shit what did you just say?" Delano stood up and asked him again. What did you just say to me about your cousin?" Delano looked scared and he was pacing back and forth in front of Gina. "Dad don't be scared. Peter can bring the dead people back if you ask him to." Delano went to the phone and called his brother and told him what Ricardo just told him, and then told him that Maria, was busy flying around the fucking room. Peter laughed "Delano we know our cat died, shit Peter went over to him and told him to get back up he wasn't ready for him to go, shit the damn cat got up and is still walking around. How's Gina and the boys doing?" Delano told him they were all okay and that the children asked to speak to their cousin and he told them to wait a minute, while his uncle went and got him. When Peter came to the phone they started taking turns talking to each other in Italian, and then Ricardo told Delano to come to the phone and touch it. When he reached for the phone it turned red hot and he dropped it and they laughed.

"See Peter can do something new" they were laughing they thought it was funny. Delano looked at Gina and she said nothing she just looked at her children and smiled. The children were excited one afternoon, they came into the house from being outside and ran up to her. "Mother guess what Maria can do now!" Gina sat down and told her to show her. She took the dead flower and blew on it and it came back to life, and she handed it to Gina and smiled. "Isn't it wonderful mother I can do something new. Isn't the flower beautiful?" Gina said yes the flower was beautiful and then told them to go and find something to do, inside the house that normal children did. Ricardo looked at her and then said "Mother it's okay, that she can do that; do you know what I can do now." She looked at him and asked "what is it that you can do now honey." He walked over to the fireplace and blew on it and the flames started burning.

Gina looked at her children and then suddenly she felt a strange feeling in her stomach. "Delano!" She called out "Delano come quickly hurry! something is going on inside of me!" Delano ran down the stairs to the sofa and asked Ricardo what was happening. He told him his brothers were talking to grandfather, he has to go now because they are about to come home. Gina told him that she was only eight months that the babies were not due yet. Ricardo looked at her and then smiled "mother they are ready now for you to hold them. If you tell them to wait they will just ask them." Gina looked at Ricardo she touched her stomach, and told them it was okay that she wanted them to wait, that she was not ready for them to come home yet." She turned and looked at Delano and told him come talk to his sons and make them behave.

Delano walked over and put his hand on her stomach, and told them to calm down that he loved them, and he too wanted to hold them, but not yet. Gina got up off the sofa then went to go upstairs and turned and asked her children was there anything else she should know? Ricardo walked up to her and smiled "Mother guess what my brothers can do." She looked at him and then asked "what can they do son?." Ricardo smiled and then said "They can become one." Gina looked at him and asked what did he mean? Ricardo said "they can walk through walls and they can join and be one person mother. Isn't it wonderful?" He asked her.

Gina looked at him then said "yes, I guess all of this is wonderful, if you say so." Gina went up stairs and sat down on her bed, and started thinking about the children and all the things she was witnessing. She began to wonder if this was truly wonderful or not. She got to thinking about whether or not she had the right to deserve children such as the one's she was birthing. She had taken many lives in her lifetime and never had she considered what she was really doing. She had wanted to know from the time she had first found out she was carrying Delano's child, was she worthy of giving life to anyone.

She sat there remembering talking to the priest and asking him could God forgive a person for being a fool and she remember his answer. "That God was not only a forgiving God that he had a way of making the wrongs of one person's life turn into rights." Was this what he was doing? The priest had told her that everyone had a purpose in life, and she began to wonder if that was really true, and if so then did it mean that she had given her children this right to possess the power they had. Had not she asked God to grant her children the right to give life, and power to bring all her wrongs to rights? She thought of all the miraculous things that her children were doing and then she asked God was she really going to witness something wonderful?

They were talking of wars and the trouble of the world and with the bombing on the World Trade Center. Gina felt in her heart, that maybe her children would not be given a chance to perform their miracle, for is not war only the gateway to death? What comes from a world fighting and hating each other? Does not love mean anything to people? Have we come to a society that all one can do is cheat and hurt ,and no one considers the price that it costs to lose love and life? Gina was full of questions, but she had no answers She realized that Ricardo had the answers but she didn't want to ask a child to help her..

Gina lit a candle everyday, and asked God to bless her children and make them do something to help the world. It had been her prayer, since the first moment she knew she was carrying life inside of her. Now she stood there looking in the mirror at her stomach, and wondering what could make her so worthy, of carrying boys, which could join and become one? What could be these children purpose she thought? Her children didn't want to play with other children they kept to themselves. They were so smart. Ricardo was already finishing with his schooling and he was now studying the stars. She wondered why he chose to study stars was there a special reason? Maria was into speaking different languages all the time. She already could speak five and Gina laughed to herself she barely could speak English. Peter's son was the same he did not wish to play with other children, but he loved animals ,and he kept bringing dead animals back to life. Peter had told Delano that he could do things that sometimes frighten him so bad that he was scared to pick his son up.

Gina laughed they were a family of sinners, giving birth to angels, was not that some kind of cruel joke? Surely God was punishing them for what they had done in their lives, by giving them children, who taught them only the value of life and love. Gina thought of how excited Maria was about flying. She loved it and as she flew by you could feel the life inside of her spreading and filling the room with the delight of her heart. Gina looked at the calendar it was now November and she was due at the end of December. She wondered if this was some kind of curse? Her son and daughter was born on Christmas day and now she was to have twins born right around the same time. What was going on? could she truly take more? for her heart now at times felt weak, when she witness some of the things the children were doing. Her heart would flutter so hard that she felt herself about to pass out.

Delano walked into the room and asked was she all right and Gina looked at him and he came and sat down next to her. He touched her stomach and smiled, and then turned and looked at her "honey I am afraid that these children, we are bringing into the world will get killed. What if someone finds out what they can do, and decide they should be killed? Gina looked at him and she shook her head. She knew she told him that these children were only on loan. "Don't you hear them telling you, that they have been together up in heaven, and that they are excited to be coming here? God would not do such a thing as to let them come down here, then have them destroyed by man. I believe in my heart, that they are here for a reason honey. I hope that I live long enough to see what they are here to do."

Delano looked at her then Ricardo and Maria came into the room. "Mother why is it you trouble yourself so with so many questions? If I tell you why we have come, will it really make all that difference to you? I think Mother, that we should not tell you yet, but Maria has something she wants to show you, I have decided that it is okay and I ask you and father to not tell anyone about what you are about to witness. Father you must not even tell Thomas, for I know you confide in him, and this is not for him to know yet. Will you give me your word father? mother promise too that you will not tell what we are about to show you?

The children stood there looking at Gina and Delano and waiting for their answer. Gina looked at Delano and she smiled and then she turned and told them that they would not tell. The children and took off their clothes, and turned around and lifted up their arms, and out of their backs came wings; like birds and they began to fly around the room. Maria turned and did the most amazing thing Gina had ever witness in her life, she disappears into a rose. Gina stood up as she saw her daughter go inside the rose, she looked at the other roses turn gold as she came back out and then she and Ricardo put back on their clothes. Gina sat down on the bed and she looked at them and she began to cry.

Maria rushed over to her mother and put her hand on her and smile "mother don't be afraid of me. I am here to help you. I promise that all of us will make it right and that we will make this place here something special." Gina looked at her child, she felt she was not worthy of such an honor as to birth these children. Ricardo came and kneel down next to his mother. He told her that the boys were not going to listen to her much longer, for they had to come to start growing it was getting close to the time when they were do what they had been conceived for.

"Ricardo is this my fault the reason you children are doing all these things? Mine and Delano's fault? Ricardo looked into his parents in the eyes and he turned, and looked at Maria, and then she came and sat on her father's lap and kissed him. "No mother it is not your fault, we are here because God told us that we had to come and make it right here. This planet is a chosen planet and everyone here has been given something special "the ability to love. Over the years mother, love has been taken away, because Satan did not want love; he only wanted to hurt and destroy. He lives here on earth you know, He has nothing to do but try to stop us he cannot touch you or us, but he does try to sometimes like with Peter. He tried to take him before he was born. Peter, is the special child, but it is the twins which will make the circle whole, and then in time mother and dad, you will see that we are only here to help bring love back, and make it all right on this planet. We live in the stars mother, and it is there that one day we will return. Mother, will you chose to come with us when we go home? Or will you decide to stay here?"

Gina looked at him she wondered why Ricardo was not asking his father the same question. She looked at him and then at Delano, and she turned and told him if she had to live her on this planet without Delano, she would not enjoy it. She would miss him and them so much, that she would die inside, therefore she would want to be with them. He smiled "mother then I grant you your wish right now. I promise that we shall all be together, and that you have nothing to worry about." Gina looked at him and smiled and then asked when were his brothers coming.

Ricardo looked at Gina then he looked at Maria and smiled "they will be here in a few weeks mom. Hey mom, do you want to know what their names are? Gina looked at him not even her and Delano, had even considered naming the children yet. "Mother their names are Michael and Gabriel. They are the chosen two, for they are the ones that will save this place. We are only here to help them mother, and we have been making a path for them to enter." Gina turned and looked at Maria she was smiling and touching Delano's face, she said "Mother guess what I think, I shall wish them to have eyes like my father. Look mother, does not his eyes have the sparkle of life in them?"

Gina turned and looked at Delano and she smiled at him "Maria I think you are right, I think your father has the most beautiful eyes, I have ever seen here on earth. I look into them and I feel all the love he has for me; and I know that if you wish, your brothers to have eyes like his, it will be a good thing." She smiled and laughed "oh mother sometimes I think that you should be a rose." Gina looked at her and asked why did she think she should be a rose? Maria said that roses were special, they had the scent of heaven in them, and that she knew her mother did too. Gina grew tired and laid back on the bed and the children came and started talking to their brothers in Italian. Gina stopped them and asked why did they always talk in Italian? was not there some reason for them speaking in that language? for their parents didn't speak it, nor could they understand it. "Mother we talk in the language that grandfather taught us for he likes to hear us. Father, did you tell mother that grandfather slept inside her for so long, that grandmother became jealous and made him go home? Delano told her no, that they had just done it. Gina looked at them and asked what were they talking about, and Delano told her that he had seen his father inside her stomach on the ultra sound, that he had to stay there to protect the boys. It wasn't until the other day when she felt so lightheaded, that he went home to be with his mother.

"Are the boys safe now without him?" She turned and looked at Ricardo and he said "yes they were very safe, that nothing could touch them, not even the breath of Satan." The children went back to talking to their brothers, Delano laid his head on Gina's breasts and they drifted off to sleep.

Have you ever considered that there are angels sitting by you? Each one of us has an angel watching over us, and they are there to take care of us, and keep us safe and out of harm if they can. Not all angels are here to keep you safe though, some come to take you back home for they miss you and cannot stand to be away from you. Then there are those who work for Satan, and they are here to help destroy you, and bring you to him. You see this world is full of angels, and yet man has not seen them, for they could not bare the fact that they couldn't control them. The spirit of God, controls Angels and only he can give them power. Satan can steal them but he cannot give them life or power. Is it not wonderful to know that you have an angel? When Ricardo said this to Peter and Delano they stood and looked at him and then smiled and told him that they were at a loss for words but agreed with him.

The twins were born the week before Christmas and on Christmas morning the family witness the most amazing thing they had ever seen. Peter and Renee and had come to town to share in the birth of the children. On Christmas morning Peter called them all down stairs and told them to come and watch what they all could do together. Gina and Delano told them they would be right down and Delano called Renee and Peter into the room, and told them that they could not tell anyone what they were about to witness. Delano pulled his brother to him and told him he loved him. Peter looked at him and said he loved him too and then they took their wives downstairs to the living room, and the children were gathered together by the fireplace.

"Father, I wish to give you and your brother, a special gift this morning" Ricardo said as he looked at Maria and she nodded and then at Peter and he nodded yes too. Peter had one twin and Maria had the other in their arms, and then Ricardo came and stood between them, then he lifted his arms to the heavens, and the children's clothes fell to the floor, and their wings came out and they flew up to the ceiling, they then turned and looked down on their parents and started chanting together. "We are here... We are here... Come to us.... Come to us... We are here... We are here come to us... Come to us!" Then in a light so bright that it nearly blinded them, they saw Ricardo and Bridget coming out of the children, and they stood in the light and smiled at them.

They were holding hands with the children, and they were all singing and laughing and talking in Italian. Delano smiled and called out to his father "Dad, I love you so much for giving me this chance at life and love." He looked down at Peter and Delano smiled, and then spoke to them. "My sons, I love you so much, and I am proud to see you taking care of the children. How are you Peter? I have never been given the chance to hold your son, so I am now being given that chance. He let go of Bridget's hand and he stepped down to the floor, and walked over to Peter and looked at him. He reached out and touched his hair and then his face, and then he pulled his son to him, and kissed him and told him he loved him more than life.

Peter was crying he didn't say anything he only looked at him. "Peter my son, I have given you your wish for a son, because you needed to know that you were loved more than life. We are so happy to watch you and Renee care for Peter, and this day we grant you the knowledge that you will not remember after this day." He turned to Gina and to Delano and told them that they would remember but they could not tell anyone what they saw, and if they gave their word that it would happen. Gina gave her word and so did Delano and then the clothes that were on Renee dropped to the floor and she turned and showed them her wings. Renee was an angel that had come to help them. Peter looked at his wife and smiled he had not even considered that she was not human.

They had been together all these years now and he had not considered the fact that she had been sent to him. She turned back around and Gina screamed, she was Renee the girl that had bumped into her and had died in the car crash. Gina fainted, and Delano caught her right before she hit her head on the floor. He looked at his father and smiled "you see Peter, you did love her and your son, and I knew that, and I asked God to let you have another chance at happiness with her." Peter looked at her and went to touch her and she flew up to the children and they all began speaking in Italian and laughing and singing together.

When Ricardo walked over to Delano he kissed him and told him he loved him then he flew up to the children and took Bridget hand, and they all talked and laughed then Renee said "good bye" and she came back down to the ground, and her clothes went back on her, and the children came down to the ground, and when the light disappeared. Peter fell to the floor and Renee walked over and kissed him, then told him to wake up. Peter looked around and then got up off the floor "hell, I missed everything! my silly but passed out." He was pouting and Delano laughed and went over and kissed his brother, and Gina walked over and pulled Renee to her, and looked at her and then smiled. The twins were crying and Gina went to them and she took one, and Renee took the other, and they went to feed them.

Chapter Nine

Ten years had passed since that Christmas morning, and the twins were expecting their eleventh birthday in a month. The children were so beautiful, that Gina often looked and smiled at them when she knew they weren't looking. She had seen America fight two wars, and so many lives had been lost. During the years she had seen Maria, bring four people back to life. The first one was a woman who a robber shot trying to take purse. The woman had her children's college fund money in the purse, and she refused to let go of it. Gina and Maria had gone shopping that day and when they came out of the shop, they witness the young man shooting the woman, and her falling to the ground.

Maria froze everyone who stood on the street except her, Gina and the young man. The woman laid dead, and he turned and saw all the frozen people, and pointed the gun at Maria and shot it. Maria caught the bullet and then she walked up and touched the woman, and she stood up and her open wound healed, and the boy screamed at what he saw. Maria then walked up to the boy and in a loud voice ordered the demon that had held this boy's mind, to leave his body and never come to earth again. Four gray clouds came out of the boy, and they flew down into the ground and Maria stomped her foot and said "Enter no one else I said be gone!" She then removed all thoughts and knowledge of what had happen from the boy, and the woman, and then went and took Gina's hand, and everyone went back to their day's business.

The second life was that of a child. Maria had been out playing in the garden and talking to her grandmother, when she heard the car strike the child, and the woman cry out in pain. She told her grandmother she would be right back, and she walked to the front of the house, and she saw the child laying there and she once again froze everyone, then she walked up to the woman and awoke her and she fell to the ground. She was a child of God, and she prayed this prayer "Jesus this is my only child, and you know how much I love him. Please heavenly father, do not let this terrible thing which has happen, be the end of his life." Maria walked up to her and she smiled at the woman and told her "because your love for your child is pure, and the love you have for my heavenly father is pure and true, I shall grant you your wish. From this day forth no harm shall ever come to your child; and he shall be in the band of angels, which fight for the glory of this planet." Maria reached down and touched the boy on the forehead, and when she touched him he open his eyes and looked at his mother and jumped up, and ran to her and then he turned and faced Maria then walked up to her; and she smiled and he said "thank you for bringing me back to her. Are you the child that the man spoke of?"

Maria smiled at him and then she said yes, and removed all knowledge from their minds of that day, of what had happen and froze them. As she walked back towards the garden everyone started back to the matters of the day, and the woman and the child went home. The third was that of an old lady, which just dropped dead, right in front of the house. The family was sitting in the living room eating popcorn when it happened. The children all got up and went to the window and Maria told the woman to get up and go for it was not her time, that her grandchildren were waiting for her. The woman stood up and she looked at her clothes then shook her head and dusted herself off and continued down the street. Maria smiled and watched her cross over, then she saw four children, a man and a woman holding hands, holler for her, and the woman put her hands around the children, and smiled at them giving each one a kiss. As she kissed each child Maria, rose a little off the ground, and then when they walked away she fell to the floor. Ricardo walked over and touched her heart, Maria woke up and they all went back to eating popcorn and talking. The fourth person she saved was that of an old man, which was homeless. Maria, Thomas, and Gina had just gotten into the car, when they saw the man walk out in front of a car, deliberately get struck and die. Maria got out of the car and froze everyone, once again then walked up to the car and said "Go back to your shape and the car mended itself. The man in the car was bleeding and Maria waved her hand, he was healed and then she reached down and touched the man, and he opened his eyes. Maria told him she understood his pain. The man had lost everything in the world that he cared for, in a car accident, and he had gone mad. Maria looked at him and told him to stand up, she smiled and then she gave him back his youth, and told him that from this day forward he had a chance to start life again. "Go and do it all over again, only this time be wiser and know that it is truly God, who watches over you, and keeps you safe." She removed all knowledge of herself, and what had happened; she waved her hands over the man, and his clothes became new, and he stood there a man, all clean and fresh. Maria smiled and then went back to the car and got in, as she did the people went back to the matters of the day.

Ricardo and his brothers were out at the airport with Thomas seeing him off. Gina had remained in the car for she was tired, and Maria was with her. Ricardo looked up at the sky and suddenly he froze, everything and his clothes dropped to the ground. Gina watched as he went up into the air and Ricardo stopped two planes from crashing, and exploding. They had been headed right at each other. He move one plane up and then the other down, and then he waved his hand over both planes, and erased all memory of what had happen. He flew back down to earth and his clothes came and went back on him. He then kissed Thomas, and told him never to tell anyone what he had seen, and Thomas told him he had his word.

The world was truly in bad shape, Russia was at war with Jerusalem, and had sent a bomb to destroy the city. Peter had been reading the bible, when he suddenly stopped, and then grabbed his mother and father's hand, and then froze everything in time, while they flew to Jerusalem. He sat his parents down on the ground, told them to cover their eyes, for the bomb was headed here, and he had very little time. He froze everything except the bomb, and when it got so close to the city, that even Renee covered her heart, she and Peter watched their son catch the bomb in his hand, and then fly up into space. Peter consumed the bomb, as it exploded and then flew back down to his parents; and once with them left Jerusalem, everything went back to as it was and no one knew what had happen.

Gina had been out in the garden and she was planting some new rose bushes, she heard the boys playing in the background. Suddenly, she didn't hear them and she turned and watched the twins join hands, and they went from being two boys into being one body, with two heads. She looked at them and then she went back to digging in the roses, and the boys returned to two separate bodies and went back to playing again.

Gina and Delano had spent many a night watching her children flying around the room and talking to their grandparents about the wonderful things they were doing here on earth. Gina felt truly blessed to have been given the chance to see her children do such wonderful things, and yet she feared for their lives and each day she would watch over and protect them. Ricardo looked identical to Delano, and at times now she often thought that he was here to do something else, but he wouldn't tell her what it was and she didn't pressure him.

Maria was so beautiful she had hair of gold, and she looked like a model, she was so tall and graceful. Maria would often disappear into the roses and then come out and look around and smile at her. Gina was beginning to gray and her face was beginning to age, she and Delano were getting up in age now, and they wondered if they would be here to see the children do what they had been sent to do. She often would go and light a candle and pray that the children would remain safe, if something happened to her and Delano. They still chose not to play or talk to other children, but they kept telling them that they would have grandchildren. They would all call and talk to Peter on the phone and every six months, they got together and joined hands, and then disappeared into the clouds.

They would be gone for the whole day, and then would return and tell them that they had been with their grandparents. Ricardo came to his mother one day while she was out in the garden, and told her to pick a rose and hand it to him. Gina looked at all the roses and then she reached way back in the back and picked the most beautiful yellow rose she had ever seen. She walked over and handed the rose to her son, and Maria flew out of the rose with a woman, and she and the woman looked at Ricardo, then at Gina. Maria smiled and said "mother this is Angel, she is Ricardo's wife."

Gina stood up and looked at her and smiled, and went and hugged her, and Angel took Ricardo's hand, and they went into the house to his room and closed the door. Maria turned and told her mother to fear not, for her first grandchild was on the way. Gina nodded her head and told her she was happy to know it, and looked at her and smiled, as Maria then flew back into the roses, and then returned with a man.

Gina stood up as they came out of the rose, and she looked at the man, and thought he was handsome. He smiled and walked over to her and kissed her on the cheek, and told Gina that he was Maria's husband, and that he had missed his wife so much. He then flew into the rose that they had come out of, and when he came back out, he had three children with him. There were two girls and a boy, and the children looked just like Maria and him. Maria walked up and she smiled and turned and said "mother this is my husband Donald, and these are my children, and she called each child one by one, up to meet their grandmother. The first child's name was Destiny, and she looked just like Maria. She kissed Gina, and told her she was happy to be home. The second girl name was Theresa, and she too kissed her grandmother, and told her she was happy to be home. The young boy came up and he introduced his self. "Grandmother I am Jerome, and I am the angel that keeps the gate to the earth safe. I am so happy to see you and meet you, for mother has told us all about you, and it is truly an honor to know, that such a woman came from this planet."

He reached over and touched Gina's hair, and it went back to gold, and her face went back to that of a young woman. Delano walked out and asked what was going on for he heard his son in the room with someone and they were making love. Maria laughed and then walked up to him and smiled, then reached out and took his hand, and then took him to meet her husband and his grandchildren; and as they met him they kissed him and hugged him tightly, and told him they were so proud to be his grandchildren. Delano looked at Gina and told her she looked just like she did the day they first met.

Theresa walked up to him and smiled, and then she blew him a kiss, and he turned back to the man that Gina had first met, then he ran to Gina and kissed her, and they turned and looked at their three grandchildren and smiled. When Ricardo and Angel came out into the garden he told his father that this was his wife, Angel, and that they were expecting their firstborn to come very soon. Delano looked at the woman and then she walked up to him and smiled and kissed him, and told him that her son would look like him and Ricardo, and that she felt honored to finally meet him. Delano never asked how or when they had been married, or how the children and them had come to be. He accepted them with open arms, and the smell of roses filled the air, and they all went into the house, and sat down to the table, and Maria spread her hand over the table, and it was filled with food from every nation and she told them to eat.

Delano stood up and he lifted his voice to the Lord and shouted "Father of all, I speak to you from my heart. Thank you for such a wonderful thing you have done for me and my wife. I promise to keep them all safe and from harm." Just then Thomas and his family came into the room, he looked at all the new faces and smiled and said "Well isn't anyone going to introduce them to my family and me?" Everyone laughed and they came and sat to the table and the children and the grandchildren began talking to each other and laughing as they ate. Thomas looked at Delano and they smiled and then began to eat too.

Ricardo and Angel gave birth to a boy, as they said they would and twelve years passed and they grew older but Gina and Delano never aged. They spent many nights playing with their grandchildren and their hearts were made glad, as each of them grew up and became men and women of great statue. Each time a child reached the age of eighteen, they flew into the rose and brought out their mate, and by the time Gina turned eighty, and Delano was then one hundred, they had ten beautiful grandchildren. Peter and Renee had one grandchild, but they never met the woman who gave birth to their grandchild, for she refused to leave heaven.

One night though she came to them in a dream, and told them to watch over her son and husband for she missed them, and that she grew anxious for them to return home to her. When Peter and Renee woke up, Renee told Peter that the woman was named Princess, and that she guarded the water of youth. He never asked more and he and Renee never aged they stayed as they were from the time they first kissed. Many years passed, and war and destruction was everywhere. Man had tried to control many things, and because of their foolish wisdom, they had caused Satan to gain control of too much. Satan stood watching the earth, one day and he decided he no longer wanted it to be. He looked up at the sun and told it to come forward slowly, for he wanted to see the terror, of the foolish people who thought he didn't exist. The sun refused to do it, but Satan reached up into the sky, and grabbed it and started to bring it down, himself inch by inch.

One night Gina was sitting on the sofa watching television, when a news bulletin flashed across the screen. She called for Delano and he came into the room, and looked at the news the sun was moving, and it was heading toward the earth. It was said that in two days the earth would be destroyed, and that nothing living would exist. It would be burned up everything that was, and man became scared, and the people were crying and calling out for someone to help them. There was turmoil in the streets, as the sun came closer. The water on the planet began to dissolve from the heat. The heat of the sun took many lives, and with each hour there could be heard great laughter coming from under the ground.

The children did not seem to be affected by what was happening, they were happy and gay. Gina watched people going back to church, and begging God to hold them, but the children said nothing they just wanted to play. When Peter and Renee said that the airplanes had quit running and that they had no way to come; Maria laughed and told them she would make sure they came in time, and for them to quit worrying so much. Peter handed the phone to Renee, and told her that Maria wanted to talk to her, and when Maria spoke she talked in Italian, and so did Renee, and no one could understand what was said.

Renee laughed and told her thank you, for she could not hear or see, for Satan had blocked her mind. Maria laughed and told her that Satan was a fool for doing all this, and that the day fast approached, that the time was coming and she hung up the phone. As the sun approached the earth it began to get so hot, that even the water began to run hot out of the faucet, and people were terrified at all that was going on. There were no more wars, all the people of the earth were coming together and begging God to have mercy on them. They pleaded for the God of the earth, to do something, and many died and fell on the ground. So many that they had no place to put the bodies, and all that remained were piles of ashes all over the world.

Strange how now color or territory, didn't matter anymore to anyone. All you could hear were the prayers. People were in the streets praying and gathering, holding hands and in every country, all over the planet the people did the same thing, they begged God for help. Gina went to the window it was so hot, and nothing had life anymore. The trees were all withered, and there was fire and flames everywhere. The water that was left on the planet was so hot, that no one could drink it, and the food was gone. Gina feared that the world she loved was coming to an end.

The President of the United States, came on the television and told the world that it was coming to an end, and he begged the people to pray harder to God to deliver them. There was no place to run, nowhere to hide, people were dropping dead on the ground. It was a site so hard to behold, that even Gina cried out in pain and prayed, that God would give the world peace and save it. The children were all laughing, and they went to her and told her that they knew she was scared, and asked her why. "Mother we are here and now is the time. Maria held up her hand and she called to Peter in the wind "come Peter, come to me and bring the family with you. She opened up her arms and out of her came Renee, Peter, and his son and grandson.

Gina fainted into Delano's arms for she could not bare it. Delano looked at Ricardo and told him that his mother was not breathing, and he felt himself beginning to lose his air. Ricardo told him not to worry, that everything was in order, and then he and the rest of the children gathered together, they took each other's hands and went outside. Ricardo looked at all the dead bodies lying on the ground, he looked at all the destruction that Satan had caused, and he and the children, began to shed their clothes and their wings came out, as they flew up toward the sun.

Hitler, and Hitler said, "Go now or forever..."

The people began to rise up off the ground and everyone looked up at the children and they were no longer a secret. They were being seen by the world. People started falling to the ground praying and thanking God for the miracle they were witnessing. As the children neared the sun, a man stepped out, and he was red and looked like fire, and he faced the children and he yelled for them to go back, and leave him alone.

The children were not afraid of him, they kept heading towards the sun, and as they got closer the earth, began to cool off, and they began to glow a brilliant white and gold glare. Gina woke up, and looked up at her children and the man in flames, and her heart feared him. The man shouted to them "Go back! Go Back! I will not let you do this! Go back I say to you or I shall destroy you!" Ricardo stepped up to the man and he shouted at him "Satan, you have had your time here on earth, and your days were numbered. This is the day I have been waiting for. You have not rights here any longer. Go now or forever regret the day you came here!"

Gina and the entire world could hear what was being said, it was like watching television and seeing a movie. Satan looked at the children and laughed "You are children, you cannot hurt me. I am stronger than you, look at all the things I have done, and he began to show the children the world; and all the destruction and death, he had caused. Then out from behind Ricardo came Peter's son, and he spoke in a loud voice "Satan, I warn you again, leave my people along or I shall destroy you, and this is my words. Be gone and leave my children alone!"

Satan laughed and he threw a fireball at the children, and as soon as it hit them, it broke up; and the fire turned to water, and fell to the earth. As each drop fell and hit earth, it began to put out the fires, that were consuming it. Satan became angry and he shouted "so you think you can stop me do you! Well this is not your place, it is mine and he called on all his angels, to come and stand with him. Up from the earth raised a host of people, and they stood behind Satan, and began to chant "Go back! Go back before we destroy you!

Maria came out from behind Ricardo, and she spoke in a voice so loud that it shook the earth "Listen to me this is your last warning. I tell you to go back and leave my people along for I grow tired of you and your ways here, and I now have had my fill!" Satan threw a great ball of fire at her, and she was hit and she flew backwards into Ricardo and Peter, and they flew back into the sun. Satan and his angels began to throw more and more fire balls at them, and as the fire balls hit the children, they began to explode and turned to water and fell to the earth. The people on the earth were standing looking up into the heavens, and they were so afraid that you could hear their hearts beating.

All you could hear down on earth was the voices of the people yelling save us "God save us! God forgive us from our sins, protect us from the wrath of Satan!" Satan heard the people down on earth, calling for God, and he started throwing fireballs down to them. As the balls hit the earth they burst and turned to water. Satan yelled out "I am Satan! This is my place leave now or I shall destroy all of you! children do you hear me leave me alone!"

It was then that the twins stepped out, and when Satan saw them he became even angrier, and he sent a fireball so large at them, that Gina screamed out. Satan turned and reached down and picked Gina up, and took her into his hands, holding her out to the children that stood before him. Renee's clothes fell off and so did Angel's and Maria's husband, and they all had wings, and they flew up and stood by the children. Renee came forward and spoke "Satan you have my child in your hands, let her go, or I shall not only destroy you, I shall make you regret the day you ever were born!"

Satan laughed and they began to squeeze the air out of Gina, Maria walked up in front of Renee. Maria told Satan to release her mother this instant, or she would do to him what no man could do! Satan laughed and he shouted at her "what do you think I am a fool? I know you are life but you cannot hurt me. You think you can do me harm you stupid bitch!" and he sent a fireball at her and Maria grabbed it with her hand, and as she let it go, it fell to earth and as it hit, it began to bring back the dead things to life. The plants and the flowers began to bloom and chant "Beware! Beware! This is the day that the Lord has made." The trees began to grow leaves of colors and the earth began to smell so sweet that Satan yelled "stop that you fool I can't stand the smell of sweetness! He sent another fireball at her.

Renee grabbed it and then she turned and looked at him and shouted "you fool do you not know who we are? you have run out of time and we all grow tired of fighting you. Stop now or this will be the last day that you shall ever see anything again!" All of the children joined hands and they shouted at the same time "we demand you to let that child go right now! Satan laughed at them then he dropped Gina and she began to drop down to the earth at such a speed that Delano feared for her and he screamed out for Ricardo to catch her before Satan killed her. Ricardo stepped out from behind and reached down and grabbed his mother, and placed her beside his father. Ricardo turned and looked at Satan and he shouted at him "This day, is the last day. It is day that I spoke of many centuries ago, and I no longer am interested in you Satan. You are a fool you have been given to much power, and I shall not allow you to have any more!" Ricardo raised his hand up, and then in a voice that was so loud that the earth shook he said "Children of Satan be gone!" Everyone who stood behind Satan was suddenly gone, and Ricardo looked like he had grown twice his size, and he turned and once again said "Satan you shall reap what you sow, for I am who I am, and you are a fool!"

Satan turned around and he had no one standing with him, he was alone and by himself. The people down on earth began to cry out, and they started singing "Glory! Glory! Lord God Almighty King of the Earth, and all that exists. Glory! Glory! Glory! Lord God Almighty, King of the Earth!" Satan looked down at all the people in the world praising God, and he became like a large ball of fire, and he yelled at them "I shall win this battle, and then I shall destroy all that ever was!"

When he finished talking the heavens open up, and there sat on a throne, sat the trinity. The light of heaven was so bright, that man could not stand to see it, and they covered their eyes, and bowed down and chanted louder with the angels, "GLORY! GLORY! LORD GOD ALL MIGHTY, HE RULES THE HEAVENS, AND HE RULES THE EARTH! NONE CAN SEE WHAT HE SEES, AND NO ONE CAN DO WHAT HE DOES! GLORY! GLORY! GLORY! LORD GOD ALMIGHTY. GLORY! GLORY! GLORY! LORD GOD ALL MIGHTY!

Satan turned and he went to throw another fireball at the children, and there stood Jacob, Isaiah, Peter and Paul, and a host of others, and Job walked up and he looked at Satan, and shook his head, and then went to join the rest. All of the angels of heaven, and on earth, came and stood around the children, and they looked at Satan. He laughed and told them that he was not afraid of them, and that he would win the battle and prove it. Satan turned and looked at God, and he yelled at him "you have to send children to do what you want. I see you do not fight me alone, well send who you will, for I killed your son, and I shall kill them too!"

It was then that the twins began to grow, and they grew bigger with each word, that came from Satan mouth. He turned and looked and they were larger than him, and he still threw a fireball at them. God stood up and then walked over to his angels and smiled at them "My children are not here to fight you Satan. They are here to stand and show the people that their prayers have been answered. You Satan have no power here. Now once again I warn you if you keep up this battle that you will lose. Have not I been good to you? Did I not allow you the right to torture my children and look at the entire world, and all the trouble you have caused."

The Lord open his gown and from within He began to show Satan all the wrongs he had done, and with each wrong the children behind him grew bigger and bigger. God turned and looked at his children and smiled "these are the chosen ones, they need not fight you Satan. But if you keep on, I shall not only let them fight you, I shall let them destroy you! Satan consider what I say now ,for I go back to my chair, and when I get there, I shall no longer be interested in anything you have to say." Satan did not listen to God, he laughed and God went back and set in the chair, and then he joined hands with his son, and his spirit, and he told the angels to prepare for battle.

The angels lifted up their shields, and they raised up their swords, and the children joined hands, and Renee went and stood behind them, and lifted up her sword, and she looked at Satan and told him in a loud voice "Children of God prepare for Battle. This is the day that the Lord has made, rejoice I say children! Rejoice and be glad, for none is greater than the Lord God Almighty." She raised her sword up and the pointed it at Satan.

Renee pointed her sword at Satan and as she did it put out his flames. Renee turned and faced the sun and told it to go back to where it belong. The sun went back to its place in the heavens and the earth shook and the people sang "Glory to God! Glory to God!" and all of the people in the world fell to their knees, and they prayed for the children to win the battle. "You were warned to not do this, and you still were a fool. Such as it is, this is the day that the Lord has made. Rejoice I say children of the earth and lift up your hands to a God that loves you!"

The people on earth began to stand up, and raise up their hands to the Lord, and chant louder and louder with the angels "This is the day that the lord has made rejoice and be glad in it! None is greater than God is! Glory! Glory! To God King of the world! Glory! Glory! To God King of the World." Satan turned and faced God he looked at him and the trinity and then declared that it was not fair for him to fight so many angels at once, was he afraid of him so much that he had to have a host of angels, to fight only one man?

The twins stepped forward, and then they joined together and became one. Gina looked at her children and screamed out to them "Fight children, I now know why you are here. Fight children for there is none greater than God! Fight children for the lives that I took, when Satan had my heart, and I knew no better! Fight children for the wrongs that I did! Fight children for the lives of the ones to still come! Fight children for the right to live free! Fight children for the right to love! Fight children for I love you and there is nothing greater than love! Fight my children and stand for my father in heaven who loves you such as me! Fight my children for we are here watching! Fight my children for he cannot win! Fight my children for this is the day! Fight my children for this is the day!

Gina began to grow a bright gold with each word that came from her mouth. Gina began to get louder and with each breath that she took the children grew stronger. She then turned and looked at Satan and she screamed at him "You are a fool to fight these children of mine, and this is the day that the world has been waiting for. I am Gina Delano, and I have come to stand before you, Satan. I was yours, and you have lost my children and me. I now stand with God, and this is your last chance! Go home and leave us alone, or this will be the day!

Satan turned and face her he looked her in the eye but Gina stood tall she was not afraid. Gina's wings came out of her back, and she went and stood behind her children. Gina ordered them to fight, and she told them she loved them, and each child emerged, and they formed a circle and they began to chant. "We are here... we are here... come to us... come to us... we are here... we are here... come to us... Come to us!" Then the heavens open up and out stepped their grandparents and their parents, and they came and stood behind Gina. Behind them stood a host of angels, and they all raised up their swords, and they shouted together "we are here... we are here... come to us... come to us!"

A great light filled the heavens, and out from behind the trinity, came a light so great that not even the angels could look at it, all were blinded, no one could see but Satan, and the twins. The earth began to sing out, the trees and the flowers, the birds and the animals, the fish in the sea, all that existed began to sing out in a loud voice "This is the day!" This is the day! Beware you fool this is the day! Satan once again laughed and he drew his sword and the twins turned to their mother, and walked up to her and spoke, "Mother, for the lives you have taken, we stand here today, and we stand for justice. We stand for peace. We stand for love! Mother we are ready, hand us your sword mother, and go back to father, and hold his hand!"

"Listen to us father, we love you very much, and this is the day that you and mother, created long ago in your hearts, when you asked God to forgive you for your sins. Father, here is your love, and we are the love of your hearts. Father do not be afraid, Mother has given us her strength. She is the key, Satan cannot touch her or anyone ever again." They waited until Gina was next to Delano and then Peter, Delano and Gina formed a circle and began to chant "Children fight for us! Children fight for us! Win the battle and come home! Win the battle and come home! Fight children, fight hard and strong! Satan, you are a fool! Look at what you have done. Children we stand ready! We claim the right to see our children fight! God we are ready and so are our children!

They looked up into the heavens and the twins joined again, and became one, only they had two heads. They turned and looked at Satan, then loudly shouted at him "Prepare to die Satan! Prepare to die! For you have caused too much harm, and you will never again run the earth." Satan drew back his sword, and came forward "I fear you not!" He said and he and the twins began to fight.

Each time their swords hit, the heavens sparkled, it was the like watching light and day join. The more they fought, the more the earth began to turn back to life. The flowers began to bloom and the water began to turn cool, and with each blow Satan struck, the twins grew in size; they became stronger, and Satan got mad, and shouted at them "I will fight till the end, and you cannot kill me, so prepare yourself for I am Satan, and I rule the planet earth. I shall win my battle with you!" Satan raised his sword back and out from behind the trinity came a voice that shook the earth and the heavens.

"Satan I have watched you grow, and become a fool. You were my chosen child, and you and you alone failed the test of time. I am, who I am, and you should have not challenged me, but for your stupid ways, I shall now let you weep what you have sowed. Satan I am not proud of you and you should have listened. Children of God this is the Day! I now give you the power that is needed to get my son into control, and trust me Satan, I am he who brought you here, and I am he who will now take you away!"

The twins stepped forward and bowed down to the great light, and when they rose back up they continued on in the battle with Satan. They fought strong and hard and the earth and the heavens shook with each blow of the swords and Satan tried with all his might to kill the twins, but his effort was in vain. As the twins fought him, they began to sing, and Satan told them to shut up and fight he could not stand the noise. The choirs of heaven, and the people of earth, and the angels, whom stood behind the children, began to sing "This is the day! This is the day! This is the day that the Lord has made!" The twins fought hard and they saw that Satan was growing tired and they had pity for him, and as they hit his sword, and Satan began to weaken, they stopped and turned to the throne, and looked at the light, then turned back and said "What do you tire Satan? Oh surely not you, for you are the one who wanted to fight! What shall we do God, let him rest?"

Satan yelled out "I need no help from you!" and Satan charged and the twins drew back their sword and cut off his head and then Satan disappeared. The angels started singing Glory! Glory! Glory! Lord God almighty King of heaven and earth!" The children all joined together, and they went up into the heavens, and the clouds closed up. There was nothing but sunshine and blue skies with stars sparkling and a rainbow of colors of every kind circled the world.

Gina and Delano and Peter looked at each other they did not know what to do. They went into the house and there inside were the children waiting for them. They ran to their mother and threw their arms around her, and told her to be patient, that they would be back soon. They looked at their father and smiled, and went and hugged him, and then they hugged Peter, and said "no one would remember them ever fighting the battle, and that all was now right in the world once again." Gina turned and asked them was Satan still alive?

Maria looked at her and smiled, then the children disappeared. Delano and Peter looked at each other, and then they turned and out of the fireplace came Renee. She walked up to Peter and touched his eyes and closed them, and then she kissed him, and when he opened his eyes he could not remember what had happen. He turned to Delano and asked what was going on, and he asked his wife where were the children, and the grandchildren. Delano looked at Gina and she looked at him, then they turned to Renee and she walked up to them and touched their eyes. When they opened them they could not remember what had happened either.

They called out to the children but no one came, Gina turned to Renee and she walked up to her and looked into her eyes. Gina then smiled and went and sat down on the sofa and she told Delano to come and sit by her until the children came home. Where are the children he asked are they outside playing? Peter walked to the window and looked out and he said he didn't see them. "But come Delano and look at how beautiful the world looks today."

Delano got up and he went and stood by his brother, Peter, and they stood there looking at the people walking around, and everyone was smiling and laughing and talking. No one remembered anything about the battle, and yet everyone knew something had happen. The world was at peace there was no fighting, and no more angry faces. Everyone was talking of the goodness of God, and the wonders of his glory. The news and the televisions all over the world were all about happy times, and they talked of freedom and peace for everyone.

Gina walked outside to the garden, and she walked over to the roses, and she reached down and picked eleven flowers, and brought them into the house, and placed them inside the water. "Come and look at how beautiful these roses are today honey. Aren't they the sweetest smelling things you have ever smelled? Delano walked over and smelled the flowers, and he agreed and then Peter came and took two flowers out, and gave them to Renee. She smiled and then she called out "Children it's time to come down, and the children came down from upstairs, and they all went and stood by their parents and hugged them.

All of a sudden the children started singing, and it was the most beautiful music that Gina had ever heard in her life. They shouted and sang of great happening in heaven, and on earth and as each child sang the flowers, that were in the vase changed to gold.

Maria started singing the most beautiful words, and Gina felt them in her soul. Finally she understood why the children were born, and why she had been given the chance. It is the most beautiful feeling of all to have your life taken into love. Gina had given up hate and misery and picked up love and happiness. She was a conqueror, and no one could stop her now. She looked over at her children and she smiled as they singed God praises. It wasn't about how you worshiped, or even about God, that they sung about. They song about freedom and life, of love and happiness and joy. The sung about a fight and the victory which was won for the people of earth. They stood a chance to win now, they could fight and stand on their own now, they were conquerors, for the glory of happiness of peace.

Gina sat down and looked at them, and her heart sung out with them, she did not know what the future held, or what tomorrow would bring, but she knew in her heart that they all stood a chance now, and she stood ready to fight, with them to the end. As the years past she watched her children turn into adults and have children of their own, and she was full of the joy of life with each birth. They had an army and when the time came for the battle to be fought again, she knew they would win again, only this time there would be no more battles to fight.

Delano and her watched as the world began to grow in peace and love. The color of skin no longer matter and everyone seem just happy to be alive and breathing. The sun no longer concern the world, it shined brighter than it had ever done, giving life and bringing joy with the sunrise and the sunset. Maria had given birth to three girls, each one had become a blessing in their own way. Diane was able to heal by touch, and she saved many lives in her lifetime. She lived to be thirty nine years old, and on her death bed she gave birth to a child, by the name of Renee.

Renee died the same day that the child was born, and Peter died two days later. Delano died the night that Ricardo's wife gave birth to a son, and she named him Delano. Gina watched the children replace them, and as they died. She watched her grandchildren become stronger and wiser, and she felt blessed and truly happy to know, that God loved her so much. Maria came to her one day and told her it was time for them to go home, she held out her hand and Gina took her hand, and she looked at all ten of her grandchildren standing in the room. To each one she kissed she gave them a blessing and told them to do what God had sent them to do.

As she kissed the last child and blessed him, the room filled with light and their clothes fell off and they open up their wings. Gina saw the heavens open up and there stood Delano waiting for her with Peter, Renee, Bridget and Ricardo and their parents and grandparents. She saw her children, which had died standing there, and then she realized what was happening. She was leaving her angels there on earth, to protect and guard, over the people, for Satan still existed he had hidden and they were busy trying to find him.

Gina asked what had happen to his head and Renee told her that he carried it for he could not put it back on he had to find a sinner to do it. Gina asked would he be able to find one but Renee did not answer her. "Gina it is time for us to go now, and we must leave say your last words to the children." Gina turned and looked at her family of angels and she told them to stand guard, and beware of the sly fool, who tried to take their lives. I know children that you are the chosen angels of God, and that he can win any battle that he chooses to fight with you. I love you and I shall miss talking to you for you now stand alone with the grace of God."

When Renee and Gina ascended up into heaven, there was a loud trumpet playing, and the clouds all shined bright; and water began to pour down from heavens, in a way that no man had ever seen before. Gina watched as her grand children spread their wings open, and made a cross and then open up their hands and reach them out over the world.

Each child stepped up and did something the first grandchild blew air out over the world, and with his breathe came life to all the dead plants, and nature returned to what it first was at the beginning. The second child walked up and held up his hands, and water flowed from them and within the water were fishes and every sea creature you could imagine. Gina watched as he filled the world with the most beautiful water she had ever seen, and she smiled and nodded her head in approval. The third grandchild came forward and open up her hands and inside of them where the flowers of life. She began to throw them all around the world filling it with a smell so sweet that Satan if he still could smell had to cover his nose.

The fourth grandchild came forward and she held in her hands so many birds, that when she opened them up they flew in every direction and filled the air with the wind of their wings. The fifth grandchild came forward and opened his arms and out poured the most beautiful rainbows that earth had ever witness, and Gina started laughing at the glory of the beauty, and the shine and the colors of life. The sixth grandchild came forward and she opened up her arms and out came the music of the angels and she filled the earth with a sweet song of love and happiness and joy.

Gina began to dance and shout for joy and the seventh grandchild came forward an open up his arms and joined in the singing he too filled the earth with song but when the eighth grandchild came forward he started dancing around the world. He started filling the earth with rhythm and praise and Gina started dancing with him. The ninth grandchild came forward and opened up the heavens and the angels came out, and started dancing and singing with them. Gina shouted Glory! Look Delano at are children and what they can do!

The tenth and final child came forward and he was dressed for battle and he held a sword in his hand, and he went and bowed before the throne of God and shouted at the top of his voice "Worthy is the Lord our God! And then he turned and opened up his arms and filled the air with victory and the Gina shouted "Yes, now I see the truth. I now know that I can rest in peace." She walked over to Delano and took him into her arms, and they started dancing around the heavens, and Renee and Peter joined them along Ricardo and Bridget.

It was the biggest party Gina had ever seen. Every one of the children had given back to the earth what Satan had taken away and it was the most beautiful sight Gina and Delano had ever seen or behold. They looked at their children and smiled and then waved good-by and as they walked with their parents and grandparents into the clouds the children returned to earth; their wings slowly went back into their backs, and their clothes raised off the ground and went back on. The children and their sibling all began to sing and laugh and slowly they went back to the days matters.

The End